Jaco

Nature in Disease

Anatiposi

Jacob Bigelow

Nature in Disease

Reprint of the original.

1st Edition 2023 | ISBN: 978-3-38230-426-3

Anatiposi Verlag is an imprint of Outlook Verlagsgesellschaft mbH.

Verlag (Publisher): Outlook Verlag GmbH, Zeilweg 44, 60439 Frankfurt, Deutschland
Vertretungsberechtigt (Authorized to represent): E. Roepke, Zeilweg 44, 60439 Frankfurt, Deutschland
Druck (Print): Books on Demand GmbH, In de Tarpen 42, 22848 Norderstedt, Deutschland

Nearly twenty years ago the Discourse on *Self-limited Diseases*, which stands at the head of this volume, was delivered before the Massachusetts Medical Society, at their annual meeting, as an expression of opinions I had been led to entertain as to the influence of treatment on the event of some morbid affections. Subsequent observation has not tended to shake these opinions; and I have had the satisfaction to believe that many of my medical friends, for whose judgment the public entertain the highest respect, have arrived at similar conclusions. As science has advanced, some revision has become necessary of this as well as of some other essays, written long ago. But the general truth of the positions then assumed has not been contradicted by later experience of competent observers in the profession.

The exclusive pursuit of any profession frequently tends to an undue exaggeration of its powers. What we have been early taught to accept on authority, and what we have been accustomed habitually to announce to others, may become engrafted on our own belief, so as to constitute an unquestioned rule of practice. The necessity is, on this account, more imperative, that inquirers for truth should divest themselves of personal considerations, and seek for rules of practice which are based on enlightened experience, and impartial and reliable evidence.

I have given the title "Nature in Disease" to the

Self-limited Diseases, which stands at the head of this volume, public opinion in this part of the country seems to have undergone progressive modification in regard to the treatment of disease. At the same time unequivocal manifestations are appearing on both sides of the Atlantic that more of forbearance, and less of troublesome interference, are required in medical practice than was formerly believed to be necessary by a majority of the profession.

BOSTON, Jan. 1, 1859.

NATURE IN DISEASE.

NATURE IN DISEASE;

ILLUSTRATED IN

VARIOUS DISCOURSES AND ESSAYS.

TO WHICH ARE ADDED

MISCELLANEOUS WRITINGS,

CHIEFLY ON MEDICAL SUBJECTS.

BY JACOB BIGELOW, M. D.

PHYSICIAN AND LECTURER ON CLINICAL MEDICINE IN THE MASSACHUSETTS GENERAL HOSPITAL; PROFESSOR OF MATERIA MEDICA IN HARVARD UNIVERSITY; PRESIDENT OF THE AMERICAN ACADEMY OF ARTS AND SCIENCES; AND LATE PRESIDENT OF THE MASSACHUSETTS MEDICAL SOCIETY.

SECOND EDITION, ENLARGED.

BOSTON:

PHILLIPS, SAMPSON AND COMPANY.

MDCCCLIX.

To

ROBLEY DUNGLISON, M. D.,

PROFESSOR OF THE INSTITUTES OF MEDICINE, IN THE JEFFERSON MEDICAL COLLEGE, PHILADELPHIA, ETC. ETC.

MY DEAR SIR :

I am sure that you will unite with me in admitting that the experience of a long professional life is the best corrective of the exaggerated estimate which we are liable to form, or imbibe, in our earlier years, as to the power of medication to control disease.

I inscribe to you this new edition of a work, — parts of which were published long ago, — in token of my recognition of the distinguished rank which you hold as one of the medical lights of our country, and of my satisfaction in knowing that you concur with me in the principles laid down in its leading chapters.

I am, dear sir,

With respect and regard,

Your friend and servant,

JACOB BIGELOW.

PREFACE

TO THE FIRST EDITION.

It is observable to many physicians that a change in the mode of regarding the treatment of disease has come over the medical world, not only in this city, but in various parts of the United States, during the last quarter of a century. In many cases a practice of watching, guiding, and trusting the salutary indications of nature, has taken the place of more active interferences of art. Those men whose medical career began at a period antecedent to that which has been named, will recollect that the course then most prevalent among the profession consisted in energetic and sometimes annoying and painful applications of supposed remedies, from the beginning to the end of diseases, whether those diseases were amenable to such treatment, or totally incapable of being influenced by them. And, in some instances, such active measures were promoted by influential teachers of medical science in the great schools of our country.

present collection of discourses and disquisitions, because a number of the principal articles in its contents bear directly on that subject. But I have taken advantage of the same occasion to incorporate in this small volume some other miscellaneous papers, chiefly on medical subjects, written or published at various times during a long and not inactive professional life. J. B.

BOSTON, Nov. 1, 1854.

PREFACE

TO THE SECOND EDITION.

THE reception given to the first issue of this collection of Discourses and Essays has been thought by the publishers to authorize the stereotyping of its pages, and the enlarging of their number with some additional articles on medical subjects of interest.

In a little work lately published, entitled "Brief Expositions of Rational Medicine," to which the reader is referred, I have endeavored to compare and define the prominent modes of practice which prevail at the present day,— the Artificial, the Expectant, the Homœopathic, the Exclusive, and the Rational.

Since the publication, in 1835, of the Discourse on

CONTENTS.

ON

SELF-LIMITED DISEASES:

A DISCOURSE DELIVERED BEFORE THE MASSACHUSETTS MEDICAL SOCIETY, AT THEIR ANNUAL MEETING, MAY 27TH, 1835.

[At the beginning of this discourse, the customary obituary notice was taken of eminent members of the society, deceased during the previous year.]

THE death of medical men is an occurrence which eminently demands our attention, for it speaks to us of our science, and of ourselves. It reminds us that we, in turn, are to become victims of the incompetency of our own art. It admonishes us that the sphere of our professional exertions is limited, at last, by insurmountable barriers. It brings with it the humiliating conclusion, that while other sciences have been carried forward, within our own time and almost under our own eyes, to a degree of unprecedented advancement, Medicine, in regard to some of its professed and most important objects, is still an ineffectual speculation. Observations are multiplied, but the observers disappear, and leave their task unfinished. We have seen the maturity of age and the ardent purpose of youth called off from the half cultivated field of their labors, expectations, and promise. It becomes us to look upon this deeply interesting subject with unprejudiced eyes, and to endeavor to elicit useful truth from the great lesson that surrounds us.

In comparing the advances which have been made during the present age in different departments of Medical science, we are brought to the conclusion that they have not all been cultivated with equally satisfactory success. Some of them have received new and important illustrations from scientific inquiry, but others are still surrounded with their original difficulties. The structure and functions of the human body, the laws which govern the progress of its diseases, and more especially the diagnosis of its morbid conditions, are better understood now than they were at the beginning of the present century. But the science of therapeutics, or the branch of knowledge by the application of which physicians are expected to remove diseases, has not, seemingly, attained to a much more elevated standing than it formerly possessed. The records of mortality attest its frequent failures, and the inability to control the event of diseases, which at times is felt by the most gifted and experienced practitioners, gives evidence that, in many cases, disease is more easily understood than cured.

This deficiency of the healing art is not justly attributable to any want of sagacity or diligence on the part of the medical profession. It belongs rather to the inherent difficulties of the case, and is, after abating the effect of errors and accidents, to be ascribed to the apparent fact, that certain morbid processes in the human body have a definite and necessary career, from which they are not to be diverted by any known agents with which it is in our power to oppose them. To these morbid affections, the duration of which, and frequently the event also, are beyond the control of our present remedial means, I have, on the present occasion, applied the name of *Self-limited diseases*; and it will be the object of this discourse to endeavor to show the existence of such a class, and to inquire how far certain individual diseases may be considered as belonging to it.

By a self-limited disease, I would be understood to express one which receives limits from its own nature, and not from foreign influences; one which, after it has obtained foothold in the system, cannot, in the present state of our knowledge, be eradicated or abridged by art,—but to which there is due a certain succession of processes, to be completed in a certain time; which time and processes may vary with the constitution and condition of the patient, and may tend to death, or to recovery, but are not known to be shortened, or greatly changed, by medical treatment.

These expressions are not intended to apply to the palliation of diseases, for he who turns a pillow, or administers a seasonable draught of water to a patient, palliates his sufferings; but they apply to the more important consideration of removing diseases themselves through medical means.

The existence of a class of diseases like those under consideration is, to a certain extent, already admitted, both by the profession and the public; and this admission is evinced by the use of certain familiar terms of expression. Thus, when people speak of a "settled disease," or of the time of "the run of a disease," it implies, on their part, a recognition of the law that certain diseases regulate their own limits and period of continuance.

It is difficult to select a perfectly satisfactory or convincing example of a self-limited disease from among the graver morbid affections, because in these affections the solicitude of the practitioner usually leads him to the employment of remedies, in consequence of which the effect of remedies is mixed up with the phenomena of disease, so that the mind has difficulty in separating them. [*Note* A.] We must, therefore, seek for our most striking or decisive examples among those diseases which are sufficiently mild not to be thought to require ordinarily the use of remedies, and in which the natural history of the disease may be observed, divested of foreign influences. Such examples are found in the vaccine disease, the chicken-pox, and the salivation produced by mercury. These are strictly self-limited diseases, having their own rise, climax, and decline; and I know of no *medical* practice which is able, were it deemed necessary, to divert them from their appropriate course, or hasten their termination. [*Note* B.]

It may appear to some that the distinction of these diseases from others is the old distinction of acute and chronic. Yet, on due inquiry, such an identification is not found to be sustained, for there are some acute diseases which, we have reason to believe, are shortened by the employment of remedies; while, on the other hand, certain chronic cases of disease are known to get well spontaneously, after years of continuance.

If the inquiry be made, why one disease has necessary limits while another is without them, the reply is not uniform, nor always easy to be made. Sometimes the law of the disease may be traced to the nature of the exciting cause. Thus the morbid poison of measles, or of small-pox, when received into the body, produces a self-limited disease; but the morbid poisons of psora and syphilis may give rise to others which are not limited, except by medical treatment.

[*Note* C.] Sometimes, also, the cause being the same, the result will depend on the part, organ, or texture which is affected. Thus, if we divide with a cutting instrument the cellular or muscular substance, we produce a self-limited disease, which, although it cannot by any art be healed within a certain number of days or weeks, yet in the end gets well spontaneously, by one process, if the lips are in contact, and by another and slower process if they are separated.* But if, on the other hand, we divide a considerable artery, we have then an unlimited disease; and the hemorrhage, or the aneurism, which follows, does not get well, except through the interposition of art.

The class of diseases under consideration comprehends morbid affections, differing greatly from each other in the time, place, and nature of their spontaneous developments; so that they may admit of at least three general subdivisions. These may be called, 1st. The *simple;* in which the disease observes a continuous time, and mostly a definite seat; 2d. The *paroxysmal;* in

* In one case, the disease is a solution of continuity; in the other, a solution of continuity and contact.

which the disease, having apparently disappeared, returns at its own periods; and, 3d. The *metastatic;* in which the disease undergoes metastasis or spontaneous change of place. In the present state of our knowledge, we have no difficulty in finding examples of each of these subdivisions. There are also other examples, in which the disease, although capable of being in part influenced by medical treatment, still retains a portion of its original intractability, and has strong relations to the class in question.

As a mode of directing our inquiries toward these diseases, we may suspect those complaints to be self-limited in which it is observed that the unwary and the sceptical, who neglect to resort to remedies, recover their health without them. We may also suspect diseases to be of this character when we find opposite modes of treatment recommended, and their success vouched for, by practitioners of authority and veracity. We may, moreover, attach the same suspicion to cases in which the supposed cure takes place under chance applications, or inconsiderable remedies; as in the empirical modes of practice on the one hand, and the minute doses of the homœopathic method on the other. Lastly, we may apprehend that cases are fatally self-limited,* when enlightened physicians die themselves of the diseases which they had labored to illustrate, —as in the case of Corvisart, Laennec, Armstrong, and others. [*Note* D.]

In proceeding to enumerate more precisely some of the diseases which appear to me to be self-limited in their character, I approach the subject with diffidence. I am aware that the works of medical writers, and especially of medical compilers, teem with remedies and modes of treatment for all diseases; and that, in the morbid affections of which we speak, remedies are often urged with zeal and confidence, even though sometimes of an opposite character. Moreover, in many places, at the present day, a charm is popularly attached to what is called an active, bold, or heroic practice; and a corresponding reproach awaits the opposite course, which is cautious, palliative, and expectant. In regard to

* In the following article on the Treatment of Disease, it has been found convenient to divide diseases into the curable, the self-limited, and the incurable. In a general sense, however, the last term falls within the second.

the diseases which have been called self-limited, I would not be understood to deny that remedies capable of removing them may exist; I would only assert that they have not yet been proved to exist.

Under the simple self-limited diseases, we may class *hooping-cough.* This disease has its regular increase, height, and decline, occupying ordinarily from one to six months, but in some mild cases only two or three weeks. During this period, medical treatment is for the most part of no avail. Narcotic appliances may diminish the paroxysm, but without abridging the disease. After hooping-cough has reached its climax, change of air sometimes appears to hasten convalescence. Also if inflammatory, or other morbid affections, supervene upon the pure disease, they may become subjects for medical treatment. With these exceptions, hooping-cough appears to be a self-limited disease.

Most of the class of diseases usually denominated eruptive fevers, are self-limited. *Measles,* for example, is never known to be cut short by art, or abridged of its natural career; neither can this career be extended, or the disease kept in the system beyond its natural duration, by the power of medicine. *Scarlet fever*, a disease of which we have had much and fatal experience during the last three years, is eminently of the same character. The reasons, which induce me thus to regard it, are the following. The writings of medical observers agree in assigning to it a common or average period of duration, and this is confirmed by the observations of practitioners at the present day. From this average duration and character there are great natural deviations, the disease being sometimes so slight as to attract the notice of none but medical eyes, and sometimes so malignant that treatment is admitted to be hopeless. The modes of treatment, which have had most testimony in their favor, are various, and opposite. By Dr. Fothergill, stimulants were relied on; by Dr. Currie, cold water; by Dr. Southwood Smith, and others, blood-letting. But it is not satisfactorily shown that either of these modes of practice has been particularly successful; for, where the writers have furnished us anything like definite or numerical results, it does not appear that the mortality was less in their hands than it is among those who pursue a more expectant practice. The post-mortuary appearances, which in many diseases furnish useful lessons for practice, are in scarlet fever extremely various and uncertain; and sometimes no morbid changes, sufficient to account for death, can be discovered in any of the vital organs, or great cavities. [*Note* E.]

Small-pox is another example of the class of affections under consideration, its approach and disappearance being irrespective of medical practice. It may, at first view, appear that inoculation has placed artificial limits on this disease. But it must be recollected that inoculated small-pox is itself only a milder variety of the same disease, having its own customary limits of extent and duration, which are fixed, quite as much as those of the distinct and confluent forms of the natural disease.

Erysipelas is an eruptive fever, having strong analogies with those which have been detailed. It is not certain that art can very materially affect either the duration or the extent of this malady. If a physician is called to a case of erysipelas, which is beginning to be developed upon a part of the face; and if he is asked, whether the disease will extend to the crown, or the neck, or to the right ear, or the left,—he cannot tell. And if he is asked to prevent it from visiting either of these places, I know of no satisfactory evidence that he can do it. Erysipelas, however, in a great number of simple, or exanthematous cases, in subjects previously healthy, gets well without any treatment; and in a great number of deep-seated and phlegmonous cases, as well as those in which vital organs are affected, it proves fatal under the most approved methods of medical and surgical practice. It is true that patients have recovered, under punctures, incisions, and cautery. It is also true that they have died under the same operations, so that it may be submitted as a doubtful point, whether we yet possess adequate evidence that erysipelas is not also a self-limited disease.

It is a question of great interest to the medical profession, to determine whether *typhoid fever* is a disease susceptible of control from medical means. On this subject no one now doubts that, if the disease is once fairly established in the system, it cannot be eradicated by art, but must complete a certain natural course, before convalescence can take place. But a question still exists, whether this disease is capable of being jugulated, or broken up, at its outset, by the early application of remedies.

It must be allowed that attacks of disease resembling those of typhoid sometimes speedily disappear during the use of remedies; but it is by no means certain that such cases are actually cases of typhoid. The diagnosis of this disease, during the first day or two, is extremely difficult, its character being simulated by different febrile and inflammatory affections; so that if a patient, under the use of remedies, succeeds in avoiding protracted disease, we are not justified in saying that the disease he has escaped was typhoid or typhus fever. Andral, whose experiments on the different modes of treatment in continued fever are very extensive, has stated, that in a number of cases, observed by him, in which the fever was sufficiently intense, the disease ceased in twenty-four or forty-eight hours, without any treatment, except that of rest and a regulated diet.*

* Clinique III. 619.

Moreover, in weighing the influence of treatment, it ought to be recollected, that during the existence of any prevailing epidemic, mild cases, partaking of a similar character to that of the reigning disease, continually appear among the less susceptible part of the community. Thus, cholera is attended by diarrhœa or cholerine, influenza by mild catarrh, small-pox by varioloid, scarlet fever by slight sore throats or ephemeral eruptions, &c. Now, although these cases are in reality modified examples of the grave diseases which they accompany, yet I believe that no well-informed physician will attribute the mildness or shortness of their character to his own particular practice.

On the other hand, it is certain that cases of real typhoid do often come under active treatment at an early stage, without being broken up, or disarmed of their appropriate consequences. This particularly happens when the disease is endemic in families, so that successive cases begin, as it were, under the eye of the attending physician, who has every possible inducement to detect and prevent them, if he can. In such families, indeed, it will sometimes happen that febrile attacks of different kinds, consequent upon fatigue and anxiety, and perhaps partaking of the typhoid character, will take place among the friends and attendants of the sick; and these may disappear speedily, under rest and evacuations. But that grave and specific typhoid fever will thus disappear, is a point of which we as yet want proof. That it sometimes fails to disappear, we have abundant proof.

Typhoid fever has, in many respects, a marked affinity with the class of eruptive fevers, which are supposed to depend on a specific morbid poison, and which no one pretends to intercept after the body has become infected with them. Scarlet fever and measles, for example, when once established, require a certain number of days to finish their course; so also does typhoid. Scarlet fever and measles can, in most cases, be had but once during life; but to this general rule there are exceptions. The same is precisely true in regard to typhoid. The contagiousness of scarlet fever is a point of dispute among physicians; and so is that of typhoid. Scarlet fever is attended by an eruption on the skin. Typhoid fever also has for one of its most constant symptoms a red, lenticular eruption, consisting of a few scattered rose-colored pimples, appearing chiefly on the trunk, from about the sixth to the nineteenth day of the disease. There also occurs, in most subjects, a minute, vesicular eruption of *sudamina*, about the neck and elsewhere. In scarlet fever, moreover, certain portions of the mucous membrane undergo morbid alterations, particularly on the tonsils, and other parts of the fauces, and these frequently degenerate into ulcers, affecting the subjacent textures. In like manner, in typhoid fever, the mucous membrane of the granular patches in the small intestines, which have been named after the anatomist Peyer, undergo morbid changes, and these changes are followed by ulcerations, and sometimes perforations of the intestine. This fact, established by the researches of Louis and other pathologists in Paris, has been abundantly confirmed by post mortem examinations made in this country during the last few years.* If it be objected to the proposed classification of this fever, that the *taches* are sometimes few in number, or wholly

* 1835.

absent: it is equally true, that the pustules of inoculated small-pox are likewise often very few, or absent; and that the eruption of scarlatina sometimes wholly fails to appear. The sore throat also in the latter disease is wanting quite as often, to say the least, as the morbid affection of Peyer's glands.

Before quitting the subject, I beg leave to introduce the opinion of one or two medical writers, in regard to the possibility of interrupting or breaking up this disease by means of art. M. Louis, of whose researches in regard to typhoid fever it is but small praise to say that they are more exact and comprehensive than those of any living writer, is of opinion that the disease cannot be thus intercepted. "Experience," says he, "has shown, that a well marked typhoid affection is not capable of being broken up."* To this testimony of one of the most

* "L'experience ayant montré, que l'affection typhoide bien caractérisée, n'est pas susceptible d'etre jugulée, ce qui n'est guere moins vrai, d'ailleurs, suivant toutes les apparences, de la peripneumonie et des autres maladies inflammatoires." — LOUIS, *Gastro-entérite*. II. 512.

Andral says, in regard to the different modes of treatment in typhus, "Quelles que soient les mèthodes employées, il est un

eminent teachers in the French metropolis it may not be amiss to add that of an American physician, whose opportunities for observing the disease in different parts of New England were extensive, and whose Essay on Typhus Fever well merits an attentive perusal. The late Dr. Nathan Smith, in the course of some remarks on the possibility of interrupting this disease at commencement, observes: "During the whole of my practice I have never been satisfied that I have cut short a single case of typhus that I knew to be such."*

Having said thus much, I leave the subject of the tractability of typhus and typhoid fever to the light of future investigation. It is but justice to state, that numerous and highly respectable authorities are declared in favor of the efficacy of art in shortening and mitigating these diseases; and it will be a source of gratification

certain nombre de cas où, sans que ces methodes y prennent part, la nature conduit la maladie à une terminaison heureuse ou funeste." —*Clinique* I. 651.

* At the time of the publication alluded to, the distinction between typhus and typhoid fevers had not been well made out. The distinction is good, though writers of authority differ on the subject.

to the friends of humanity and science, should it ultimately be settled, that the active treatment now usually pursued at the commencement of cases is instrumental in lessening their duration, severity, or danger.

Among the morbid affections which have now been enumerated may be found sufficient examples of continued diseases which receive limits from their own nature, and not from the interference of art. Whether the number of these diseases may not be augmented by additions from among other fevers and acute inflammations, I am not prepared to decide. It is difficult, however, to withhold the belief that a more extended inquiry must probably serve to multiply, rather than diminish, the number of maladies to which this character will be found appropriate.*

We come next to a second order of self-

* There is not room here to discuss the question whether Pneumonia and other acute inflammations fall under the category of self-limitation. Blood-letting, in proper cases, lessens the severity and danger of these diseases. But it is not apparent that it greatly abridges their duration. Dysentery may be accounted a self-limited disease.

limited diseases, of which the term *paroxysmal* is sufficiently descriptive. This term applies to certain morbid affections, which occur in fits or paroxysms, leaving the patient comparatively well in the intervals, at the same time that the paroxysms themselves can neither be foreseen, prevented, nor, as far as we know, materially abridged in their duration. At the head of this subdivision stands *Epilepsy*, a disease which has long been eminent as an opprobrium of medicine, and for which, it is believed, the healing art has not yet devised a cure. The first attacks of epilepsy, especially while there is any doubt as to the nature of the malady, are usually made the subjects of active and various treatment. But after the recurring paroxysms have established the character of the disease, if active medical practice is persevered in, it is rather to satisfy the anxiety of friends than the judgment of the practitioner.

Angina pectoris, appropriately called by Dr. Good, Sternalgia, is a paroxysmal disease, which in many cases controls its own movements. The anatomical character of this disease is not uniform, and, I may add, the same is true of its medical treatment. And in this place it may be proper to state that various incurable lesions of the heart, lungs, brain, and other viscera, do not apparently destroy life by a regular, undeviating march; but that, as far as their outward phenomena afford evidence, they seem to proceed by alternate fits and pauses, undergoing, in their progress, all states except that of retrogradation. This is apparently true in regard to tubercle, carcinoma, ossification, hypertrophy, and some other morbid alterations. It is also even true in regard to old age itself.

Thirty years ago we might have added *gout* to the opprobrious list under consideration. But as we may now be said to possess the means of shortening the paroxysms, by the use of certain acrid narcotics, and as an abstemious life goes far towards lessening the frequency and violence of the recurrence, we may be justified in withdrawing gout from the place it would otherwise occupy. [*Note* F.]

The diseases of mania and melancholy, asthma, when it depends on emphysema of the lungs, gravel in the kidneys, and the symptoms produced by ascarides in the rectum [*Note* G], furnish other examples of maladies which manifest themselves in unforeseen paroxysms. Cases which bear the names of all the above diseases are undoubtedly relieved, and sometimes even removed by medicine; but it is equally true that other cases are wholly intractable, both as to their recurrence, their duration, and their susceptibility of much change from medical treatment. And it will come to the recollection of many practitioners, that they have, in the course of their lives, believed themselves to have cured these diseases, when in fact they have only witnessed the spontaneous subsidence of a paroxysm.

The last subdivision of our subject includes what may be called *metastatic* diseases. By this term I wish to express certain morbid affections, which pass by metastasis from one part of the body to another, for the most part independently of artificial influence. Of this kind are certain *cutaneous* affections, more especially some which are chronic and hereditary. Many persons pass a considerable portion of their lives in alternate annoyance from a disease of the skin, and from its vicarious substitute in some internal organ.

Others again are afflicted with hemorrhagic or purulent *discharges*, which at times disappear only to be succeeded by equally troublesome affections in a different part. *Gonorrhœa* cannot be prevented from occasional metastasis of inflammation, and *mumps* are sometimes found to undergo the same transition. But perhaps the most remarkable example of a metastatic disease is found in *acute rheumatism*. This morbid affection often begins to discover itself in a limited and comparatively unimportant part of the system. From thence, in grave cases, it travels by successive migrations from joint to joint, and from limb to limb, till it has visited nearly all the great articulations of the body. It also attacks the organs of sense, and the viscera which are essential to life. During the course of these migrations the attending physician cannot foretell at any given stage what part will be next invaded by the disease, neither can he protect any part from being thus invaded; nor can he control the period during which the disease will reside in any particular part previously to its next metastasis. Nevertheless acute rheumatism is susceptible of great palliation though of little abridgment, and, after having run out its career, terminates in spontaneous recovery; not, however, in some cases, until it has laid the foundation of serious organic derangements, especially of the heart.

I forbear to dilate on the structural lesions of different organs, many of which can only be cured by the extirpation of the part in which they reside, thus sacrificing the integrity of the body to the preservation of life; and in which extirpation cannot avail, when the seat of the disease is in a vital part. I also pass over the pestilential epidemics of plague, yellow fever, malignant dysentery, and cholera; diseases about which the medical profession have great differences of opinion, and of which thousands die annually, though hundreds of volumes have been written for their preservation. [*Note* H.]

It may perhaps appear that the views which have now been taken of the power of medicine, in so large a class of diseases, are gloomy and discouraging, and that an unworthy tribute is paid to the labors of those physicians who have patiently studied and ardently acted for the benefit of humanity. Such views, however, are

4

far from being the object of the present discourse. Were it permitted by the compass of the subject under consideration, it would be a very grateful task to enumerate those maladies of the human frame, over which we have reason to believe that medicine has obtained decisive influence. To a medical audience, it is unnecessary to recall the instances of pain relieved, spasms controlled, inflammations checked [*Note* I], and diseased associations broken up, under limitable diseases, by the agency of the healing art. Were there no other trophy for the medical profession to boast, it is sufficient to know that the diseases of small-pox and syphilis alone would have entailed misery and extermination on a large portion of our species, had not medical science discovered the prevention of the one, and the successful management of the other.

But that the usefulness of our profession may extend, our knowledge must go on to increase; and the foundation of all knowledge is truth. For truth then we must earnestly seek, even when its developments do not flatter our professional pride, nor attest the infallibility of our art.

To discover truth in science is often extremely difficult; in no science is it more difficult than in medicine. Independently of the common defects of medical evidence, our self-interest, our self-esteem, and sometimes even our feelings of humanity, may be arrayed against the truth. It is difficult to view the operations of nature, divested of the interferences of art, so much do our habits and partialities incline us to neglect the former, and to exaggerate the importance of the latter. The mass of medical testimony is always on the side of art. Medical books are prompt to point out the cure of diseases. Medical journals are filled with the crude productions of aspirants to the cure of diseases. Medical schools find it incumbent on them to teach the cure of diseases. The young student goes forth into the world, believing that if he does not cure diseases, it is his own fault. Yet when a score or two of years have passed over his head, he will come at length to the conviction that some diseases are controlled by nature alone. He will often pause, at the end of a long and anxious attendance, and ask himself how far the result of the case is different from what it would have been under less officious treatment than that which he has pursued; how many in the accumulated array of remedies, which have supplanted each other in the patient's chamber, have actually been instrumental in doing him any good. He will also ask himself whether, in the course of his life, he has not had occasion to change his opinion, perhaps more than once, in regard to the management of the disease in question, and whether he does not, even now, feel the want of additional light.

Medicine has been rightly called a conjectural art, because in many of its deductions, and especially in those which relate to the cure of diseases, positive evidence is denied to us. We are seldom justified in concluding that our remedies have promoted the cure of a disease, until we know that cases exactly similar in time, place, and circumstances, have failed to do equally well under the omission of those remedies; and such cases, moreover, must exist in sufficient numbers to justify the admission of a general law, on their basis. Nothing can be more illogical than to draw our general conclusions, as we are sometimes too apt to do, from the results of insulated and remarkable cases; for such cases may be found in support of any extravagance in medicine; and if there is any point in which the vulgar differ from the judicious part of the profession, it is in drawing premature and sweeping conclusions from scanty premises of this kind. Moreover, it is in many cases not less illogical to attribute the removal of diseases, or even of their troublesome symptoms, to the means which have been most recently employed. It is a common error to infer that things which are consecutive in the order of time have necessarily the relation of cause and effect. It often happens that the last remedy used bears off the credit of having removed an obstruction, or cured a disease, whereas in fact the result may have been owing to the first remedy employed, or to the joint effect of all the remedies, or to the act of nature, uninfluenced by any of the remedies. We see this remarkably exemplified in recoveries from amenorrhœa, and from various irregularities of the alimentary canal.

An inherent difficulty, which every medical man finds to stand in the way of an unbiased and satisfactory judgment, is the heavy responsibility which rests upon the issue of his cases. When a friend, or valuable patient, is committed to our charge, we cannot stand by, as curious spectators, to study the natural history of his disease. We feel that we are called on to attempt his rescue by vigorous means, so that at least the fault of omission shall not lie upon our charge. We proceed to put in practice those measures which on the whole have appeared to us to do most good; and, if these fail us, we resort to other measures, which we have read of, or heard of. And at the end of our attendance we may be left in uncertainty whether the duration of sickness has been shortened, or lengthened, by our practice, and whether the patient is really indebted to us for good or evil. In the study of experimental philosophy, we rarely admit a conclusion to be true, until its opposite has been proved to be untrue. But in medicine we are often obliged to be content to accept as evidence the results of cases, which have been finished under treatment, because we have not the opportunity to know how far these results would have been different, had the cases been left to themselves. And it too frequently happens that medical books do not relieve our difficulties on this score, for a great deal of our practical literature consists in reports of interesting, extraordinary, and successful results, published by men who have a doctrine to establish, or a reputation to build. "Few authors," says Andral, "have published all the cases they have observed, and the greater part have only taken the trouble to present to us those facts which favor their own views."* A prevailing error, among writers on therapeutics, proceeds from their professional or personal reluctance to admit that the healing art, as practised by them, is not, or may not be, all-sufficient, in all cases; so that on this subject they suffer themselves, as well as their readers, to be deceived. Hence we have no disease, however intractable or fatal, for which the press has not poured forth its asserted remedies. Even of late we have seen unfailing cures of cholera successively announced in almost every city, in which that pestilence unchecked has completed its work of devastation!

* Bien peu d'auteurs ont publié tous les cas qu'ils ont observés, et la plupart ne se sont empressés de nous transmettre que les faits que caressaient leurs idées. — *Clinique* III. 618.

It is only when, in connection with these flattering exhibitions, we have a full and faithful report of the failures of medical practice, in similar, and in common cases, setting forth not only the truth, but the whole truth, that we have a basis sufficiently broad to erect a superstructure, in therapeutics, on which dependence may be placed. Such, it must give the friends of science gratification to observe, is a part of the rigid method which characterizes the best examples of the modern French school; and such, it is not difficult to foresee, must ultimately be the only species of evidence on this subject, to which the medical profession will pay deference.

It appears to me to be one of the most important desiderata in practical medicine, to ascertain, in regard to each doubtful disease, how far its cases are really self-limited, and how far they are controllable by any treatment. This question can be satisfactorily settled only by instituting, in a large number of cases, which are well identified and nearly similar, a fair experimental comparison of the different active and expectant modes of practice, with their varieties in regard to time, order, and degree. This experiment is vast, considering the number of combinations which it must involve; and even much more extensive than a corresponding series of pathological observations; yet every honest and intelligent observer may contribute to it his mite. Opportunities for such observations, and especially for monographs of diseases, are found in the practice of most physicians, yet hospitals and other public charities afford the most appropriate field for instituting them upon a large scale. The aggregate of results, successful and unsuccessful, circumstantially and impartially reported by competent observers, will give us a near approximation to truth, in regard to the diseases of the time and place in which the experiments are instituted. The *numerical* method employed by Louis in his extensive pathological researches, and now adopted by his most distinguished contemporaries in France, affords the means of as near an approach to certainty on this head, as the subject itself admits. And I may add, that no previous medical inquirer has apparently submitted to the profession any species of evidence so broad in its foundations, and so convincing in its results, as that which characterizes the great works of this author on Phthisis and Typhoid fever.

In regard to acknowledged self-limited diseases, the question will naturally arise, whether the practitioner is called on to do nothing for the benefit of his patient; whether he shall fold his hands, and look passively on the progress of a disease which he cannot interrupt. To this I would answer,—by no means. The opportunities of doing good may be as great in these diseases as in any others; for, in treating every disease, there is a right method and a wrong. In the first place, we may save the patient from much harm, not only by forbearing ourselves to afflict him with unnecessary practice, but also by preventing the ill-judged activity of others. For the same reason that we would not suffer him to be shaken in his bed, when rest was considered necessary to him, we should not allow him to be tormented with useless and annoying applications in a disease of settled destiny. It should be remembered that all cases are susceptible of errors of commission, as well as of omission, and that, by an excessive application of the means of art, we may frustrate the intentions of nature when they are salutary, or embitter the approach of death when it is inevitable. What practitioner, I would ask, ever rendered a greater service to mankind, than Ambrose Paré, and his subsequent coädjutors, who introduced into modern surgery the art of healing by the first intention? These men with vast difficulty succeeded in convincing the profession, that, instead of the old method of treating incised wounds by keeping them open with forcible and painful applications, it was better simply to place the parts securely in their natural situation, and then to let them alone. In the second place, we may do much good by a palliative and preventive course, by alleviating pain, procuring sleep, guarding the diet, regulating the alimentary canal,—in fine, by obviating such sufferings as admit of mitigation, and preventing or removing the causes of others, which are incidental, but not necessary, to the state of disease. In doing this, we must distinguish between the disease itself, and the accidents of the disease, for the latter often admit of relief, when the former does not. We should also inquire whether the original cause of the disease, or any accessory cause, is still operating, and, if so, whether it can in any measure be prevented or removed; as, for example, when it exists in the habits of life of the patient, in the local atmosphere, or in the presence of any other deleterious agent. [*Note* K.] Lastly, by a just prognosis, founded on a correct view of the case, we may sustain the patient and his friends during the inevitable course of the disease; and may save them from the pangs of disappointed hope on the one side, or of unnecessary despondency on the other.

It will be seen that, in the foregoing remarks, a low estimate has been placed on the resources of art, when compared with those of nature. But I may be excused for doing this in the presence of an audience of educated men, and the members of a society, whose motto is *Naturâ duce*. The longer and the more philosophically we contemplate this subject, the more obvious it will appear that the physician is but the minister and servant of nature; that, in cases like those which have been engaging our consideration, we can do little more than follow in the train of disease, and endeavor to aid nature in her salutary intentions, or to remove obstacles out of her path. How little, indeed, could we accomplish without her aid! It has been wisely observed, by Sir Gilbert Blane, that "the benefit derivable to mankind at large, from artificial remedies, is so limited, that, if a spontaneous principle of restoration had not existed, the human species would long ago have been extinct."*

The importance and usefulness of the medical profession, instead of being diminished, will always be elevated, exactly in proportion as it understands itself, weighs justly its own powers, and professes simply what it can accomplish. It is no derogation from the importance of our art, that we cannot always control the events of life and death, or even of health and sickness. The incompetency, which we feel in this respect, is shared by almost every man upon whom the great responsibilities of society are devolved. The statesman cannot control the destinies of nations, nor the military commander the event of battles. The most eloquent pleader may fail to convince the judgment of his hearers, and the most skilful pilot may not be able to weather the

* Medical Logic, p. 49.

storm. Yet it is not the less necessary that responsible men should study deeply and understandingly the science of their respective vocations. It is not the less important, for the sake of those whose safety is, and always will be, committed to their charge, that they should look with unbiased judgment upon the necessary results of inevitable causes. And while an earnest and inquiring solicitude should always be kept alive, in regard to the improvement of professional knowledge, it should never be forgotten that knowledge has for its only just and lasting foundation a rigid, impartial, and inflexible requisition of the truth.

NOTES.

Note A.

The difficulty of discriminating between the symptoms of disease, and the effects of treatment, has undoubtedly led to much erroneous practice, so that we cannot be too careful or vigilant, in watching the consequences of our own remedies. For a long time the effects resulting from an excessive use of mercury were mistaken for the phenomena of syphilis. The arterial reäction, described by Marshall Hall, which sometimes follows excessive blood-letting, has been confounded with the arterial action of disease requiring further depletion. Constitutional irritation, produced or kept up by an inordinate use of vesicatories and other counter-stimulants, has been made a reason for the further continuance of those applications. Much acute and unnecessary suffering has been caused by the prolonged application of sinapisms to the tender skins of infants, and the limbs of dying patients. The pains of hunger, resulting from a too-restricted diet, are most keenly felt by convalescents from sickness; yet we sometimes see the cries of infants, arising from this cause, mistaken for signs of disease, and met by the practitioner with medicines, and further restrictions. I do not speak of these things as common occurrences, yet they have been sufficiently so, to render it obvious that circumspection, on the part of the practitioner, is necessary to avoid them.

Note B.

The vaccine vesicle might, if it were desired, be extirpated by the knife or caustic, although, if the vesicle be sufficiently developed to excite notice, the surgical remedy would be at least as bad as the disease. In regard to medical remedies, I have had occasion to observe their inefficiency in cases where inflammatory diseases, requiring treatment, have occurred during the progress of cowpox. The depletive remedies employed for the former diseases did not affect the progress of the vaccine vesicle. When this vesicle is slow and diminutive, it is commonly owing to the coëxistence of some other cutaneous affection.

In regard to mercurial salivation, although the treatment proposed by Dr. Pearson and others may have been reiterated in many volumes, yet I believe that most practitioners of experience find themselves obliged to rely upon time and palliatives, aided by the withdrawal of the cause.

Note C.

The modern introduction of the non-mercurial treatment in syphilis might almost lead us to consider this malady, also, as among the self-limited diseases. Although syphilis, as it existed in the days of Mr. Hunter, appears to have yielded to mercury alone, so that this eminent author regarded it as one of the distinguishing traits of the disease, that it had no tendency to spontaneous recovery; yet the experience of the last twenty years has shown that syphilis, as it now exists in all its prominent varieties, has been cured, in many thousands of cases, by a treatment in which no mercury in any shape is employed. Nevertheless, the treatment by the anti-phlogistic method. which has been substituted, requires, in order to be successful, more or less depletion, abstinence, and positive rest, conjoined occasionally with other remedies. So that the disease still undergoes efficient treatment; and, indeed, when it is wholly neglected, as it sometimes is by the abject and the reckless, it results in the most deplorable consequences, of which our hospitals and almshouses furnish sufficient and frequent examples.

Note D.

Corvisart died of a disease of the heart; Laennec and Armstrong of pulmonary consumption. Other examples may be found of persons who were writers on the diseases of which they afterwards died.

Note E.

Ulceration in the tonsils and palate is the most common lesion in scarlatina, but the other morbid appearances discovered in autopsies of cases of this disease are exceedingly various and uncertain. Among those which I have observed, or which have been noticed by my medical friends in this city, are ulcerations in the larynx, and inflammation of the mucous membrane of the trachea and bronchiæ. In one case of thirty-six hours' duration, the chief morbid appearance, in addition to the ulcerated throat, was an extensive peritonitis with effusion of coagulating lymph lining most of the abdominal cavity.

Serous effusions in and upon the brain have been occasionally noticed, but most frequently in the secondary forms of the disease. In the child of an eminent physician in this city, whose case and autopsy I witnessed, there was slight ulceration of the tonsils, but no lesion of any important viscus could be detected, though diligently sought for by our best pathological anatomists. Two similar cases have been stated to me, and I find them also noticed by some writers on the disease. In these cases the poison of the disease seems to destroy life, without exciting inflammatory action.

Family predisposition appears to influence the tendency to mortality in scarlatina. In some cases the children of a family all die in rapid succession. A predisposition to take the disease seems also affected by the same cause, so that it sometimes operates during the same season upon members of the same family residing in different places, without personal intercourse.

The latent period between the inception and development of this disease appears subject to great variation. I knew a patient to be taken with scarlet fever in forty-eight hours after arriving in this country by a passage of forty days from Europe. In this instance, as no case existed in the ship, the latent period must have been less than two days, or more than forty.

Scarlatina and some other eruptive fevers reciprocally affect the development of each other. During the prevalence of measles and scarlet fever in this city, in the winter and spring of 1832, a considerable number of cases occurred, in which the two diseases, each preserving its own distinctive character, were successively passed through by patients, without quitting their beds, yet the diseases were in no wise blended, or intermixed. In the family of a lady residing in Tremont Place, five individuals had scarlet fever, and three of them measles, nearly at the same time. The circumstances are interesting. One child had measles first, the disappearance of which was immediately followed by scarlatina; both diseases proved mild, and were completed in about twenty days. Another child had severe scarlatina with a bad throat, the ulcers of which were not healed before the sixteenth day. After this the patient remained stationary, with a quick pulse, and without return of appetite or strength, for several days more, when the eruption of measles appeared under the cuticle which was desquamating from scarlatina, and passed through its regular course. A third child in the same family was affected in a more singular manner. The eruption of measles appeared first, with slight catarrhal symptoms, and continued one day. It then vanished, and was in two days succeeded by scarlet fever. This lasted about a week, and when the patient was expected to get well, the crimson eruption of measles reäppeared, and lasted three days more. In these cases the two diseases, though probably coëxisting in the body at the same time, and in the last case decidedly so, were never extant at once in an active or characteristic form. There was no reason to suppose that the intensity of either disease was diminished, or aggravated, by the presence of the other.

Scarlet fever exists in some cases where its presence is not suspected, as the following cases, selected from a number of similar ones, may show. A child, previously well, was taken in fits at night, and died on the following morning. As the disease was not epidemic at the time, the nature of the complaint was not suspected till a few hours before death, when another child coming out with the eruption, this circumstance led me to an examination of the throat of the first, which was found ulcerated. In another case, a child was affected with a very troublesome rheumatic stiff neck. On inquiry, it was ascertained that a scarlet efflorescence had existed on the preceding week, of which the rheumatism was doubtless a sequel, though the nature of the eruption had not been apprehended.

The sequelæ or secondary effects of scarlet fever are extremely various. Rheumatic affections are among the most common. Dropsical effusions are frequent, both in the cellular texture and in large cavities. Anasarca and ascites are not of uncommon occurrence. I have seen hydrocele, which disappeared spontaneously in a few weeks, and hydrocephalus, which proved fatal. Troublesome indurations of the parotid and submaxillary glands often occur, and may, or may not, be followed by suppuration. A fatal induration of the whole anterior neck is sometimes met with. This I have seen both in the primary and secondary disease. A purulent or sanious discharge from the ears occasionally follows scarlet fever, and sometimes continues long enough to destroy the organic texture, and with it the sense of hearing, in one or both ears. Erysipelas and roseola are among the other appearances which I have seen to supervene upon this uncertain disease. Fortunately, however, the largest portion of cases are attended with no sequelæ, or with such as disappear spontaneously in their own time, without permanent injury to the patient.

Note F.

We have sufficient evidence that many cases of gout, both in this country and Europe, have had their paroxysms abridged by the use of colchicum, and different species of veratrum. Some individuals are fortunate enough to obtain this effect under a moderate dose, which only affects the bowels. But in most persons it is necessary to take enough of the medicine to produce vomiting and temporary prostration, before the desired result can be obtained. This effect is sometimes so severe that many patients prefer the disease to the remedy, and in fact the practice is hardly warranted in the case of very feeble or aged persons.

Three cases have occurred to me, in which gout has disappeared altogether under an entire abstinence from spirituous and fermented liquids. In one of these it is now thirteen years since a paroxysm occurred, and in another seven years, the individuals both enjoying good health, and leading active lives. The third case was that of a gentleman of this city, lately deceased at seventy-six years of age, who had suffered more than twenty years with gout, and was reduced to use crutches. After commencing a course of entire abstinence, the paroxysms began to abate in violence, and for the last seven years of his life he assured me he had not felt the sensation of gout. In his last illness a slight chiragra occurred after taking a dose of tincture of rhubarb. Some other cases are now in the progress of trial, with apparent alleviation of the disease.

I have been told by others that this plan of treatment has in some instances failed to be followed by relief, and very probably this may be true; but such instances have not yet come under my personal observation, where the experiment has been fairly made in the acute disease.

Note G.

The natural history of the small ascarides is curious, and not well understood. Many individuals are infested with them in childhood, but get rid of them as they advance in years. Some, however, are troubled with them during the whole of a long life, though they are represented as less annoying after middle age than before. They most commonly appear periodically, both in children and adults, after intervals of from three to six weeks. During the intervals they are neither felt nor seen in the discharges. Their periodical return is announced by a sense of itching and burning at the extremity of the rectum, felt principally in the evening, sometimes producing tumefaction, and eruption of the neighboring skin. This irritation continues to recur every evening for perhaps a week, or more, and then ceases. During this time the worms are discharged alive and active in every alvine evacuation. Cathartics and enemata bring away vast numbers of them, but without diminishing the annoyance occasioned by those which remain behind. At length they spontaneously cease to appear, the irritation subsides, cathartics no longer bring them to light, and the inexperienced practitioner flatters himself that the evil is remedied. Nevertheless, after a few weeks, they again return in undiminished numbers, attended by the same phenomena as before. Whether the new race are cotemporaries of the old, or descendants from them, it is not easy to tell; but the latter supposition seems most probable.

It is commonly believed that the principal residence of ascarides is in the rectum, because they are most felt there. They have been found, however, in other parts of the alimentary tube. Many patients, immediately after a cessation of the annoyance in the rectum, are visited by pain in the epigastrium, attended with costiveness and clay-colored discharges. This state continues for two or three days, and is then followed by a bilious diarrhœa. I have repeatedly known these consecutive events to occur with great regularity for half a dozen years, so much so that my inquiries are generally directed towards this cause, when children have complained of epigastric pains at regular periods. Whether, in these cases, the worms ascend to the duodenum and mouth of the biliary duct, or whether the whole is an affair of sympathy, future autopsies may perhaps determine.

The nidus of these animals, and perhaps the food also, appears to be the mucus which lines the alimentary canal. Buried in this substance, they resist the effect of the most violent cathartics and vermifuges, oil of turpentine and croton not excepted. If it be permitted to derive an hypothesis from the phenomena which they exhibit, it would be, that during a greater part of the time they remain quietly embedded in this mucus, deriving from it their habitation and nourishment, being at the same time secured from the effects of the peristaltic motion by this and by the adhesive power of suction; but that at certain periods, perhaps at their generating seasons, they issue forth from this covert, and mingle themselves in the contents of the alimentary canal; in consequence of which they are liable to be expelled with the common mass.

I have known ascarides to be eradicated by a severe dysentery. In some cases they have been totally removed by large injections of oil, particularly of lamp oil. But more frequently they resist these and most other remedies for a series of years. A temporary palliative may always be found in small injections of weak salt water, or even of an ounce or two of cold water.

Note H.

I would by no means undervalue the exertions which have been made, and are still making, by indefatigable and distinguished men, for the control of what are called pestilential epidemics. I would only be understood to state that no one method of treatment, in the diseases enumerated, appears to have acquired sufficient credit with the profession generally, to be turned in their hands to any great practical account. The records of medical literature show that a period of ten years has seldom elapsed without the annunciation of some effectual mode of practice, in some one of these diseases. And, what is more, the amount of evidence with which these statements are supported, and the pathological skill with which the indications are explained, seem sometimes sufficient to shake the incredulity of the most sceptical. Nevertheless, after a certain term of years, the diseases are found to be fatal as before, and fresh innovations in practice take the place of the old, and excite confidence anew among the sanguine and ardent members of the profession. The truth is, that no epidemic is equally malignant in all seasons and places; and, from some unknown cause, the laws which affect its tendency to death or recovery are essentially different in different climates at the same period, or in the same climate at different periods. This fact must be known to those who have personal experience in regard to these diseases, or who are conversant in their epidemic history. Reliance, therefore, cannot be justly accorded to any mode of treatment which has not had the testimony of a large number of years in its favor, and this also under a proper variety of situations and circumstances. Were it otherwise, these diseases, in the hands of the medical profession, would long ago have ceased to be pestilences.

Note I.

I am aware that some of the most distinguished French pathologists of the present day incline to the opinion that many acute diseases, or at least inflammations, are incapable of being shortened in their duration, by art. [See marginal note, page 30.] The opposite opinion prevails very generally in this country and in England, and it would be premature to consider the question as decided, until it has been submitted more extensively to the test of comparative numerical results. It is certain that the most distressing symptoms of acute inflammations are often arrested at once by remedies. This happens, for example, from blood-letting in croup and pleurisy, and from opium in strangury and dysentery. If, however, the disease is fully established before the application of remedies, it usually goes on to complete its course, and in that case the remedies are palliatives only. And if remedies be applied in the incipient stage, an uncertainty hangs over our diagnosis, for the supposed pleurisy may have been rheumatism, and the supposed croup may have been catarrh, or laryngismus; for even the physical signs require a certain maturity of development in disease to render them satisfactory. Leaving, then, as undecided, the question of positive duration in acute inflammations, we do not risk much in asserting that their character is often essentially modified by treatment, so that they are more easily supported by the patient, and the apparent danger attending them diminished. We must wait for the modern spirit of *accurate* inquiry to furnish a further light on this subject.

Note K.

As examples, it may be stated that the salivation produced by mercury gets well of itself, provided the original cause is discontinued. An issue made by caustic, or otherwise, gets well after the original cause has ceased to operate; but if an accessory cause is present, such as the pressure of an irritating foreign substance, it then fails to heal. The local atmosphere may be considered as an original, or an accessory cause, in those diseases which are benefited by change of climate or situation. A long train of diseases might be mentioned, which are brought on, or kept up, by injurious habits of life, and are relieved or cured, not by medicines, but by a removal of the habit under which they have been, or continue to be, induced. Such are the diseases which attend on sedentary life, intemperate indulgences, lactation, insalubrity of diet, &c.

Sometimes a disease, the cause of which is not removed, may disappear in consequence of a new habit, by which the system becomes capable of bearing with impunity the influence of this cause; as in sea-sickness.

ON THE

TREATMENT OF DISEASE:

AN INTRODUCTORY LECTURE, DELIVERED BEFORE THE MEDICAL CLASS AT THE MASSACHUSETTS MEDICAL COLLEGE IN BOSTON, NOVEMBER 3, 1852.

OF the sciences which have most occupied the time and labor of mankind, a certain number lead by their investigations to clear and positive results, and enlarge the amount of human knowledge by the discovery and promulgation of absolute truth. Another portion lead only to results which are probable or presumptive in their character, and which furnish to mankind rules of action, in cases where better lights cannot be obtained. To the former class has been given the name of exact sciences, and to the latter the name of presumptive or conjectural sciences. Mathematics form an exact science, on the conclusions of which, when once known, there can be no difference of opinion. In like manner, chemistry and mechanics, astronomy and portions of natural history, are examples of exact sciences, the demonstrations of which, when once made clear, may afterwards be modified and enlarged, but are never fundamentally shaken. On the other hand, the important sciences of ethics and politics, of commerce and finance, of government, and speculative theology, are inexact in many of their principles, as is proved by the widely different constructions under which men receive and apply them to practice.

It would at first seem that the exact sciences were those most worthy the cultivation of intelligent minds, inasmuch as they lead to satisfactory, and therefore to gratifying, results; and because, in their more elevated departments, they involve and require some of the highest reaches of the human intellect. But in the opinions of mankind, as evinced by their practice, the opposite judgment prevails, and probably nine tenths of the labor of educated and intellectual men are employed on studies which are, in their nature, uncertain and conjectural.

The cause of this great ascendency in the

attention given to the inexact sciences, is to be found in the vast and paramount importance of their subjects, and also in the difficulty of consummating their great ends. It is much more important to mankind to know how to avoid anarchy and crime, war, famine, poverty and pestilence, than it is to know that the planet Saturn has a ring, or that a lily has six stamens, that light can be polarized, or that potass can be decomposed. Yet, while the latter propositions are susceptible of absolute demonstration, the former processes, which bear directly on human happiness or misery, are frequently removed beyond our foresight or control. The wisest men often fail to influence the destinies of states, families, and individuals, and the shrewdest calculators are baffled in regard to a coming crop, a pecuniary crisis, a glut in the commercial market, or a change in the public morals. Nevertheless, the wise man, conscious of superior talent, and the philanthropist, desirous of the public weal, and even the interested man, who looks to his personal advantage and progress, must give themselves and their energies to studies which involve the immediate wants of their fellow-men, even though their best directed efforts should fail of the desired results. And the simple reason is, that, if the best qualified minds decline to undertake this task, it will most assuredly be assumed by the ignorant and presumptuous.

Preëminent among the inexact and speculative sciences stands *practical medicine*, a science older than civilization, cultivated and honored in all ages, powerful for good or for evil, progressive in its character, but still unsettled in its principles; remunerative in fame and fortune to its successful cultivators, and rich in the fruits of a good conscience to its honest votaries. Encumbered as it is with difficulty, fallacy and doubt, medicine yet constitutes one of the most attractive of the learned professions. It is largely represented in every city, village and hamlet. Its imperfections are lost sight of in the overwhelming importance of its objects. The living look to it for succor; the dying call on it for rescue.

The greatest boons and the most important objects presented to our aspirations in this life, are not to be approached through paths which are straight and unmistakable. The avenues to most of them are shadowed by doubts or clogged with incessant obstacles. Next to the spiritual welfare of men, the preservation of their lives, the peace and safety of their communities, the acquirement and preservation of their worldly goods are among the objects which take strongest hold on their desires. Yet grave doubts are justifiable, whether any precise means have yet been agreed upon by which these desirable ends can with certainty be attained. And if any one deems it a reproach on medicine that its cultivators have not arrived at a common faith and practice, let him consider whether the laborers in other fields, however honest their intentions, are agreed in their theological creeds and political platforms.

Considering the great importance of the objects of medicine, the frequent and earnest appeals made for its assistance, and the vast sums annually expended in its remuneration, it is not surprising that disappointment and complaint often follow the failures, necessary or unnecessary, of medical practice. "Man is of few days and full of trouble." Yet, in the face of this acknowledged truth, he requests and expects that his physician will provide him with many days, and remove at least his bodily troubles. This expectation on his part is reasonable or otherwise, according to the circumstances under which it is made. It is unreasonable, if his case is helpless, and he is merely paying the debt of suffering and death which his mortal nature exacts. But it is reasonable and proper, if his complaint is of a curable kind, or if, whether curable or not, his physician has claimed and vaunted the power to remove it.

Most men form an exaggerated estimate of the powers of medicine, founded on the common acceptation of the name, that medicine is the art of curing diseases. That this is a false definition, is evident from the fact that many diseases are incurable, and that one such disease must at last happen to every living man. A far more just definition would be, that medicine is the art of understanding diseases, and of curing or relieving them when possible. Under this acceptation our science would, at least, be exonerated from reproach, and would stand on a basis capable of supporting a reasonable and durable system for the amelioration of human maladies.

Every young man, who proposes to become a member of the medical profession, should ask himself whether he considers medicine a liberal and honorable science, to be followed for the good it may do to mankind, or as a dishonest trade, to be pursued for the purpose of profiting himself by the deception of his fellow-men. If he accepts his profession in the first sense, he will strive to understand his science in all its bearings, and practise it with conscience and fidelity; if in the latter, he will put his conscience aside, and study only the low arts which entrap the credulous and unwary.

With the trade of medicine I have nothing to do. Knowing that I address an ingenuous and cultivated audience, composed mainly of young men who are looking forward to an honest and honorable place in professional life, I make no apology for proceeding to express my belief of the manner in which medicine should be practised and disease treated, for the reciprocal benefit of him who gives, and of him who receives its aids.

Let no one deceive himself by believing that success, stable, permanent, honorable success, can be attained without knowledge of the great principles of the profession and science of medicine. This knowledge must consist in an accurate acquaintance with the structure and offices of the human body, and the laws of its healthy condition. After these follows the science of pathology, involving the great and fundamental art of diagnosis, by which the diseases of the human body are detected, and distinguished rightly from each other. The power of distinguishing diseases lies at the root of all correct and enlightened practice, and without it all medical action is empirical and fortuitous. There is no more pernicious error than for a physician to believe that he can prescribe safely for the symptoms of a sick man, without understanding, in some measure, the nature of his disease. Symptoms are of various import, according to the seat of their origin and the nature of their causes; and if taken alone without a correct interpretation of these attendant considerations, they often lead to a wrong result, or to no result at all. A patient not unfrequently sends for a physician on account of a certain symptom which is distressing him, and which may be, for example, a pain in the abdomen, or in the head. Now, a pain in the abdomen may arise from colic or peritonitis, from rheumatism or neuralgia, from dysentery, from calculus, carcinoma or strangulation. And, in like manner, a pain in the head may arise from a multitude of different and even opposite causes. Now it is well known that the kind of treatment which is effectual in one case, is pernicious in another; and he who prescribes for the symptom irrespectively of the cause, is quite as likely to do mischief to his patient as good, and quite as likely to destroy life as to save it.

If the question be asked, what makes a great physician, and one who is appealed to by his peers, and by the discerning portion of the public, for counsel in difficult cases, I would answer, that *he is a great physician who, above other men, understands diagnosis.* It is not he who promises to cure all maladies, who has a remedy ready for every symptom, or one remedy for all symptoms; who boasts that success never fails him, when his daily history gives the lie to such assertion. It is rather he, who, with just discrimination, looks at a case in all its difficulties; who, to habits of correct reasoning, adds the acquirements obtained from study and observation; who is trustworthy in common things for his common sense, and in professional things for his judgment, learning and experience; who forms his opinion positive or approximative, according to the evidence; who looks at the necessary results of inevitable causes; who promptly does what man may do of good, and carefully avoids what he may do of evil. Examples are rare of this perfection, yet, for an approach to such a standard of professional excellence, I would venture to direct your remembrance to the venerable ex-professor, fortunately yet among us, of the theory and practice in this University.

Every citizen, whose capacity is able to reach the ordinary affairs of life, is aware that the persons most capable of discharging the common offices, or of exercising the common arts and duties of life, are the individuals who have, by talents, education and practice, become EXPERTS in those arts and duties;—and that, on the other hand, those persons who profess to have acquired knowledge by intuition, to have become learned without labor, and to have arrived by short cuts at results and qualifications which demand years of preparatory training, must be incompetent and treacherous sources of reliance. And it is the general admission of this truth which gives support and confidence to the various professions, arts and callings, to which men devote their lives.

A little machine called a watch is carried about by most persons, and when this machine has stopped or is out of order, they do not lay their own ignorant hands upon it, but submit the case to the skill of an expert, who is known to be qualified to judge and act in such cases. It is the duty of this artist, when applied to, to examine the interior of the watch, to ascertain, by the use of his skill, in what part the disease is situated, and to apply to that part the appropriate remedy. If a spring or a chain is broken, it must be restored; if the wheels are out of gear, they must be put in place; if the hands only have caught, they have only to be liberated, and if the pivots are dry and rough, they must be oiled or cleaned; —and, lastly, if the watch has had a destructive fall, if it has been crushed by being trodden on, if it has lain a month in the salt water, or if it is worn out by running steadily for threescore years and ten, then the case is incurable, and the only palliative advice which the practitioner can render is, that the owner should procure a new watch, or reconcile himself to do without one.

But suppose there resides in the place a watch-doctor who prescribes for symptoms, and who, among other things, has a remedy for the symptom of stopping, and that this remedy consists in a certain kind of friction, shaking, or manipulation, an ointment applied to the outside, or an invisible particle of some nugatory substance inserted into the inside; and suppose that one or two watches in a hundred which had stopped by accident, should by accident resume their motions under such treatment, could anything but the most unmitigated folly draw the inference that such a person is entitled to become the accredited horologer to the community?

What is so conspicuously true in the common business of life, is only an example of what is more vitally true in the practice of medicine. If a man has had the misfortune to get a shot or a stab in his body, he does not need a doctor who administers a specific dose or a sovereign plaster for holes in the body; he wants a man who can tell him whether the wound has passed inside or outside of his peritoneum, and whether it is requisite for him to make his will, or to make arrangements for pursuing his journey.

But the prescribing for symptoms in the dark is not the only instance in which false logic has entered into medical reasoning. It is not less absurd to suppose that disconnected events, which have closely followed each other, have therefore a necessary dependence upon each other. Shrewd, practical men do not thus govern themselves in the common affairs of life. A merchant, about to send a ship to sea, endeavors to find a captain to take charge of her who understands navigation, who can keep his run and determine his place, who studies the weather and is on the lookout for a lee shore, and who in emergencies can judge whether it is necessary or not to cut away the masts or throw over the cargo. But suppose a man appears, and such have been, who announces that he has a specific bottle of oil with which he cures tempests, and by pouring a teaspoonful of which upon the waves, the storm is speedily made to cease! Would any prudent owner intrust his vessel to such a man, and on such grounds, even though he should produce a hundred certificates that storms had stopped in half a day or half an hour after the application of his remedy? For these certificates, if true, would only prove that, in a certain number of cases, a result had followed by accident, which common sense, and, if necessary, a thousand opposite cases, would show had nothing to do with the pretended cause.

What would be true of the apparent or alleged cure of a tempest at sea, is no less true of the pseudo-cures which every day take place in diseases which are self-limited, paroxysmal or recidivous in their character. There are doubtless living many men who believe themselves to have been cured half a dozen times of various diseases, of fevers and inflammations, of neuralgia, rheumatism, gout and asthma; and each time perhaps by a different remedy, but who, on the next imprudence or returning period, are destined to find themselves feverish, neuralgic, gouty, or asthmatic still.

Deceptions in medicine are occasioned not only by the dishonesty of charlatans, but quite as often by the well-meaning credulity of other practitioners, whose intellect is impulsive, or whose education has been unduly curtailed. It is so flattering to a man's self-love to believe that his chance shots have sometimes taken effect, that physicians of regular position may pass their lives in mere speculative and random efforts at curing diseases, shutting their eyes against their own failures, and not allowing themselves to consider that in a certain portion of successful cases which they had failed to understand, the disease in truth got well without, or perhaps in spite of, their misdirected and embarrassing practice.

Medicine is a great good and an unquestionable blessing to mankind, when it is administered by discriminating and intelligent hands with sincerity and good judgment. It disappoints expectation, and fails to accomplish its mission, when the agent who dispenses it falls into the mistaken resource of professing infallibility, and of raising hopes which he knows not how to accomplish. No man is deemed to be safe in his worldly affairs who is afraid to look into his own pecuniary condition. Neither is a physician safe in his practice or his reputation, who is afraid to face the case of his patient in all its bearings. That man is most to be relied on who looks calmly and understandingly at the emergency before him, who knows the import of signs, and deduces from them the probable tenor of coming events; who is aware of the great truth that all men must die, but is also aware of the more gratifying truth that most sick men recover; and who, in particular exigencies, inquires of his reason and his knowledge, in which of these two immediate categories his patient is placed, and how far the event of the case is within his control. He will then interfere or he will wait, he will act or he will forbear, as he only knows how who can form a correct verdict from the evidence before him, and who knows the immeasurable good or harm which hangs on medical practice.

The vulgar standard of medical character depends very much on the supposed successful result of cases. But this is not the true standard, for the best physicians as well as the most popular practitioners often lose their patients, and even their own lives, from common diseases; while, on the other hand, the most injudicious treatment and the most reckless exposures are not unfrequently survived. Laennec and Bichat, two of the most distinguished lights of modern medicine, died of the very diseases they were themselves investigating. Preissnitz, the prince of modern empirics, himself a robust peasant, died of premature disease at the age of fifty-two, in the midst of his own water-cure. It is well known that the most thronged and popular places of resort for grave, difficult and intractable cases, are those from which there are most funerals. On the other hand, men support life in certain cases under every extreme of opposite treatment, under ultra-depletion and ultra-stimulation, under heroic practice and nugatory practice, under "hot drops" and cold douches, under drachm doses of calomel and imponderable doses of moonshine. Clot Bey, and his two or three associate Frenchmen, entered a plague hospital at Cairo in the height of the epidemic. They shut themselves up in the concentrated atmosphere of the infection, they remained in bed in contact with dying patients, they wore the shirts of those who had just expired, they inoculated themselves with the secretions of pestilential buboes,—and all to no purpose. They were alive some years afterwards, and quarrelling with each other for the glory of their hair-brained enterprise. Four thieves in the plague at Marseilles freely prosecuted their robberies in the infected houses of the dead and dying; and the aromatic vinegar, which has immortalized their prophylactic practice, was very probably an impromptu invention brought forward by them to procure their exemption from punishment.

The humility which we may learn from the limited influence of our art on the health and lives of mankind is probably a far safer guide to a correct practice, than the fanatical confidence with which unenlightened ultraists of every sect carry out their respective dogmas. In a sphere of action where some good may always be done, and where much harm often is done, and "fools rush in where angels fear to tread," it is well to consider some of the rules which may lead an honest inquirer after truth to the nearest attainment to a correct judgment and practice.

Supposing, what I would fain wish might always happen, that the physician is duly and thoroughly imbued with knowledge of his science, the first great question, which presents itself in every case or emergency, is that which involves the diagnosis. This being established, the practitioner is enabled to avail himself of the lights of reason and experience in regard to a correct course of therapeutic proceeding. But it often happens that the nature of the case cannot be made out in one, or two, or three interviews with the patient, and we are obliged to wait for the gradual development of diagnostic symptoms, as a judge and jury in a like case would be expected to postpone, or wait for the arrival of witnesses. It is a mistaken pride which leads physicians to commit themselves by an oracular guess at first sight, which the events of the succeeding day may show to have been erroneous. Moreover, if, from the obscure character of the case, or the imperfection of our science, diagnosis is impossible, we should then so generalize our treatment that we may include what is possible of good, and exclude what is probable of harm.

Having settled, as well as our means admit, the pathological condition of our patient, the next question is that which regards the probable tendency of the disease if left to itself. Attention to this point is of high importance, since it will prevent us from neglecting our patients in grave and dangerous affections, as well as from annoying them with useless appliances in short, safe or unimportant cases. Many diseases are insidious in their origin. The nervous imbecility which has its foundation laid in modern schools, the slight cough and evening flush which herald approaching phthisis, soon get beyond the reach of medical means, unless seasonably detected by the wary eye of the practitioner. A simple discharge from the ear may terminate in deafness, and an ulcer of the cornea in loss of sight. A protracted intermittent at length undermines the health, and neglected syphilis ends in a miserable death. Cases like these require prompt and energetic interference on the part of the practitioner. On the other hand, diseases which are light in themselves, and tend to speedy recovery, as common catarrh, hooping-cough, varicella, and a host of other things, if they occur in healthy subjects, and are not complicated with graver affections, may safely be left to themselves, or treated with the mildest remedies and cautionary measures.

Another most important question, exercising the hopes and fears of every practitioner, from its connection with reputation, safety and life, is that which relates to the curability of diseases. Is the disease amenable to medical treatment, or not? If the case is of a recoverable character, and happily a great majority of our cases are so, the physician should anxiously and carefully have recourse to the recorded authorities of his science, and to his own personal experience. In doing this he should beware of implicitly trusting those who have published only the favorable side of their practice, preferring to build up a temporary reputation rather than to promulgate unpopular truths. And, in analyzing his own experience, he should equally beware of hasty generalizations, of impressions made by remarkable examples, rather than by aggregates of well observed and duly arranged cases, from which alone impartial and correct inferences are to be drawn.

In accordance with such views, we shall find many cases which are, for the most part, capable of being arrested or broken up by the interposition of remedies. Thus, the grave and various symptoms which result from an overloaded stomach are at once removed by the action of an emetic, or sometimes of a laxative; colic in like manner yields to opium or to purgatives; syphilis is cured by mercury, and sometimes without it; and certain inflammatory attacks apparently yield to seasonable depletion. Moreover, in other cases which cannot be thus arrested, but which, from their nature, must run a destined course, it is generally admitted that the safety of the patient may be promoted, or perhaps the duration of the case abridged, by remedial treatment. This is believed to be true in regard to evacuations at the commencement of febrile and inflammatory diseases, and to a multitude of other remedies applicable in various cases. But on this subject it is extremely difficult to obtain decisive and satisfactory knowledge. It involves a question, the settlement of which is to be approached by extensive and contrasted numerical observations, a large portion of which yet remain to be made, although we have valuable contributions and examples on many subjects.

On the other hand, when we know that a case is self-limited or incurable, we are to consider how far it is in our power to palliate or diminish sufferings which we are not competent to remove. Here is a most important field for medical practice, and one which calls for an exceedingly large portion of the time and efforts of every physician. When we consider that most diseases occupy, from necessity, a period of some days or weeks, that many of them continue for months, and some for years, and finally that a large portion of mankind die of some lingering or chronic disease, we shall see that the study of palliatives is not only called for, but really constitutes one of the most common, as well as the most useful and beneficent employments of a medical man.

In the use of efficient remedies, much depends upon deciding the proper stage or time to which their employment is applicable. Some curative agents can with propriety be used only at the outset of the diseases, and if this opportunity is lost, the remedies are afterwards less effectual, and perhaps even injurious. Venesection, in the early stage of certain acute diseases, may be productive of great good; in the middle stages it is of less benefit, or of none at all; and in the latter stages it is injurious and inadmissible. On the other hand, wine and opiates, which are strongly contra-indicated in the first stage, are afterwards not only tolerated with impunity, but in certain cases are taken with decided benefit.

But, gentlemen, the agents which we oppose to the progress of disease may, by excessive or ill-timed application, become themselves the pregnant sources of disease. Every prudent practitioner is bound to consider the effect and tendency of the remedy he is using, and to inquire whether the means employed to counteract the existing disease are not, in their turn, likely to produce evil to the patient; and, if so, whether the evil will be greater or less than the disease for which they are administered. The sudden healing of an old ulcer, issue or eruption, may be followed by symptoms more serious in their character than those which have been removed. Many remedial processes, if employed in excess, or with injudicious frequency, result in permanent injury to the patient. The habitual use of active cathartics, although attended with temporary relief, seldom fails to bring on or aggravate a permanent state of costiveness. Large and often repeated blood-letting tends to the establishment of debility and anemia in some subjects, or of reäction and plethora in others. Opium and other narcotics are in themselves, if abused, fertile sources of disease. The modern crying evil of polypharmacy and over-medication is profitable to the druggist, habitual to too many physicians, and annoying, if not detrimental, to most patients.

On account of these and similar considerations, much discretion is needed on the part of the physician to enable him to judge rightly of the kind of treatment which it may be safe and proper to employ, and of the degree and amount of that treatment, and of the requisite length of time for its continuance. Medical practice, in many cases, points to the direct substitution of a positive good for a positive evil; but unfortunately, in other cases, it admits only of a choice between evils; and in these cases not only the knowledge and experience, but also the judgment and common sense of the practitioner, are put in indispensable requisition to lead him to a correct issue.

It is wrong to suppose, as is often done, that the opportunities for doing good in medicine are limited to the effect of specific remedies, or to the application of drugs and instruments. The enlightened physician surveys the whole ground of his patient's case, and looks for the presence of any deleterious agencies or unremoved causes of disease. Many morbid affections, which have resisted powerful remedies, cease speedily on the discovery and removal of their sustaining cause. This is the case with various specific complaints produced by particular drugs and stimulants when habitually used. A child is often sick from an error in the diet, health or habits of the nurse or mother. An individual frequently suffers from the quality and quantity of his habitual food or drink, or of his exercise, air, occupation, or clothing. The starved infant and the overfed gourmand, the drunkard and the ascetic, the pale student and the emaciated seamstress, require removal and reform, not drugs and medicines. A patient dies of phthisis in a confined office or a damp northern climate, who might have enjoyed long life in an active occupation or a more pure and temperate atmosphere. On the other hand, men fall victims to the fevers and abdominal diseases of the south and west, who might have escaped disease by a timely removal to the north. It is as necessary in many cases that the physician should inquire into the situation, diet, habits and occupation of the patient, as that he should feel his pulse or explore his chest. It often happens that the disordered state of the one cannot be corrected until the other has been previously set right; and a little dietetic instruction, or even moral advice, is more serviceable than a technical prescription.

In regard to their duration, their probable issue, and their susceptibility of relief, the physician may profitably divide his cases into three classes; those which are curable, those which are temporarily self-limited, and those which are incurable.* In the first class, or that of curable diseases, are to be included those morbid affections which we know, or have reason to believe, are under the control of remedies, so that they can be arrested, or abridged, in duration. For the most part, acute inflammatory diseases, when not of fatal intensity, are mitigated by depletion and the antiphlogistic regimen, more or less ac-

* See note, page 21.

tively enforced, according to the degree of violence. Spasmodic diseases, on the contrary, are influenced by opiates, antispasmodics and tonics, and by the removal of their cause, when it can be discovered and remedied, as in the case of dentition, indigestible food, &c. Sympathetic diseases are to be addressed through the medium, organ, or texture, which is primarily affected. Thus, a headache depending upon a disordered stomach, or a hysteric affection upon irregularity of the uterine function, are to be treated under this view of the subject. Hemorrhages and other morbid discharges are to be dealt with by removing the cause when practicable, by diminishing vascular activity, or by quieting the discharging surfaces with opiates, or contracting them with astringents. There is one class of curable diseases which are controlled chiefly by specific remedies, being in some instances suspended, in others radically removed. Thus, gout is relieved by colchicum, and intermittents, it is believed, by quinine. Scabies is cured by sulphur, syphilis by mercury, goitre, as we are informed, by iodine, and various chronic eruptions by arsenic and corrosive sublimate. The foregoing examples will serve to illustrate, not only the power of medicine, but also the great variety of grounds which should govern medical practice, and the importance of an intelligent diagnosis, as well as a knowledge of therapeutic means.

In the next subdivision, or that of self-limited diseases, we include those "which receive limits from their own nature, and not from foreign influences, and which, after they have obtained foothold in the system, cannot in the present state of our knowledge be eradicated or abridged by art, but to which there is due a certain succession of processes, to be completed in a certain time, which time and processes may vary with the constitution and condition of the patient, but are not known to be shortened by medical treatment." Examples are abundant, and are found in typhus and typhoid fever, measles, small-pox, hooping-cough, dysentery, and many other diseases of lighter or graver character.*

It is with regret that we are obliged to acknowledge the existence of a third class, that of incurable diseases, which has been recognized in

* See marginal note, page 31.

all ages as the *opprobrium medicorum*. It includes the long train of internal morbid degenerations, malignant and chronic, by tubercle and granulation, by atrophy and hypertrophy, softening and hardening, scirrhus, encephalosis, ossification, concretion, contraction and dilatation, with their various consequences of phthisis, emphysema, dropsy, epilepsy, paralysis, and a multitude of intractable disorders, in which organs are disabled, functions destroyed, and life itself rendered incapable of continuance.

It is obvious that in the three foregoing classes of disease very different modifications of treatment are required. In curable diseases, our remedial measures should be prompt and energetic in proportion to the emergency of the case, and the certainty of benefit which is to follow their employment. In self-limited diseases, our treatment must be of the expectant character. It consists in doing what we can for the comfort and safety of the patient, avoiding useless and troublesome applications, watching against accidents and complications, and waiting for the salutary operations of nature. In those maladies which are in their nature incurable, we are obliged to confine ourselves to the palliation of suffering, and the removal of causes which may aggravate the disease.

Such, I believe, is the true exposition of the powers and duties of every medical man. The dignity of our science, and the responsibility of our profession, require that we should form just views of the extent of our capacity and duty, and that we should not shrink from avowing them to the world. Our science, imperfect as it is, has achieved as much as any similar science for the prevention, alleviation and removal of the evils which it combats. Let us not bring it into disrepute, by pretending to impossibilities, by asserting what cannot be proved, and by professing what human art is unable to accomplish. A new era will dawn upon medicine when its faithful and enlightened cultivators shall more constantly devote their time and their efforts to enlighten the public mind in regard to the true mission and powers of their science; and when they shall leave to charlatans and fanatics the doubtful and dishonest game of unfounded professional pretension.

PRACTICAL VIEWS

ON

MEDICAL EDUCATION.

PUBLISHED BY VOTE OF THE MEDICAL FACULTY OF HARVARD UNIVERSITY IN 1850.

THE undecided state of public opinion in regard to some of the fundamental points in a course of medical education, including among other things the portion of the term of pupilage proper to be spent in attendance on lectures, is thought to justify a further consideration of the subject. In some of its relations, this subject has already been discussed, in the Transactions of the American Medical Association for 1849, in two reports, pages 353 and 359, to which the reader is particularly referred. The following condensed, but more general view of the subject of medical education is now respectfully submitted to the members of the Association.

Medical instruction should be adapted to the power of students to receive and retain what is communicated to them, and should be confined to what is important to them in their subsequent life.

In modern times the constituent branches of medical science are so expanded, that they are not acquired by any physician in a lifetime, and still less by a student during his pupilage. The same is true even of many individual branches. It is not, therefore, to be conceded that "a scheme of scientific instruction should embrace the whole science, and no part should be omitted;" nor that "a well-digested plan of lectures embraces all that is to be known and taught." Medical science has at this day become so unwieldy, and contains so much that is unnecessary, at least to beginners, that the attempt to explain to students the whole is likely to involve the result of their learning but little.

In Chemistry, at the present time, a thorough adept is unknown. No man living knows all the recorded facts, or all that is to be known and taught, in that science. Organic chemistry alone fills large volumes, though yet in its infancy.

In Materia Medica there are some thousands of substances and their compounds, which possess what is called a medicinal power. Yet it is not probable that any physician effectively reads the one half, or remembers one quarter, or employs in his yearly practice one tenth, of the contents of the common dispensatorics.

In Pathology, so complicated and various are the conditions attendant on the individual forms of disease, and their relations with idiosyncrasy, temporary condition, and external agency, with organic lesions and functional disturbances, that few of the most experienced pathologists can be said to understand their whole science, or to be always competent to its successful application.

In Etiology, the theoretical literature of causes has spread itself out to an extent which is burdensome and unprofitable. It is true, that "man, from his nature, is subject to suffering, disease, and death;" but it is not equally apparent that "the causes by which these conditions are produced are ascertainable." We know nothing of the vehicle of cholera or influenza, nor is it probably in the power of any physician, by any art or application of his knowledge, to produce in a given healthy man a case of common pneumonia or of acute rheumatism, of diabetes or Bright's kidney, of hypertrophy or of cancer, or even of a common boil, or wart.

In Therapeutics, many hundred volumes exist, such as would not have existed, could a knowledge of the cure of diseases be made so easily tangible that it could be spread before the student in the three or five years of his pupilage.

In Anatomy, general and special, microscopic and transcendental;—in Physiology, with its intricate ramifications;—in Surgery, of which several subordinate specialities constitute distinct living professions; it is not to be admitted that the means or time of any ordinary course of lectures can furnish full and complete instruction. Certainly it must be difficult to arrange a course of lectures on any of the extensive sciences which now constitute medicine, if it be indeed true that "the teachers are not justifiable in suppressing any portion."

It is the business of lecturers in medical schools to condense and abridge the sciences which they respectively teach, to distinguish their essential and elementary principles, to sift carefully the useful from the superfluous, and to confine the scope of their teachings, as far as possible, to what is true and profitable, and likely to be remembered and used by their hearers. It is unfortunately too true, that, "in an extended system of instruction, there is much that the student will not master, much that will have escaped his attention, much which he ought to know that he has not learned." The remedy appears to be, to teach him well what he can and should master, and briefly to point out to him the sources, fortunately abundant, from which he may obtain the rest.

Much injury is done to the cause of true learning by medical assumption, amplification and exaggeration, by premature adoption of novelties, and by tenacity of theories, personal or espoused. Students, in all former years, have expended much time in learning what it afterwards cost them both time and trouble to unlearn;—in acquiring, not merely the truths of science, but the crude announcements and plausible doctrines of sanguine or ingenious men. How much time has been wasted, in some of our distinguished seminaries, in acquiring the visionary and now neglected theories of Rush and Broussais!

The most commonly exaggerated branch of medical science is therapeutics. Enlightened physicians well know that many diseases are incurable, and that others are subject to laws of duration which cannot be interrupted by art. Yet students sometimes return from medical schools persuaded that their instructors know how to cure a large part of these diseases, and that, if others are less fortunate, it is attributable to their own fault.

Medical teachers should keep pace with the progress of their respective sciences. Yet, in their haste for the promulgation of novelties, they should not omit to give the proper consideration to the older and more settled principles of science. Medical men are liable to commit the error of adopting premature opinions, unsound practice, and inconvenient changes of language and nomenclature, sometimes from a love of display, and sometimes from a want of self-reliance, and a fear of being thought behind the literature of their time.

The length of a course of lectures is not the

measure of its value to the student. A course of lectures should not outlast the curiosity of its hearers, nor their average pecuniary ability to attend. Custom in this country has generally fixed the limits of these things at about four months. A comprehensive and judicious course, confined to the enforcing of necessary points, is far more profitable than a more discursive course to a wearied and diminishing audience.

Lectures are chiefly wanted to impress by demonstration the practical branches of science, and they are most effective in places where the facilities for such demonstrations can be commanded. Anatomy requires extensive exhibitions by the teacher, and personal dissections by the student. Chemistry and Materia Medica require illustrations by specimens and experiments. Pathology needs the aid of autopsies, museums and the clinical demonstrations of large hospitals. A knowledge of Obstetrics is not perfected without apparatus and practice. Surgery is acquired by witnessing numerous operations, surgical diseases, illustrated explanations, and by personal practice on the dead body. Physical exploration is wholly demonstrative. A knowledge of auscultation can no more be acquired from books, or abstract lectures, than a knowledge of music, or of individual physiognomy.

The intermediate period between lectures should be spent by students in active and original study, approved and confirmed by regular recitations, and by such opportunities as can be commanded for practical, personal experience. Private schools for small classes, and the private teaching of individuals who are suitably qualified and situated, are more advantageous for two thirds of the year, than either the fatiguing jostle of overcrowded rooms, or the listless routine kept up by the survivors of a passive class.

The usefulness of a medical school depends not so much on the length of its session as upon the amount of education, preliminary and ultimate, which it requires, the fidelity with which it exacts its own professed requisitions, and the train of healthy exertion, active inquiry, and rigid, methodical, self-regulating study, to which it introduces its pupils. The longest lectures are of little use to students who want a common education, and whose medical education does not qualify them afterwards to observe, to inquire, and to discriminate. The exacted evidence of three years of well-conducted study is better than the exhibited ticket of a six months' course.

The subjects most important to be well taught in medical schools are the elementary principles which constitute the framework of medical sciences, and the mode of thought and inquiry which leads to just reasoning upon them. After these, most attention should be given to selecting and enforcing such practical truths as will most certainly be wanted by the young practitioner in his future career of responsibility.

The things to be avoided by medical teachers are technicalities, which are unintelligible to beginners,—gratuitous assumptions and citations of doubtful authorities,—prolix dissertations on speculative topics,—excessive minuteness in regard to subjects which are intricate and but little used, and therefore destined to be speedily forgotten. To these may be added controversies, superfluous personal eulogiums and criminations, and all self-exaggeration, personal or local.

REPORT ON HOMŒOPATHY:

MADE TO THE COUNSELLORS OF THE MASSACHUSETTS MEDICAL SOCIETY IN FEBRUARY, 1854.

THE committee appointed by the Counsellors of the Massachusetts Medical Society, to consider the resolution of the Essex North District Society,* and also that of Dr. Spofford, in relation to the subject of Homœopathy, beg leave to Report: —

That the Massachusetts Medical Society was incorporated mainly for the purpose of establishing a proper standard of medical education, and of insuring a competent degree of knowledge among those who should be authorized to practise the profession of medicine in this Commonwealth, and they are not aware that the

* These resolutions contemplated dissolving the connection of Homœopathists with the Society.

Society possess any power to coërce men, after they have been thus educated and qualified, to embrace, or renounce, any theoretical opinions, or modes of practice, which they may innocently believe, or which, not believing, they may think it proper to profess.

In medical science there are certain fundamental laws relating to the structure and functions of the body, and the morbid changes to which it is subject, also regarding the signs by which those changes are discovered, — upon which all well-educated physicians are agreed. But in certain provinces of medical science such fundamental laws, owing to the imperfection of our means of knowledge, cannot at the present time be established. This is the case with Therapeutics, or the art of treating or curing diseases, in which the evidence required by science is difficult to obtain, and in regard to which writers and teachers, sects and individuals, and even the same individual in the course of an ordinary lifetime, may without dishonesty entertain great diversities of opinion.

The tendency of modern observation is such as to lead us to the belief that disease is less frequently under the control of remedial treatment than it was formerly supposed to be. Where observations are impartially made by competent persons, it is found that people recover, and also that they die, under all the ordinary modes of treatment. And the evidence collected from sources which are worthy of reliance is not so abundant or satisfactory as to convince a reasonable man that any general system of practice can be relied on for the cure of all cases. Hence, it is not surprising that diversities, contrasts, and even extravagances in practice, are embraced by the sanguine, the credulous, the uninformed and the interested, frequently based upon no better authority than accident, imperfect observation, or defective power of judgment in the party who adopts them.

The broadest division which has been recognized for centuries, in the treatment of disease, is that which resolves the whole subject into the active and the expectant modes of practice. The first employs various interfering agencies in the management of the sick,—the last waits more on the unassisted course of nature,—and both have long had their exclusive advocates.

To the last of these divisions Homœopathy really, though not avowedly, belongs. Its character is, that, while in reality it waits on the natural course of events, it commends itself to the ignorant and credulous by a professed introduction into the body of inappreciable quantities of medicinal substances. Now the nugatory effect of such quantities is demonstrated by the fact that in civilized life every person is exposed to the daily reception, in the form of solution, dust or vapor, of homœopathic quantities of almost every common substance known in nature and art, without any appreciable consequences being found to follow. And the pretended exactness with which such nominal doses are administered by homœopathic practitioners is doubtless a fallacy, capable of producing in the living body no other effects than those which charlatanry has in all ages produced in the minds and bodies of imaginative patients.

It is a fact much older than the institution of this Society, that visionary systems of practice have replaced each other in the faith of multitudes, at least several times in a century. And this will probably be the case, so long as practical medicine continues to be, what it now is to a great extent, a theoretical and conjectural science. At the present period, among the sects usually called irregular, the homœopathic sect prevails to a considerable extent in this country and in Europe. In the United States it is exceeded only by the sect called Botanic, or Thompsonian practitioners, which at the present time appears, of the two, to number most disciples. It is not probable that the faith of either of these sects will be displaced by a return of their followers to any more enlightened or rational creed. Nevertheless, it is safe to predict that they will both be superseded in the course of time by other systems, not more rational or probable in themselves, but possessing the attraction of greater novelty, or urged upon the credulous with greater adroitness. When the world, and especially the unenlightened part of it, shall be settled in their opinions on other sectarian subjects, we may anticipate unanimity of opinion among them in the science of practical medicine.

But it is not only to expectant medicine, in the form of its counterfeit, homœopathy, that the censure of prejudice and credulity is to be attached. The opposite system of active practice, carried to the extreme usually called heroic, is alike chargeable with evil to the patients, whenever it becomes the absorbing and exclusive course of the practitioner. Physicians are too often led to exaggerate the usefulness of the doctrines in which they have been educated, and especially of those by the exercise of which they obtain their daily bread. In such cases habit gets the ascendency over enlightened judgment, and the man of routine, or of narrow views, asks himself, from day to day, what drug or what appliance he shall next resort to, instead of asking the more important question, whether any drug or any appliance is called for, or is properly admissible in the case.

In Medicine, as in the other inexact sciences which deeply concern the welfare of mankind, enough has been learned to show that extreme measures, either of omission or of commission, are not, when systematized as a whole, productive of benefit or safety to mankind.

It is quite probable that the prevalence, at times, of eccentric and ultra-sectarian doctrines in medicine, is attributable to the exaggerated value attached by physicians themselves to incessant activity in practice, and an assumption of credit for particular modes of medication, to which, as such, they are not entitled. There is often a want of openness in the intercourse of physicians, both enlightened and ignorant, with their patients, who are requested to believe that their cure depends not in any degree on the salutary influences of nature and time, but in the rigid enforcement of a prescribed routine of practice, either active or formal, as the case may be. And when opposite modes of treatment are urged upon the public by different practitioners with reasonings equally specious, it is not surprising that patients should sometimes adopt that which is least troublesome in its operation. Neither is it surprising that they should sometimes embrace even a deception, which absolves them from their allegiance to an unnecessarily severe or troublesome course of treatment.

An honest and independent practitioner, and especially a member of the Massachusetts Medical Society, should never be induced to give his counsel, or his aid in any shape, to empiricism and dishonesty, whether it occur among those who are within or without the pale of its membership. And no consideration of gain or notoriety should induce those, whose age or standing cause them to be resorted to for consultation, to lend their influence or countenance to encourage either the delusions of those who are honest, or the practices of those who are not.

If quackery, individual or gregarious, is ever to be eradicated, or even abated, in civilized society, it must be done by enlightening the public mind in regard to the true powers of medicine. The community must be made to understand that there are certain things which medicine can do, and certain other things which it cannot do; that some diseases are curable by active interference, and others by time and nature alone; that true medical skill lies in discrimination and prognosis, and judicious adaptation of management, more than in assumed therapeutic power, in regard to special agents; and that he who professes to cure by medicine a self-limited fever is as much an impostor, or deluded man, as he who pretends to do the same thing with a fractured bone or incised wound. Nothing so much shakes the confidence of mankind in the medical profession as unfulfilled promises; nothing so much strengthens this confidence as fair dealing exhibited in an earnest requirement and fearless expression of the truth. Such a course, by commending itself to the sensible and enlightened, may be expected, sooner or later, in some measure to influence the unreasonable and ignorant, — much sooner, indeed, than a warfare carried on in the arena of empiricism with its own weapons.

ON

THE MEDICAL PROFESSION AND QUACKERY.

AN INTRODUCTORY LECTURE, DELIVERED AT THE MEDICAL COLLEGE, BOSTON, NOVEMBER 6, 1844.

I AM about to address myself to an audience of young men, a class of persons who, in our new and active country, assume an influence, and wear a responsibility, unknown in the older communities of Europe. The sparse character of our population, the call for active and efficient men, the sure market which exists for talents, and even for common ability and prudence, have given a national precocity to our youth, and a readiness in adapting themselves to new and difficult spheres of action. I have heard foreigners speak with surprise of the arrival, in distant ports of Europe or India, of American ships commanded, not as is usual by weather-beaten veterans, but by beardless striplings. The signs of our mercantile houses bear often the names of very young men, and the avenues of our professions are so crowded with them, that perhaps no regulation is more liable to be infringed than that which requires that professional candidates shall be twenty-one years of age. Young men command the ranks of our military corps and swell our political meetings. Their voice is heard among us in the periodical press and in the halls of legislation.

These precocious habits of our country have of course been felt in the medical profession. In most of the schools of Europe medical honors are not conferred until after a novitiate of four, and more frequently five years, during which an extensive circle of sciences is obliged to be mastered, and to be approved by a series of strict examinations. Not only are the essential branches of medicine required to be fully understood, but they must be preceded by a knowledge of the subsidiary sciences, and must also be confirmed by practical and clinical experience.

With us, on the other hand, the short period of three preparatory years devoted to regular study and lectures may be said to constitute nearly the sum total of a medical education; for the collateral requirements are so small that their acquisition is often effected during the same three years which are applied to the other branches. And a young man, who has learned to read and write, issues from the village school, or perhaps from the counter or the plough, and in three years is licensed, and declared competent to exercise the multifarious profession of medicine and surgery in all its departments. As it often happens in this and similar cases, the newly-approved candidate sends forth his anxious glance, directed not always to his own deficiencies or the means of supplying them, but to that common goal and object of a young man's inquiry, which is to fill up the measure of his practical aspirations — an opening. By the timely decease of some elderly practitioner, or by the fortunate discovery of a rising settlement, in some distant State, or on some promising water-power, he finds himself, perhaps at short notice, installed, under virtue of the acquiescent silence of the small community in which he lives, the constituted physician of the place. In one month, perhaps in one week, he may be called upon to diagnosticate organic lesion in a case of life and death, or to treat the most formidable convulsive disease. He may be summoned to tie the femoral artery, or to decide and act in a case of placental presentation. There may be no consulting physician within many miles, at least none who can arrive in season for the emergency.

The safety, then, and probably the lives of the unfortunate constituents of this young man will depend upon the question whether he has or has not been truly educated, whether his mind and hand have been adequately trained for the great occasions that await him. It is not enough that he has suffered three years to expire while taking his ease in the office of a city physician, nor that he has passed a corresponding time in following the rounds of a country practitioner. It is not enough that he has carelessly read the works of approved authors, and has squeezed through the customary academic examination. If he has done only this, it is more than probable that failure awaits on himself and disaster upon his patient. But if his studies have been methodical, and conducted with an eye to practical application; if he has concentrated his attention upon necessary points; if he has felt the earnest interest which, more than anything else, imprints truth on the remembrance; if he has gathered up and arranged his resources in reference to coming emergencies; if he has gone over in anticipation the difficulties of his profession, and planned his own mode of extrication,—then he will find that inexperience does not involve failure, and that youth is not an insurmountable barrier to success. He will recollect that the most eminent physicians and the most successful operators have had their first cases. He will perhaps also remember that some of the most distinguished men in history have emerged from obscurity while yet in youth; that not only warriors, like Alexander and Napoleon, but statesmen, like Pitt and Fox, and philosophers, like Davy and Bichat, had achieved some of their proudest laurels at the very entrance of manhood.

Let it not be supposed, however, that I am an advocate for the premature assumption, by young men, of the responsibilities of our profession. Every medical student is to be considered unfortunate, who, by reason of poverty, or the stress of other circumstances, is obliged to hurry his probationary period to an early termination. Too much time and attention are not often bestowed on the business of preparation for practice. The oldest and the best physicians have had frequent cause to regret that they were not better educated. But the superficial student, who rarely has the time and the will to repair his early deficiencies, is haunted through life by a round of perplexity and embarrassment, and degraded by a sense of his own incompetency.

It should be borne in mind that there is no period of life in which time can be so conveniently spared from lucrative pursuits as in youth. After a man has attained to the age of thirty, it is commonly of very little consequence to him, as far as his fame and yearly receipts are concerned, whether he had commenced practice at the age of twenty-one or of twenty-four. But as far as he may prize a quiet conscience and freedom from anxiety, the later age is incomparably the most secure. I would advise any young man, who has completed his education at the end of his minority, that he should devote two additional years, and, if practicable, a still longer period, to availing himself of such advantages, both in study and practice, as may prepare him for his future duties. And when, as it often happens in our community, narrow circumstances require that a young man should live by his own exertions, this state of things, instead of being a motive that he should crowd himself prematurely into the ranks of the profession, encumbered with debt, and bare of acquirements and of means, is rather an imperative reason that he should at once begin by resolving to devote twice the customary number of years, if necessary, to the double purpose of keeping himself in an independent position, and of placing himself at length, in point of maturity of knowledge, on a par with his more favored competitors.

It may not be improper, in this place, to offer you scme suggestions as to the mode in which students may advantageously appropriate the time of their pupilage in reference to the science which they expect to acquire. Medical literature has become so vast a subject, that the undirected student is apt to be lost in the maze of books and sciences which seem equally to press upon his attention. And he is likely to fall into the pernicious error of thinking that he must read a great deal, even though he remembers little. The true object of a medical pupilage should be, not to read, but to study, to observe, and to remember; not to pass superficially over the writings of celebrated men, but to select those compendiums of the several sciences, which contain a condensed view of their essential and elementary facts, which separate the wheat from the chaff, and offer what is fundamental and useful, within a compass which is capable of being impressed on the memory. Most of the constituent sciences which are nominally included in a modern medical education, are now so extensive, that the cultivation of any one of them may afford abundant occupation for a common lifetime. Passing over the more elementary branches, I may instance the theory and practice of medicine, the literature of which is a vast magazine of rubbish, with a few gems imbedded in it, accumulated in all time since the origin of writing, and in such excess that no country in Europe could probably furnish even a catalogue of its own modern books. The history of this extensive science contains a mixture of much that is bad with much less that is good. And although in medical research the still small voice of truth has from time to time made itself heard for a season, yet it has as often been drowned by the dogmas of the visionary and the clamors of the interested. During the present century a host of theorists and gratuitous reformers have replaced each other on the arena of medical controversy. But we have seen that while a truth in medical science, like the import of the physical signs for example, struggles its way through opposition and distrust into general adoption, — an unfair and unfounded assumption rarely survives long the life of the individual whose own eloquence and obstinacy were necessary to force it for a time upon the public attention.

If we could purge the sciences of pathology and therapeutics from the writings of men who wrote merely because they had a reputation to acquire or a doctrine to establish; and could confine these sciences to the results attained by those who sought directly and impartially for the true and the useful; it is probable that the whole subject would be brought within the comprehension, not only of every physician, but of every medical student. And from the recent mode of conducting medical investigations, which has commenced and is gradually gaining foothold in all civilized countries, we may hope, in our own day, to see near approaches to this desirable result.

Every medical man, whether student or physician, owes a threefold duty, to himself, to his competitors, and to his patients. To himself he owes the cultivation of habits of order and perseverance, a love of honesty, and a desire of knowledge. No man is successful in a learned profession who does not cultivate a methodical disposition of his time. The neglect of an hour, the omission of an engagement, and the postponement of what is necessary for what is unimportant, have ruined many a good intention and many a promising prospect. Lord Chesterfield says that the Duke of Newcastle lost half an hour in the morning, and spent the whole day in running after it. This is a true expression of the career of a busy but inefficient man. He who is always driven, always in a hurry, always late, and always with deficiencies to be made up, is very likely to be always a failure. It is well known that the responsibilities of society are best and most easily discharged by those who estimate the value of small portions of time, who do things strictly in their proper season and place, who provide against contingencies, and distribute their day in reference to what is, as well as to what may be, required of them.

But the best ordered arrangement of time, and the most punctual habits of attention, do not always succeed in our profession, except through perseverance, and often through long suffering. The public, especially in cities, are slow in giving their confidence to strangers and to young men. The late Dr. Physick, of Philadelphia, asserted that during the first three years of his practice he did not pay for his shoe-leather; and a late very eminent physician of this city once informed me that he did not earn his own board during three times that period. The conservative principle which retards the reception of young men into lucrative business, is the foundation of their security in after life, for medical practice would not be worth having, in a community whose love of change should lead them to desert their former friends and counsellors, to run after every new-comer. Physicians usually come on to the stage and move off of it in company with the generation to which they belong. In a large city, a young physician, except under circumstances of peculiar patronage or necessity, does not usually obtain employment from families who are much in advance of himself. But these families and their medical attendants pass away, and he and his cotemporaries become the standing practitioners of their time. A preparatory period in the meantime elapses, during which the candidate for future honors has usually enough to do to perfect his knowledge, to fill the gaps in his experience, and to give proofs to the community around him that he possesses aptitude for the common affairs of life.

Every physician is an inquirer during life, and continues to learn something up to the last year in which he may happen to study or practise. As the science advances, moreover, every intelligent practitioner is obliged to replace some of his former opinions with others which he finds to be better substantiated. We should be careful, therefore, not to pledge ourselves unnecessarily to medical opinions which are founded on equivocal or imperfect testimony. The public sentiment attaches a kind of disgrace to frequent changes and recantations, and it ought also to do the same to the course of any man who, for the sake of consistency with himself, continues to maintain an erroneous and exploded opinion. Both these extremes are avoided by the physician who reserves his assent to any new opinion until the evidence of the case is satisfactorily made out.

One of the most difficult virtues for a physician to cultivate is a just and proper deportment towards his professional brethren. As in all professions in which men live by their heads rather than their hands, business is liable to be overdone, and a candidate who has not acquired all the occupation that he wishes, is apt to regard his competitors as stumbling-blocks, to be gotten rid of by fair means or foul. Hence arise the jealousies, calumnies, and open hostilities so often entertained, which injure all the parties concerned, and lower the estimation of the profession with the public. Harmony and a proper *esprit du corps* may uphold the dignity of even an inferior profession; but the public rarely respect any class of men, the members of which have no respect for each other. A friendly intercourse with those whom we approve is productive of pleasure and advantage, and a gentlemanly forbearance towards those with whom we do not agree will show that we are above jealousy. A man is always to be suspected, who tells you that he is surrounded with enemies; and one who is an habitual calumniator of others forces upon his hearers the conviction that they in their proper turn are to come in for their share of his animadversions.

I doubt if physicians do not sometimes injure themselves and their cause by showing too great a sensitiveness in regard to the temporary inroads of irregular practitioners. Quackery, whether carried on by the audacious enterprise of an individual impostor, or upheld by the trumpeting of a fanatical sect, is to be considered a necessary evil inherent in the constitution of society. It exists in every walk and occupation of life by the exercise of which men procure bread. The pettifogger in law, the Millerite lecturer in theology, the demagogue in politics, the system-monger in education, and the wonder-worker upon the brains and bowels of infatuated audiences,—what are all these but quacks moving in their respective spheres, and fattening upon the credulity of dupes? A certain portion of mankind are so constituted that they require to be ridden by others, and if you should succeed in unhorsing a particular impostor, it is only to prepare the saddle for a fresh and more unflinching equestrian. It is not good policy to say or to write too much in regard to the pretensions of impostors. A celebrated author observes that "many a popular error has flourished through the opposition of the learned."* By throwing the gauntlet at an insignificant man, you at once raise him to the dignity of being your competitor, and acknowledge him as a "foeman worthy of your steel." And if you discover uneasiness, resentment, or ill-temper, the public conclude that you are influenced by your private interests. Besides, when you have entered the arena of controversy, you will probably find that the quack, who has his all

* Macintosh.

at stake, can afford more breath and time than you can conveniently spare from your other occupations, and in an active warfare, he may acquire two partisans to your one. It is not long since the exhibiter of a stuffed mermaid succeeded in drawing down the popular indignation on an unfortunate naturalist, who had ventured to declare that it was made of a fish and a monkey. The public generally require time to get disabused of a favorite error; and, if too abruptly assailed, they will sometimes hold on to it, as the traveller did to his cloak when attacked by the north wind.

In your demeanor in regard to quacks, you should keep aloof from them, and trouble yourselves little about them. Admit the general fact, that the race always do and must exist in society; that they are wanted by the credulity of a particular class of minds; that the fall of one dishonest pretender, or one visionary sect, is sure to be replaced by the elevation of another; therefore it little concerns you to know what particular imposition has the ascendency at any given time. When you are interrogated in regard to a specific subject of this kind, you should make a reasonable, cogent and dispassionate answer, always avoiding the appearance of warmth, and especially of self-interest; and you may be sure that a majority of the public will be on the side of truth. As far as my observation extends, three quarters at least of the families in Boston and New England are in the hands of regular practitioners. The remaining fraction, more or less, consists partly of minds so constituted that they require the marvellous as a portion of their necessary food, and partly of unfortunate beings, suffering the inevitable lot of humanity, who, having failed to obtain relief from the ordinary resources of medicine, seek for temporary encouragement in the dishonest assurances of any who will promise to cure them. The first class is the dog in the fable, catching at shadows; the last is the drowning man, catching at straws.

Above all, if you would discountenance quackery, take care that you become not quacks yourselves. Charlatanism consists not so much in ignorance, as in dishonesty and deception. In your intercourse with patients, cultivate a spirit of fidelity, candor and truth. Endeavor to understand yourselves and your science, weigh justly your own powers, and profess only what you can accomplish. If you announce to your patients that you will cure incurable diseases, or cut short those which have a necessary period of duration, you do not speak the truth; you merely blind your patient, while you throw the die for a fortuitous result, a game at which the veriest mountebank may at any time beat you. The profession as a body are often unpopular with a large and sagacious part of the community, because they so frequently disappoint the expectations they have allowed themselves to raise. You may safely undertake and promise to cure diseases which you know to be curable, to alleviate others which you know to be not so, and to perform what art and science can do towards conducting doubtful and dangerous cases to a happy issue. But this is all you can accomplish or promise. The skilful mariner may steer his ship through a dangerous navigation, but he cannot control the wind nor arrest the storm. Nor would he gain reputation by professing to do so.

It is hardly necessary that I should counsel you not to neglect your patients, when you can do anything for their welfare and security. Neglect of outward attentions is not, I think, a very frequent sin of physicians, inasmuch as their interest very obviously lies in a different course. But many practitioners fall into the opposite error of over-attention to their patients, of making them long, tedious or superfluous visits, of hampering them with strict and complicated instructions, and especially of over-drugging them with remedies. There are some patients, it is true, who like to be bled, blistered and physicked; but the number is small, and in most cases both the instinct of the child, and the discretion of the grown man, cause them to revolt against nauseous and painful inflictions. When, therefore, you are called to take charge of a case, ask yourselves how great is the danger, and what is the probable tendency of the disease, if left to itself. If life is in question, and you have reason to believe that the patient may be rescued by prompt and energetic remedies, you should not hesitate to employ them. But in common, trivial and safe cases, such as afford a large part of a physician's occupation, you should not allow a habit, or a hobby, to lead you into the blind routine of always thinking that you must make your patients worse before they can be better. I believe that much of the medical imposition of the present day is sustained in places where practice has previously been over-heroic, and because mankind are gratified to find that they and their families can get well without the lancet, the vomit and the blister, indiscriminately applied; and because the adroit charlatan transfers the salutary influences of time and nature to the credit of his own less disagreeable inflictions.

It is the duty of physicians to elevate their profession, by maintaining in their individual character a high moral rectitude, a just and honorable conduct, a devotedness to the welfare of their patients, and an unceasing effort to improve themselves and their science. If this course is pursued by medical men, they can hardly fail of becoming useful and respected members of society. There is no country in the world in which the avenues to respectability and distinction, to competency, and even to wealth, are more open to physicians, than in the United States. It has been observed that in England no medical man is ever permitted to attain the aristocratic rank, which belongs to birth, and which is occasionally accorded to eminence in the military, political, legal and financial professions. But in our country there is no post of honor or emolument, and no situation of influence and distinction, which our history does not show to be within the reach of our profession. But it is not to political or extra-professional preferment that the true physician should look. He should rather be contented to build up his own character within his own sphere, as a man of knowledge, fidelity and honor. The respect of the community, and the attachment of friends, will always attend on him who loves truth for its own sake, pursues knowledge that he may be able to benefit others, and deals justly with his fellow-men, consenting that they, in turn, should deal justly with him.

ON

GOUT AND ITS TREATMENT.

GOUT, technically known by the names of Arthritis and Podagra, is a painful, inflammatory disease, appearing by paroxysms, affecting chiefly the smaller joints, but liable to change its seat to various more important organs. It is hereditary in its character, and affects the luxurious more than the laboring and abstemious classes. It seldom occurs in children, but makes its appearance most commonly in middle or advanced life, and affects men more frequently than women.

The most common place for the primary attack of gout is in the first joint, or ball, of the great toe of one foot. The patient, in many cases without previous indications of illness, is surprised at being awakened in the middle of the night, or a little later, by intolerable pain in that joint, with much febrile heat and restlessness, commencing, perhaps, in a slight chill. The toe-joint soon becomes swollen, tense and red. Sometimes the ankle, heel, or instep is similarly affected. There is exquisite tenderness on the slightest pressure or motion of the part. This state of things continues from six to twenty-four hours, after which a remission of pain takes place, with gentle perspiration, and tendency to sleep. The inflamed joint, however, continues to increase in swelling, and at length becomes œdematous and shining. On the following night the pain and fever return, and so continue to do for a week, more or less, during which there is thirst, want of appetite, costiveness, and scanty high-colored urine depositing a red or lateritious sediment on cooling.

The paroxysm lasts ordinarily from three to ten days, at the end of which time the pain suddenly terminates, as if by magic. The joint continues swollen and œdematous for a few days, with itching and exfoliation of the cuticle, but the patient returns to his accustomed health with perhaps an unwonted degree of vigor and alacrity.

A precursory stage in most persons takes place in advance of the paroxysm. It is marked by a deranged state of the appetite and digestion, by heartburn, nausea, flatulence, and offensive alvine discharges, also by languor, headache, low spirits and disturbed sleep.

The first paroxysm of gout is the almost certain prelude to others, which are to follow after an interval of some months or years, according to the predisposition and habits of life of the patient. Some persons escape with two or three paroxysms only during life; others have an annual visitation, and others are attacked once in two or three months. The frequency of the paroxysms goes on increasing, until in some patients there is hardly any respite, unless for a few months in summer. The later paroxysms, however, are often more supportable, but the general health is more impaired than in the earlier attacks.

In the later attacks both feet are liable to be affected in succession, and the inflammation, after having left one foot, may return to it again. The small joints of the hand are also subject to the invasion, constituting the variety of gout called *chiragra.* In inveterate cases there is scarcely any joint of the body which may not participate in the extension of the disease. Effusion generally takes place into the synovial cavities and adjacent cellular tissues.

When the disease has become thus confirmed it is usually called *chronic gout.* This commonly follows the acute form, but in some cases may become gradually established without it. In chronic gout the affected limbs are disabled for exercise, they become painful at night, interrupting sleep, and are moved by the patient with difficulty and caution. There is also a general deterioration in the strength and spirits, the patient looks worn, sallow and haggard, the digestive powers are deranged, and there is often palpitation and dyspnœa.

When the disease has existed for a certain length of time, there appears in some persons, but not in all, a deposit of calcareous concretions, known by the name of *chalk-stones,* situated mostly in the cellular tissue, between the outside of the joint and the skin. Sometimes, however, they penetrate the fibrous textures and the cavities of the joints. These concretions are fluid, or semifluid, when first effused, but become gradually solid by the absorption of their fluid parts. They finally become hard and friable, resembling common chalk in their appearance. In their more fluid state they are formed of hydrated lithate of soda, but the solid concretions consist mainly of lithate of soda, with some phosphate of lime.

The chalky concretions are liable to grow with the return of every paroxysm. In bad cases the skin finally gives way, and a chalky serous fluid is discharged. This is afterwards replaced by a kind of chalky pus, and in this manner a part of the chalk escapes, but never the whole, owing to its entanglement in the cells and textures. Persons have been known to write their names with the denuded chalk protruding from the knuckles. Sometimes the apertures close over and cicatrize, but are liable to break out again during subsequent paroxysms. Chalk-stones are most common in the joints of the hands and feet, which they distort in an unsightly manner. They may, however, appear in any part which happens to be the seat of gouty inflammation.

Persons who are subjects of gout are also liable to gravelly complaints, and to calculus both of the kidneys and bladder. The urine is found not only to contain urea and the other solids in excess, but deposits lithic acid and lithate of soda. The nephritic complaints generally supervene after the gout has lasted some time, and the paroxysms of the two complaints rather alternate than coincide with each other.

In regard to the causes of gout, it is, in the first place, an hereditary disease. A majority of persons affected with it can trace the predisposition to their parents or ancestry. It does not follow, however, that all the children of gouty progenitors have the disease. It sometimes leaps over one generation and appears in the next, and it is frequently kept off, in those who are disposed to it, by an active and abstemious life. When gout and gravel affect the same person, it often happens that some of the children inherit the one, and some the other disease, alone.

Gout rarely if ever appears before puberty. In the statistical accounts collected by Sir C. Scudamore, it appears that the greatest number of first attacks came on between the ages of thirty and forty. But, although the number which began in persons above forty was somewhat smaller, it is evident that, if averaged upon the whole number of persons actually living, above that age, the proportion would be greater.

Gout occurs more frequently in men than in the female sex. Yet women are by no means exempt from it, and in them it is most apt to appear after the cessation of the catamenia. The stout and corpulent, of both sexes, are more liable to it than those of the opposite conformation.

The cause which is undoubtedly most active in the production of gout is a luxurious life, with the free use of vinous liquors. Persons who take little exercise, and indulge largely in the pleasures of the table, especially in animal food and fermented drinks, are the most common subjects of the disease. Among persons who are addicted to the excessive use of alcoholic liquids, it is observed that gout occurs much more frequently in those who consume wine and malt liquors, than in those who are intemperate in distilled spirits. The disease is more common in England than in this country, and occurs much more frequently among the wealthy and luxurious, than among the poorer and laborious classes.

There are various exceptional forms, under which the gouty diathesis may become apparent in the system. Sometimes the viscera become deranged, without obvious affection of the joints, constituting *irregular* or concealed gout. Thus the digestive tube may be affected with nausea, want of appetite, pain, flatulence, costiveness, or diarrhœa, acid eructations, and even vomiting. In the thorax are sometimes felt pain, dyspnœa and palpitation, and in the head, vertigo, diminution of sight and hearing, with headache, and sometimes numbness and lethargic heaviness. The spirits are excessively dejected, and the mind peevish and irritable. Sometimes the gouty inflammation attacks the eye, the fauces, or the urethra, producing symptoms imitative of various diseases.

The name of *retrocedent* gout is applied, when the disease, by a sudden metastasis, disappears at once from an inflamed joint, and attacks some internal organ with violent and alarming symptoms. The part most commonly seized is the stomach, in which there is sudden pain, with perhaps nausea and vomiting, and great anxiety and distress. The heart may also be attacked with syncope and urgent dyspnœa, or the brain with symptoms of apoplexy and paralysis.

The prognosis of gout is not unfavorable in the early stages, and so long as it keeps to the extremities. But the retrocession of the disease to the stomach, the heart, or to the brain and its membranes, is fraught with considerable danger. The prevalent notion that gout secures an immunity from other diseases is now generally admitted to be founded in error. All that can be said to be true is that many anomalous symptoms, both local and constitutional, which depend on concealed or atonic gout, and which may have harassed the patient for a long time, suddenly give way when the gout declares itself in the form of a regular paroxysm in the foot.

In its diagnosis gout is principally liable to be confounded with rheumatism. The following circumstances will serve to distinguish them. Gout affects the small joints, principally of the great toe. Acute rheumatism attacks chiefly the large ones, and often many at a time. In gout the inflamed joint is of a vivid red color, it afterwards becomes œdematous, and ends with peeling off of the cuticle. In rheumatism the joints are less red, and the cuticle does not desquamate. Gout is more paroxysmal in its character, and alternates with intervals of ease more than rheumatism. The chalky deposits are characteristic of gout, the acid perspirations of rheumatism. Gout is hereditary, affects the luxurious and indolent, and appears after puberty. Rheumatism is less distinctly hereditary, and may affect persons of all ages, classes and occupations.

The above diagnostic marks appear to me to constitute a legitimate distinction between the diseases of gout and rheumatism. It is but just, however, to state that these distinctive characters are liable to numerous exceptions, and that some of the best French pathologists, such as Chomel, Grisolle and Requin, deny the diversity of the two diseases. And experienced physicians are sometimes at a loss to which of these forms of disease they shall assign particular cases which exhibit the characteristics of both.

The treatment of a first paroxysm of gout may be expectant and palliative, for it is not certain how soon spontaneous resolution will arrive, and the patient, not without reason, is taught from day to day to look for relief and restoration to health. Little, therefore, need be done except to open the bowels with some effectual laxative, and to apply flannel with camphorated oil, or some opiate liniment. But when paroxysms are protracted and very painful, or return with progressive severity, relief must be sought from such means as are in our power. Many expedients have been resorted to, a large portion of which are liable to serious objections. Immersion of the foot in cold water has afforded great relief to the pain, but is liable to drive the gout to vital organs. Bleeding has been found to mitigate the inflammatory action, but is inadmissible except in the most robust and plethoric. Leeching the affected joint is an useful palliative, but even this has its limits of expediency. Various purgative mixtures have in turn obtained and lost a specific reputation.

The remedy which, in the present century, has taken precedence of all others is Colchicum. This drug, supposed to be the basis of a French gout medicine called *eau medicinale*, has justly acquired reputation for the power of putting an immediate stop to the paroxysm. Five grains of the powdered root, or three of the powdered seeds, or from thirty to forty minims of the wine of colchicum root, may be taken three times in a day by a vigorous adult. If the medicine is good, it commonly purges in twenty-four hours, and sometimes produces vomiting, with prostration of strength, small pulse, and cold perspiration. These effects give evidence of the full action of the medicine, but are not always necessary to the cure of the gouty paroxysm. They disappear after the colchicum is omitted.

But the arresting of the paroxysm does not involve the cure of the disease. This more important result requires the avoidance of the cause of the evil. The prevention of future paroxysms can only be expected from a careful and rigidly abstemious regimen; and this course, I am happy to believe, will be found effectual in a great majority of cases. I have known various examples of persons who had been severely and repeatedly attacked with gout, yet who have been able to ward off subsequent attacks indefinitely, by combining a life of exercise with total abstinence from vinous and stimulating drinks. This method does not always succeed in confirmed chronic gout, but in preventing the returns of the acute disease it is eminently successful. And although in certain cases, where the structure and secretions have become radically changed by the arthritic diathesis, there is little hope of perfect cure from any treatment, yet in the early, and sometimes even in the advanced stages of this malady, the recurring paroxysms are postponed, mitigated, or totally prevented by entire abstinence from vinous and alcoholic stimulants. I have the happiness to be able to allude to various cases of gentlemen well known in this city, in some of whom gout has been hereditary, in others of long duration and great severity, as in those already cited on page 57, in whom an almost perfect exemption from gout, of indefinite continuance, has followed an entire avoidance of stimulating liquids.

APHORISMS ON CHOLERA.

On the first appearance of Cholera in the United States, in 1832, much alarm was felt throughout the country in the prospect of a new and unknown epidemic, the devastating effects of which had made themselves severely felt in other parts of the world. The following short article, published in the *Boston Daily Advertiser* of August 20, 1832, was one of various communications offered to allay the general apprehension prevalent at the time.

1. When a disease, which is pervading the habitable world, appears in a particular country, the inhabitants of that country must make up their minds to face it, or fly before it.

2. If the whole population should abandon their business, and spend their time in flying from place to place, it is certain that as many would run into the disease as would run out of it, and the aggregate of distress and mortality would be infinitely increased.

3. If, by common consent, the whole population should continue their customary occupations and intercourse, without shrinking from the presence of the disease, their prosperity would hardly be diminished, and the sum of mortality, in a given term of months or years, would hardly, if at all, be increased.

4. No country has a right to expect uninterrupted prosperity. Of the scourges which occasionally visit nations, the cholera is one of the slightest.

5. A year of cholera is a less evil than a year of bad government. It is not probable that all the death and suffering which cholera has inflicted upon France has been so detrimental to that country as six months of Napoleon's administration, or one of his campaigns.

6. A year of cholera is a less evil than a year of intemperance. Twenty years ago more life and labor was sacrificed in the United States to ardent spirits than the cholera has consumed in any civilized country of Europe. At the present day, cholera, without intemperance, would be but a shadow of what it now appears.

7. If in any civilized country cholera becomes

a grievous calamity, it is chiefly because the imprudence, the terror, and the selfishness of citizens render it so.

8. History shows that, in times of general pestilence, mankind, in proportion to the state of ignorance and ferocity, have given vent to their bad passions in misguided acts of cruelty and strife. In the middle ages, to obtain satisfaction for this infliction of Providence, they massacred Jews and burnt witches. In modern times they assail municipal governments, attack public charities, mob physicians, and write newspaper calumnies.

9. It is not worthy of a humane and enlightened age, that friends, or that cities, should renounce intercourse with each other, on account of a calamity which must speedily become common to all exactly in proportion to their capacity to receive it.

10. Should the cholera continue to prevail for three years throughout this continent, it would cease to interrupt either business or recreation. Mankind cannot always stand aghast, and the wheels of society at length would no more be

impeded by it than they now are by the existence of consumption, of old age, or of drunkenness.

11. When the cholera arrives in a place, it behoves every active and healthy citizen to make his will, and make his peace with God. Having done this, he should go about his ordinary affairs fearlessly, industriously, prudently; avoiding no situation whatever into which duty may call him. Facts render it certain that, as far as cholera is concerned, there are ninety-nine chances in a hundred he will find himself alive and well at the year's end.

ON THE

TREATMENT OF INJURIES

OCCASIONED BY

FIRE AND HEATED SUBSTANCES.

BEING PART OF A BOYLSTON PRIZE DISSERTATION FOR 1812.

THE application to living textures of substances which are heated beyond a certain temperature, is followed by the phenomena of pain and inflammation. The pain is of a peculiar kind, resembling that from the continued application of fire to the part; the inflammation has a great tendency to suppurate, and often leaves a contracted cicatrix.

The communication of an excess of caloric to animal bodies, whether living or dead, is followed by certain changes. Of the fluids some are coagulated, others are decomposed, or even vaporized, if the heat be sufficient. The solids are in a greater or less degree expanded, disorganized, or decomposed; according to their susceptibility of change and the quantity of caloric received. These processes in the living body being incompatible with its healthy condition, a morbid state of the part affected necessarily ensues. This state is marked by pain, redness, swelling, vesication, suppuration, or mortification; according to the degree and extent of the injury suffered.

The distressing effects of these injuries, when they exist in an extensive degree, are exceeded by few diseases. Very dangerous cases often occur in children, whose clothes are accidentally kindled; in intoxicated persons, who fall into the fire; and in those exposed by conflagrations, or by explosions of gunpowder, steam-boilers, and the inflammable gases of mines. The peculiar appearance of a burnt surface has commonly been supposed to require a peculiar treatment; and many practitioners, instead of resorting to the general remedies of inflammation, have placed their reliance on the supposed powers of specific remedies. In this way different and opposite modes of treatment have been adopted, whose apparent success or failure at different times has occasioned disputes respecting their comparative efficacy. After a variety of trials have been made, and a multitude of cases detailed, the practice still remains undecided; and methods of treatment diametrically opposite enlist nearly an equal number of advocates.

The two modes of treating burns and scalds, which have recently acquired the greatest share of notice, are those of Mr. Kentish and of Sir James Earle. The former of these consists in the use of stimulant, the latter of cooling, applications.

Mr. Kentish recommends that the injured surface be in the first place washed and bathed with rectified spirit of wine, spirit of turpentine, or some similar application, which has been previously heated as far as it can be borne with the finger. After this bathing has been repeated two or three times, the whole is then to be covered with plasters made of common basilicon or resinous ointment, thinned to the consistence of a liniment with spirit of turpentine. This dressing is to be continued for twenty-four hours, after which its place may be supplied with some less stimulating substance, such as proof spirit or laudanum, with the coldness taken off. At the end of forty-eight hours, Mr. K. observes, the inflammation will generally be found to have disappeared, at which time the part may be dressed with camphorated oil, with Goulard's cerate, or with cerate of lapis calaminaris.

The internal treatment recommended by Mr. Kentish is also stimulant. Wine, ale, alcohol or laudanum, are advised to be used according to circumstances.

Sir James Earle, in a publication, entitled "An Essay on the Means of lessening the Effects of Fire on the Human Body," defends a mode of treatment directly the reverse of the former. This consists of the antiphlogistic regimen internally, together with the application of cold in the form of water, snow, or pounded ice, to the part affected. Sir Walter Farquhar and Dr. Kinglake advocate the same mode of procedure; and the cases related to substantiate the happy effect of the cooling treatment are not less numerous than those in favor of the terebinthinate remedies.

The disputes on the comparative efficacy of the foregoing plans of treatment have been agitated with so much warmth and so little impartiality, that the reader of them is like to end his inquiries in scepticism rather than conviction. Inconsistent and opposite facts are often stated, and the same cases distorted to prove both points of the dispute. For instance, the remarkable case of Boerhaave, who was violently scalded by the bursting of Papin's digester, and who got well under copious bleeding and purging, is cited by one as an instance of a speedy and fortunate cure, and by another as a tedious and difficult recovery, which might have taken place in half the time under a different mode of treatment. The source of this uncertainty seems, firstly, to consist in making practical deductions from individual or insulated cases, which do not afford sufficient room for a comparison of the effect of different remedies. Such is the idiosyncrasy of different constitutions, and so deceptive the appearance of different injuries, that it is often impossible to pronounce in what degree two cases resemble each other, and in what degree any application has actually expedited or retarded the cure. According to the caprice or prejudice of practitioners, the account of a case may be warped and colored in such a manner as to prove any point of a dispute that is wished. For example, should any one come forth as the advocate for a *negative mode* of treating burns, which should consist in letting them alone, or in leaving the process to nature, there is no doubt that in due time he would be able to collect a sufficient number of apparently satisfactory cases to answer all his purposes. The multitude of cases brought forward by Mr. Kentish and his opponents, in the aggregate, seems only to prove that oil of turpentine and cold water are both salutary, and both pernicious, according as the practitioner who watched their influence was under the prejudices of a favorable or unfavorable nature toward either application. A second ground of error is likewise contained in the supposition that a single and specific mode of treatment can be accommodated to all states and degrees of the injuries occasioned by fire.

It is obvious that many more cases may yet be detailed, which will not bring the question, in the least, nearer to a decision. Though a series of observations, by a faithful and intelligent practitioner, is entitled to respect, yet when two such courses present us with results diametrically opposite, we are justified in doubting the validity of the ground on which they are founded.

It occurred to me, that, could a measure be devised of inflicting two equal burns on corresponding parts of the same animal, which should afterward be treated with different applications, a chance would be afforded of testing the comparative efficacy of these applications. With this view the following experiments were instituted, which, though not so numerous and complete as could have been wished, will not, it is hoped, be thought altogether inapplicable to the object for which they were attempted.

EXPERIMENT I.

The two ears of a full-grown rabbit were immersed in water, heated near to the boiling point. Particular care was taken to immerse both ears at the same instant, to plunge them to the same depth, and to withdraw them together. In this way two scalds were obtained, as nearly as possible equal; since they were inflicted by the same substance at an uniform temperature, applied for an equal extent and length of time to parts corresponding to each other, equidistant from the centre of circulation, and both appertaining to the same subject. The animal was now suspended on his back, with his right ear immersed in a vessel of warm water, at about 100° of Fahrenheit; the left in a vessel of cold water, having its temperature reduced by ice. In this way they continued for three quarters of an hour, the temperature of both vessels being kept as regular as possible by the occasional addition of warm water and of ice. The two ears were then wiped dry and covered with common resinous ointment.

2d day. — The right ear, to which warm water had been applied, was red and opaque, but the skin remained sound; the left was evidently more inflamed, and contained several small vesications and excoriations. The heat of both was somewhat above the natural standard.

3d day. — The cuticle had separated from both ears to some extent, but most from the left, to which the cold application had been made. A small slough likewise separated from this ear.

4th day.—Additional portions had separated from both ears, but most from the left.

From the fifth to the eighteenth day both ears continued in a state of ulceration. The tip of the ears having been the first part immersed, and the last withdrawn, was of course the most intensely scalded, and sloughed off from both to some extent. The left ear, which had undergone the cold treatment, suffered most by gangrene, and was several days later than the other in healing.

EXPERIMENT II.

The two ears of a rabbit were immersed in scalding water as formerly. The right ear was covered as far as it was scalded with the stimulating ointment of Mr. Kentish, made of basilicon, thinned to the consistence of a liniment with oil of turpentine. To the left ear was applied a saponaceous liniment, composed of equal parts of lime-water and olive-oil.

Three hours afterward the ears were examined. The heat of both was much increased, but that of the right, to which the spirit of turpentine had been applied, was evidently greatest. The pain of this ear was likewise evinced by the animal lopping it or laying it on its back, while the other was carried upright. Some small blisters had risen on this ear, but none were observed on the other.

2d day.—Both ears were preternaturally warm and red, the right continuing more so. They were now covered with resinous ointment.

3d day.—A part of the tip of the right ear separated, and some of the remainder appeared destitute of sensation. The left was red and inflamed, but with no appearance of mortification.

4th and 5th days.—More of the right ear came off. The left was ulcerated, but without any appearance of gangrene.

6th—8th days.—The ulceration continued without any slough from the left ear. About the ninth day, the weather, which had been temperate, became cool; and the ears, which were kept moist by the ointment and their own discharge, became constantly cold. To this circumstance I attributed the formation of a considerable slough, which came from the right ear about the tenth, and from the left on the fourteenth day. Both ears soon after healed.

EXPERIMENT III.

The ears of a rabbit being equally scalded as before, the right was covered with Mr. Kentish's ointment, while the left was immersed in cold water with ice for three quarters of an hour. The left was then covered with basilicon, which ointment on the second day was applied to both.

2d day. — The right ear was blistered, and discharged a considerable quantity of serum or pus. The left was in a similar situation, but in a less degree.

3d day. — Both ears were in a state of suppuration, but the right much the worst; the discharge from this ear being general, from the other partial.

The right ear continued to appear the worst during the recovery, which was not complete before the thirtieth day. The loss of substance by sloughing was not great from either ear, but was least from the left.

EXPERIMENT IV.

A fourth rabbit was dipped in the same manner with the others; afterwards one ear was immersed in water, the other in proof spirit at the temperature of the room. The scalds, however, proved to be slight, as nothing ensued but a trifling redness and opacity in the parts immersed, which disappeared in two or three days, and nearly at the same time from both. This experiment would not have been mentioned, did it not serve to show the ground for fallacy, which arises from comparing the cases of different individuals. Had the result of this case been contrasted with any of the former, on presumption that the injuries received were equal, a very erroneous deduction might have been the consequence.

The foregoing experiments were conducted on a plan, which, I conceive, were it pursued to a considerable extent, would approach as near to demonstrative certainty as any subject in conjectural science of medicine is capable of arriving. A desire of the truth, however, obliges me to state the difficulties which remain, and which may seem to detract something from the weight of the experiments. The ear, which was the part subjected to experiment, is composed chiefly of cartilage and skin; it is remote from the centre of circulation, and its powers of life comparatively feeble. *Possibly* a different mode of treatment may suit this part from that which agrees with muscles and cellular substance. This is not to be considered as very probable, since the living animal fibre is apt to exhibit similar phenomena in any part of the body under the influence of the same disease. If any peculiarity existed in the ear, it was probably that of being less susceptible of the action of stimuli. A trial would have been made with some more central part, had the operation been equally convenient. A second imperfection in these experiments was caused by the accession of cold weather, which apparently occasioned a more extensive gangrene than would have ensued under the use of the remedies without this circumstance. It did not, however, occur during the first days, so that the following appearances may be considered as free from fallacy.

1st. The evident increase of heat, pain, redness,

vesication, and gangrene, following the application of oil of turpentine. Ex. II. and III.

2d. The increase of most of the same appearances, where cold water was used in contrast with warm. Ex. I.

As comparative cases come within the plan of these remarks, the following case, in which different remedies were applied to the same subject, is extracted from the Medical and Physical Journal, vol. XVIII., page 209.

"Samuel James, aged forty, had his face, hands and back most severely burnt by the explosion of hydrogen gas in a coal mine. The cold application was used to the face and hands; the warm oil of turpentine, according to Mr. Kentish's plan (originally recommended by Heister), was applied to the back, and dressed afterward with unguent, resinæ flav. softened down with the same: in order to try which mode of treatment afforded the most immediate ease to the patient, as well as the most expeditious cure. According to the patient's own account, the pain of the hands and face was immediately relieved by the cold application; but he complained of the oil of turpentine occasioning a smarting sensation on the back for five or six hours. This mode of dressing was continued for the space of two days; but, observing a considerable degree of inflammation remaining from the terebinthinate application, that dressing was changed for the neutralized cerate, which the patient did not observe, his eyes being closed by the great tumefaction of the face; but he expressed the utmost satisfaction from the superior comfort he felt in that dressing compared with the former. The next day the back appeared much less inflamed, continued gradually getting better, and was cured in three weeks. 'I am confident,' says Dr. Evans, the relater of the case, 'the back would have gotten well sooner under the cooling plan of treatment; for the patient constantly complained of the great heat in the part during the application of the oil of turpentine.'"

In a variety of cases which have occurred under my own observation, it has not been practicable to contrast the effects of different dressings; so that little of a decisive nature can be gathered from them. In one case, however, which I witnessed, of a very severe and extensive burn in a child aged ten years, which was occasioned by the clothes taking fire, and which afterward terminated fatally, the application of the oil of turpentine in the form of a liniment produced the most violent aggravation of pain, which did not cease before the patient was thrown into convulsions. Instances of the same effect have been mentioned to me by several medical friends.

Most writers, who appear as principal advocates of any mode of practice, feel obliged to produce something like a theory or rationale, which shall account for, or at least apply to, the facts and phenomena adduced. Accordingly, Mr. Kentish and the others have not omitted to back their catalogue of cases with a train of reasoning illustrative of the propriety of their special applications. Of these the two principal are entitled to a separate attention.

OF THE STIMULANT PLAN.

In defence of the oil of turpentine and other stimulant applications, Mr. Kentish states the following as a *law of the system:* "That any part of the system having its action increased to a very high degree, must continue to be excited, though in a less degree, either by the stimulus which caused the increased action, or some other having the nearest similarity to it; until, by degrees, the extraordinary action subsides into the healthy action of the part." It has also been urged, by supporters of the plan, that a lesser stimulus, as the oil of turpentine, is comparatively *sedative* in its operation on a part violently excited by a burn. The above reasoning may amuse the imagination, but does not satisfy the judgment. The analogy of almost every subject in medicine and surgery teaches us that a part already highly irritated receives no benefit from an additional stimulus, which must tend only to increase the sum of the irritation. If a man bruise his finger, do we, by way of expediting the cure, proceed to bruise it again, but with less violence, because "it must continue to be excited in a less degree," "until the extraordinary action subsides into the healthy action of the part"? Or if a man has received an hundred lashes, shall a surgeon prescribe ninety more, because ninety lashes are less stimulating than an hundred, and therefore comparatively sedative? The propriety is just the same, when we irritate with acrid spirit of turpentine a part already suffering violent pain and inflammation, as well as inereased sensibility, from a burn. Though the spirit of turpentine applied to a healthy surface is less injurious than fire, yet, if we apply the one to a part already injured by the other, we only infliet a double evil, or produee an aggregate of the mischief of both.

With regard to the internal stimulant plan of Mr. Kentish, it is advocated on a ground not less exceptionable. He assumes it as a faet that "a healthy, vigorous man" suffers less by a burn, of the same extent, than "a man of an irritable habit;" and from thenee he infers that strength resists the ill consequences of these injuries, while weakness promotes them; and that therefore, in all cases, "we should make the system as strong as we ean immediately on the attaek." Whether this prineiple be just may very properly be questioned, sinee it is an admitted fact that, from ordinary mechanical injuries, a vigorous, plethoric man suffers a higher degree of inflammation, than one whose strength and quantity of blood are less, and whose powers of reäction of course are more feeble. When a eommen injury takes plaee, whieh is capable of producing inflammation and symptomatic fever, depletion and the antiphlogistic regimen are resorted to as preventives; and this in a greater or less degree, according as the subject is more or less plethoric. For instance, if a vigorous man receive a contusion on any part of his body, so violent as to endanger suppuration or gangrene, we prevent or mitigate these symptoms by blood-letting, purging and abstinence. Now, if the same man had received a burn on the same part, endangering the same symptoms, ought our practice to be different? Is the system so revolutionized as to require opposite treatment, because an injury is caused by fire instead of mechanical violence? Or is a stout and plethoric patient, with a full, hard and frequent pulse, to be stimulated with brandy and laudanum, because his fever originated in a burn? It is certainly the height of empiricism to prescribe a specific mode of treatment for a disease merely from its name. A rational treatment is always dependent on circumstances, and is stimulant or sedative, according to the constitution of the patient, the state of the pulse, and the condition of the system.

OF THE COOLING PLAN.

Sir James Earle and Dr. Kinglake, the former in his Essay, and the latter in the Medical and Physical Journal, have advocated a mode of treatment precisely opposite to that of Mr. Kentish; yet, like him, they seem to have erred in pursuing a favorite remedy to extremes. The general and continued application of cold to a part injured by a burn or scald, is resorted to, from a belief of its tendency to abstract the excess of caloric from the part, and to restore the equilibrium. This belief is a just one, so far as it applies to the application of cold for a short time, immediately after the injury from a heated substance is received; but the continued application of it for hours and days, on the same principle, is altogether unphilosophical, and has been sufficiently refuted in the treatise of Mr. Kentish. Every particle of caloric communicated to the living body by a hot substance may be abstracted in one minute by plunging the part affected in cold water; and, if this immersion be continued, the temperature will soon be reduced below the natural standard. It is true that, on withdrawing the affected part, its temperature will soon rise to the former pitch; but this increased temperature can be nothing more than animal heat, a little increased by the violent *action* of the part, as happens in most cases of inflammation. As to the common phrase of "killing the fire," by which is meant only the relief of pain that takes place at the commencement of resolution or suppuration, this cannot be hastened by cold applications, except in slight cases which admit of resolution; whereas, in cases where blisters have arisen, and suppuration is about to take place, its progress is only retarded by the employment of cold.

With regard to the antiphlogistic regimen nothing more need be said than that its use or omission must be determined altogether by the state of the system.

It may be proper in this place to say something respecting the use of alcohol, ether, and proof spirit. These substances are often recommended in a vague manner, without reference to the mode of their application, although on this circumstance depends their efficacy. If a part of the body be washed with cold spirit, or a thin cloth wet with spirit be applied, the rapid evaporation which takes place renders the effect powerfully refrigerant. On the contrary, if the part be immersed in spirit, or the spirit be applied warm, or with a thickly folded cloth, its operation is unquestionably that of a stimulant.

After considering at length the opposite extremes of treatment which have been adopted, the result of both reason and experiment appears to be that the two extremes are alike injudicious when pursued in their full extent, and neither of them suited to the varieties of burns and of constitutions. An intermediate plan of treatment, which shall vary according to circumstances, and be dependent on the degree and state of disease, is undoubtedly the most deserving of attention.

In slight burns, where no vesications take place, and where resolution appears practicable, we should resort to cooling applications, either water or of spirit; since in this way the most speedy relief is generally given to the pain, and likewise, as in other inflammations, resolution is accelerated. The preparations of lead, or any other discutient, may be added when thought proper. In all cases of burns and scalds it may be expedient to make one application of cold water as soon as possible after the injury, to abstract the heat from the clothes, skin, &c., and prevent the spreading of its effects.

In more violent burns, attended with blisters and acute pain, a permanent relief is to be expected only from suppuration. This is promoted, as in other cases of suppurative inflammation, *not* by acrid stimulants, *not* by snow and ice, but by mild emollients and warm fomentations or poultices. Though cold applications, by benumbing the nerves, may afford a temporary relief of pain, yet this returns with equal or increased violence when these applications are discontinued; so that they must be persevered in for a long time, until tardy suppuration appears in spite of them, before effectual relief is given. In the first experiment on the rabbits, the ear which was immersed in cold water fared worse than its fellow, which was dipped in warm. In the treatment of burns tending to suppuration, perhaps no application is better than a liniment of lime-water and oil. This is very gently soothing and astringent, and by its saponaceous quality unites with the discharge, and is thus more generally and equally applied than any unctuous substance would be in its place.

In very violent burns, where the life of a part is destroyed, or where the inflammation is so great as to render mortification to a considerable extent probable, our treatment must depend on the state of the system and the appearance of the part. If marks of active inflammation are present, with increased heat and force of circulation, a sedative and depleting plan is to be followed, until the violent action has abated. On the contrary, if the inflammation be of the passive kind, with diminished action of the part, and atony and prostration of strength in the system, we may then depend on stimulants and antiseptics. It can be only in burns of this kind that Mr. Kentish's method of treatment is admissible in any extent.

In the subsequent treatment of burns, if exuberant granulations arise, they may be repressed by gentle astringents, by pressure, or by escharotics. Mr. Kentish recommends powdered chalk; but this I have found insufficient when mixed with a third part of burnt alum. Pure alum answers the purpose perfectly well. The separation of sloughs is facilitated, according to Mr.

Kentish, by introducing powdered chalk into the cavities between them and the living parts.

The contraction of the cicatrix is often an unpleasant consequence of burns. It may be obviated in a degree by a proper position of the cicatrizing part. Sometimes the contraction is so great as to impede circulation; in which case it is necessary to divide the newly-formed skin in different places, thus allowing it room to expand.

ON THE

BURIAL OF THE DEAD.

The interest which the author has felt in the Cemetery at Mount Auburn, the first of its kind in the United States, has in a measure grown out of his personal connection with its foundation and subsequent development. The project of Mount Auburn was originally conceived, the preparatory meetings called, the land selected and engaged, and the larger public structures, the gate, chapel, tower and iron fence designed, by himself at different times.* The pleasure of witnessing, through so many years, the progressive improvement of this beautiful spot, has been enhanced by the interest and active coöperation of many of our distinguished and valued citizens.

While the subject was of recent agitation, the following Address was delivered at the hall of the Masonic Temple, before the Boston Society for the Promotion of Useful Knowledge.

The manner in which we dispose of the remains of our deceased friends is a subject which,

* Historical notices of Mount Auburn have been published by Thacher, Walter, Dearborn, and others, also in the *Daily Advertiser*, Sept. 9, 1851, and the *Boston Atlas*, Sept. 16, 1851.

within the last few years, has occupied a greater share than formerly of the public attention in our own vicinity. It involves not only considerations which belong to the general convenience, but includes also the gratification of individual taste, and the consolation of private sorrow. Although, in a strictly philosophical view, this subject possesses but little importance, except in relation to the convenience of survivors; yet so closely are our sympathies enlisted with it, so inseparably do we connect the feelings of the living with the condition of the dead, that it is in vain that we attempt to divest ourselves of its influence. It is incumbent on us therefore to analyze, as far as we may be able, the principles which belong to a correct view of this subject; since it is only by understanding these, that we may expect both reason and feeling to be satisfied.

The progress of all organized beings is towards decay. The complicated textures which the living body elaborates within itself begin to fall asunder almost as soon as life has ceased. The materials of which animals and vegetables are composed have natural laws and irresistible affinities, which are suspended during the period of life, but which must be obeyed the moment that life is extinct. These continue to operate until the exquisite fabric is reduced to a condition in no wise different from that of the soil on which it has once trodden. In certain cases art may modify, and accident may retard, the approaches of disorganization, but the exceptions thus produced are too few and imperfect to invalidate the certainty of the general law.

If we take a comprehensive survey of the progress and mutations of animal and vegetable life, we shall perceive that this necessity of individual destruction is the basis of general safety. The elements which have once moved and circulated in living frames do not become extinct nor useless after death; they offer themselves as the materials from which other living frames are to be constructed. What has once possessed life is most assimilated to the living character, and most ready to partake of life again. The plant which springs from the earth, after attaining its growth and perpetuating its species, falls to the ground, undergoes decomposition, and contributes its remains to the nourishment of plants around it. The myriads of animals which range the woods, or inhabit the air, at length die upon the surface of the earth, and, if not devoured by other animals, prepare for vegetation the place which receives their remains. Were it not for this law of nature, the soil would be soon exhausted, the earth's surface would become a barren waste, and the whole race of organized beings, for want of sustenance, would become extinct.

Man alone, the master of the creation, does not willingly stoop to become a participator in the routine of nature. In every age he has manifested a disposition to exempt himself, and to rescue his fellow, from the common fate of living beings. Although he is prodigal of the lives of other classes, and sometimes sacrifices a hundred inferior bodies to procure himself a single repast, yet he regards with scrupulous anxiety the destination of his own remains; and much labor and treasure are devoted by him to ward off for a season the inevitable courses of nature. Under the apprehension of posthumous degradation, human bodies have been embalmed, their concentrated dust has been inclosed in golden urns, monumental fortresses have been piled over their decaying bones; with what success, and with what use, it may not be amiss to consider.

I have selected a few instances, in which measures have been taken to protect the human frame from decay, which will be seen to have been in some cases partially successful, in others not so. They will serve as preliminaries to the general considerations which are connected with the subject.

One of the most interesting accounts of the preservation of a body, the identity of which was undoubted, is that of the disinterment of King Edward I. of England. The readers of English history will recollect that this monarch gave, as a dying charge to his son, that his heart should be sent to the Holy Land, but that his body should be carried in the van of the army till Scotland was reduced to obedience.

He died in July, 1307, and, notwithstanding his injunctions, was buried in Westminster Abbey in October of the same year. It is recorded that he was embalmed, and orders for renewing the cerecloth about his body were issued in the reigns of Edward III. and Henry IV. The tomb of this monarch was opened, and his body examined in

January, 1774, under the direction of Sir Joseph Ayloffe, after it had been buried four hundred and sixty-seven years. The following account is extracted from a contemporaneous volume of the Gentleman's Magazine.

"Some gentlemen of the Society of Antiquaries, being desirous to see how far the actual state of Edward First's body answered to the methods taken to preserve it, obtained leave to open the large stone sarcophagus, in which it is known to have been deposited, on the north side of Edward the Confessor's chapel. This was accordingly done on the morning of January 2, 1774, when in a coffin of yellow stone they found the royal body in perfect preservation, inclosed in two wrappers; one of them was of gold tissue, strongly waxed, and fresh, the other and outermost considerably decayed. The corpse was habited in a rich mantle of purple, paned with white, and adorned with ornaments of gilt metal, studded with red and blue stones and pearls. Two similar ornaments lay on the hands. The mantle was fastened on the right shoulder by a magnificent *fibula* of the same metal, with the same stones and pearls. His face had over it a silken covering, so fine, and so closely fitted to it, as to preserve the features entire. Round his temples was a gilt coronet of fleurs de lys. In his hands, which were also entire, were two sceptres of gilt metal; that in the right surmounted by a cross fleure, that in the left by three clusters of oak leaves, and a dove on a globe; this sceptre was about five feet long. The feet were enveloped in the mantle and other coverings, but sound, and the toes distinct. The whole length of the corpse was five feet two inches."

This last statement, it will be observed, is the only point in which the narrative appears to disagree with history. We are generally given to understand that Edward I. was a tall man; and that he was designated in his own time by the name of Long-shanks. Baker, in his Chronicle of the Kings of England, says of him that he was tall of stature, exceeding most other men by a head and shoulders. I have not been able to find Sir Joseph Ayloffe's account of the examination, and know of no other mode of reconciling the discrepancy, but by supposing a typographical error of a figure in the account which has been quoted.

Edward I. died at Burgh-upon-Sands, in Cumberland, on his way to Scotland, July 7, 1307, in the sixty-eighth year of his age.

Another instance of partial preservation is that of the body of King Charles I., who was beheaded by his subjects in 1649. The remains of this unfortunate monarch are known to have been carried to Windsor, and there interred by his friends without pomp, in a hasty and private manner. It is stated in Clarendon's History of the Rebellion, that when his son, Charles II., was desirous to remove and reïnter his corpse at Westminster Abbey, it could not by any search be found. In constructing a mausoleum at Windsor, in 1813, under the direction of George IV., then Prince Regent, an accident led to the discovery of this royal body. The workmen, in forming a subterraneous passage under the choir of St. George's Chapel, accidentally made an aperture in the wall of the vault of King Henry VIII. On looking through this opening it was found to contain three coffins, instead of two, as had been supposed. Two of these were ascertained to be the coffins of Henry VIII., and of one of his queens, Jane Seymour. The other was formally examined, after permission obtained, by Sir Henry Halford, in presence of several members of the royal family, and other persons of distinction. The account since published by Sir Henry, corroborates the one which had been given by Mr. Herbert, a groom of King Charles' bedchamber, and is published in Wood's Athenæ Oxonienses.

"On removing the pall," says the account, "a plain leaden coffin presented itself to view, with no appearance of ever having been inclosed in wood, and bearing an inscription, 'King Charles, 1648,' in large, legible characters, on a scroll of lead encircling it. A square opening was then made in the upper part of the lid, of such dimensions as to admit a clear insight into its contents. These were, an internal wooden coffin, very much decayed, and the body carefully wrapped up in cerecloth, into the folds of which a quantity of unctuous matter, mixed with resin, as it seemed, had been melted, so as to exclude, as effectually as possible, the external air. The coffin was completely full, and, from the tenacity of the cerecloth, great difficulty was experienced in detaching it successfully from the parts which it enveloped. Wherever the unctuous matter had insinuated itself, the separation of the cerecloth was easy; and, where it came off, a correct impression of the features to which it had been applied was observed. At length the whole face was disengaged from its covering. The complexion of the skin of it was dark and discolored. The forehead and temples had lost little or nothing of their muscular substance; the cartilage of the nose was gone; but the left eye, in the first moment of exposure, was open and full, though it vanished almost immediately; and the pointed beard, so characteristic of the period of the reign of King Charles, was perfect. The shape of the face was a long oval; many of the teeth remained; and the left ear, in consequence of the interposition of the unctuous matter between it and the cerecloth, was found entire.

"It was difficult, at this moment, to withhold a declaration, that, notwithstanding its disfigurement, the countenance did bear a strong resemblance to the coins, the busts, and especially to the picture of King Charles the First, by Vandyke, by which it had been made familiar to us. It is true that the minds of the spectators of this interesting sight were well prepared to receive this impression; but it is also certain that such a facility of belief had been occasioned by the simplicity and truth of Mr. Herbert's Narrative, every part of which had been confirmed by the investigation, so far as it had advanced; and it will not be denied that the shape of the face, the forehead, the eye, and the beard, are the most important features by which resemblance is determined.

"When the head had been entirely disengaged from the attachments which confined it, it was found to be loose, and without any difficulty was taken out and held up to view. The back part of the scalp was entirely perfect, and had a remarkably fresh appearance; the pores of the skin being more distinct, and the tendons and ligaments of the neck were of considerable substance and firmness. The hair was thick at the back part of the head, and in appearance nearly black. A portion of it, which has since been cleaned and dried, is of a beautiful dark brown color. That of the beard was a redder brown. On the back part of the head it was not more than an inch in length, and had probably been cut so short for the convenience of the executioner, or perhaps by the piety of friends soon after death, in order to furnish memorials of the unhappy king.

"On holding up the head to examine the place of separation from the body, the muscles of the neck had evidently retracted themselves considerably; and the fourth cervical vertebra was found to be cut through its substance transversely, leaving the surfaces of the divided portions perfectly smooth and even,—an appearance which could have been produced only by a heavy blow, inflicted with a very sharp instrument, and which furnished the last proof wanting to identify King Charles the First."

The foregoing are two of the most successful instances of posthumous preservation. The care taken in regard to some other distinguished personages has been less fortunate in its result. The coffin of Henry VIII. was inspected at the same time with that of Charles, and was found to contain nothing but the mere skeleton of that king. Some portions of beard remained on the chin, but there was nothing to discriminate the personage contained in it.

During the present century, the sarcophagus of King John has also been examined. It contained little else than a disorganized mass of earth. The principal substances found were some half-decayed bones, a few vestiges of cloth and leather, and a long rusty piece of iron, apparently the remains of the sword-blade of that monarch.

The rapidity with which decomposition takes place in organic bodies depends upon the particular circumstances under which they are placed. A certain temperature and a certain degree of moisture are indispensable agents in the common process of putrefaction, and, could these be avoided in the habitable parts of our globe, human bodies might last indefinitely. I shall be excused for dwelling a short time on the influence of some of these preservative agents. Where a certain degree of cold exists, it tends powerfully to check the process of destructive fermentation, and, when it extends so far as to produce congelation, its protecting power is complete. Bodies of men and animals are found in situations where they have remained frozen for years, and even for ages. Not many years ago, the bodies of some Spanish soldiers were found in a state of perfect preservation among the snows of the Andes, where they were supposed to have perished in attempting to cross those mountains, nearly a century ago; their costume and some historical records indicating the probable period of their expedition. At the Hospice of the Grand St. Bernard in the Alps, some receptacles of the dead are shown to travellers, in which, owing to the effect of perpetual frost, together with the lightness of the atmosphere, but little absolute decay has taken place in the subjects deposited during a lapse of years. But the most remarkable instance of preservation by frost of an animal body, is that of an elephant, of an extinct species, discovered in 1806 in the ice of the polar sea, near the mouth of the river Lena, by Mr. Michael Adams. This animal was first seen by a chief of the Tonguse tribe, in the year 1799, at which time it was imbedded in a rock of ice about one hundred and eighty feet high, and had only two feet, with a small part of the body, projecting from the side, so as to be visible. At the close of the next summer, the entire flank of the animal had been thawed out. It nevertheless required five summers, in this inclement region, to thaw the ice so that the whole body could be liberated. At length, in 1804, the enormous mass separated from the mountain of ice, and fell over upon its side, on a sand-bank. At this time it appears to have been in a state of perfect preservation, with its skin and flesh as entire as when it had existed antecedently to the deluge, or during that condition of the globe which placed animals apparently of the torrid zone in the confines of the Arctic circle. The Tonguse chief cut off the tusks, which were nine feet long, and weighed two hundred pounds each. Two years after this event, Mr. Adams, being at Yakutsk, and hearing of this event, undertook a journey to the spot. He found the animal in the same place, but exceedingly mutilated by the dogs and wolves of the neighborhood, which had fed upon its flesh as fast as it thawed. He, however, succeeded in removing the whole skeleton, and in recovering two of the feet, one of the ears, one of the eyes, and about three quarters of the skin, which was covered with reddish hair and black bristles. These are now in the museum at St. Petersburg.

The foregoing facts are sufficient to show that a low degree of temperature is an effectual preventive of animal decomposition. On the other hand, a certain degree of heat combined with a dry atmosphere, although a less perfect protection, is sufficient to check the destructive process. Warmth, combined with moisture, tends greatly to promote decomposition; yet, if the degree of heat, or the circumstances under which it acts, are such as to produce a perfect dissipation of moisture, the further progress of decay is arrested. In the arid caverns of Egypt the dried flesh of mummies, although greatly changed from its original appearance, has made no progress towards ultimate decomposition during two or three thousand years. It is known that the ancient Egyptians embalmed the dead bodies of their friends, by extracting the large viscera from the cavities of the head, chest and abdomen, and filling them with aromatic and resinous substances, particularly asphaltum, and enveloping the outside of the body in cloths impregnated with similar materials. These impregnations prevented decomposition for a time, until perfect dryness had taken place. Their subsequent preservation, through so many centuries, appears to have been owing, not so much to the antiseptic quality of the substance in which they are enveloped, as to the effectual exclusion of moisture.

In the crypt under the cathedral of Milan travellers are shown the ghastly relics of Carlo Borromeo, as they have lain for two centuries, inclosed in a crystal sarcophagus, and bedecked with costly finery of silk and gold. The preservation of this body is equal to that of an Egyptian mummy, yet a more loathsome piece of mockery than it exhibits can be hardly imagined.

It will be perceived that the instances which have been detailed are cases of extraordinary exemption, resulting from uncommon care, or from the most favorable combination of circumstances, such as can befall but an exceedingly small portion of the human race. The common fate of animal bodies is to undergo the entire destruction of their fabric, and the obliteration of their living features in a few years, and sometimes even weeks, after their death. No sooner does life cease, than the elements which constituted the vital body become subject to the common laws of inert matter. The original affinities, which had been modified or suspended during life, are brought into operation, the elementary atoms reäct upon each other, the organized structure passes into decay, and is converted to its original dust. Such is the natural, and, I may add, the proper destination of the material part of all that has once moved and breathed.

The reflections which naturally suggest themselves, in contemplating the wrecks of humanity which have occasionally been brought to light, are such as lead us to ask, of what possible use is a resistance to the laws of nature, which, when most successfully executed, can at best only preserve a defaced and degraded image of what was once perfect and beautiful? Could we, by any means, arrest the progress of decay, so as to gather round us the dead of a hundred generations in a visible and tangible shape, — could we fill our houses and our streets with mummies, — what possible acquisition could be more useless, what custom could be more revolting? For precisely the same reason, the subterranean vaults and the walls of brick, which we construct to divide the clay of humanity from that of the rest of creation, and to preserve it separate for a time, as it were for future inspection, are neither useful, gratifying, nor ultimately effectual. Could the individuals themselves, who are to be the subjects of this care, have the power to regulate the officious zeal of their survivors, one of the last things they could reasonably desire would be that the light should ever shine on their changed and crumbling relics.

On the other hand, when nature is permitted to take its course, when the dead are committed to the earth under the open sky, to become early and peacefully blended with their original dust, no unpleasant association remains. It would seem as if the forbidding and repulsive conditions which attend on decay were merged and lost in the surrounding harmonies of the creation.

When the body of Major Andre was taken up, a few years since, from the place of its interment near the Hudson, for the purpose of being removed to England, it was found that the skull of that officer was closely encircled by a network, formed by the roots of a small tree which had been planted near his head. This is a natural and most beautiful coïncidence. It would seem as if a faithful sentinel had taken his post, to watch, till the obliterated ashes should no longer need a friend. Could we associate with inanimate clay any of the feelings of sentient beings, who would not wish to rescue his remains from the prisons of mankind, and commit them thus to the embrace of nature?

Convenience, health and decency require that the dead should be early removed from our sight. The law of nature requires that they should moulder into dust, and the sooner this change is accomplished, the better. This change should take place, not in the immediate contiguity of survivors, not in frequented receptacles provided for the promiscuous concentration of numbers, not where the intruding light may annually usher in a new tenant to encroach upon the old. It should take place peacefully, silently, separately, in the retired valley, or the sequestered wood, where the soil continues its primitive exuberance, and where the earth has not become too costly to afford to each occupant at least his length and breadth.

Within the bounds of populous and growing cities, interments cannot with propriety take place beyond a limited extent. The vacant tracts reserved for burial-grounds, and the cellars of churches which are converted into tombs, become glutted with inhabitants, and are in the end obliged to be abandoned, though not perhaps until the original tenants have been ejected, and the same space has been occupied three or four successive times. Necessity obliges a recourse at last to be had to the neighboring country, and hence in Paris, London, Liverpool, Leghorn, and other European cities, cemeteries have been constructed without the confines of their population. These places, in consequence of the sufficiency of the ground, and the funds which usually grow out of such establishments, have been made the recipients of tasteful ornament. Travellers are attracted by their beauty, and dwell with interest on their subsequent recollection. The scenes which, under most other circumstances, are repulsive and disgusting, are by the joint influence of nature and art rendered beautiful, attractive, and consoling.

The situation of Mount Auburn, near Boston, is one of great natural fitness for the objects to which it has been devoted. Independently of its superior size, it may be doubted whether any spot, which has been set apart for the same purposes in Europe, possesses half the interest in its original features. In a few years, when the hand of taste shall have scattered among the trees, as it has already begun to do, enduring memorials of marble and granite, a landscape of the most picturesque character will be created. No place in the environs of our city will possess stronger attractions to the visitor. To the mourner it offers seclusion amid the consoling influences of nature. The moralist and man of religion will

> "Find room
> And food for meditation, nor pass by
> Much, that may give him pause, if pondered fittingly."

We regard the relics of our deceased friends and kindred for what they have been, and not for what they are. We cannot keep in our presence the degraded image of the original frame; and if some memorial is necessary to soothe the unsatisfied want which we feel when bereaved of their presence, it must be found in contemplating the place in which we know that their dust is hidden. The history of mankind, in all ages, shows that the human heart clings to the grave of its disappointed wishes, that it seeks consolation in rearing emblems and monuments, and in collecting images of beauty over the disappearing relics of humanity. This can be fitly done, not in the tumultuous and harassing din of cities, not in the gloomy and almost unapproachable vaults of charnel-houses; but amidst the quiet verdure of the field, under the broad and cheerful light of heaven, where the harmonious and ever-changing face of nature reminds us, by its resuscitating influences, that to die is but to live again.

ON THE

DEATH OF PLINY THE ELDER.

[From the Memoirs of the American Academy of Arts and Sciences, vol. vi.]

It is commonly represented by authors and compilers that Pliny the elder, who died during an eruption of Vesuvius in the year of Christ 79, perished by suffocation from the exhalations of the volcano; and a great preciseness of expression on this subject has been perpetuated by most writers who have touched upon it in modern times.

In the preface of Broterius to the Life and Writings of Pliny, it is said: "Flammis et flammarum prænuntio odore sulphuris exanimatus est." Mason, in Smith's Greek and Roman Biography, says: "He almost immediately dropped down, *suffocated*, as his nephew conjectures, by the vapors." In Lemprière's Classical Dictionary the same is stated: "He soon fell down, *suffocated* by the thick vapors that surrounded him." Rees' Cyclopædia, art. PLINY, has a similar statement: "In his flight he was *suffocated*, being then in the fifty-sixth year of his age." Cuvier, in the *Biographie Universelle*, thus particularizes the closing scene: "Deux esclaves seulement restèrent aupres du malheureux Pline, qui périt *suffoqué* par les cendres et par les exhalaisons sulfureuses du volcan." Simond, in his Tour in Italy, says of Pliny at Stabiæ: "Although not much nearer to Vesuvius than Naples is, he there met his death, from mere *suffocation* probably, as his body was afterwards found externally uninjured." Sir Charles Lyell, in his Principles of Geology, says of Pliny: "In his anxiety to obtain a nearer view of the phenomena, he lost his life, being *suffocated* by sulphureous vapors."

The only authentic and contemporaneous narrative extant of the death of Pliny, and that on which subsequent opinions are necessarily founded, is that contained in the letter of his nephew, Pliny the younger. After an examination of this celebrated epistle, it appears to me highly probable that the elder Pliny got his death not from suffocation or asphyxia, as is commonly believed, but from some more specific and natural disease. The following is a part of the translation by Mr. Melmoth of this epistle:

"In the mean while, the fire from Vesuvius flamed forth from several parts of the mountain with great violence, which the darkness of the night contributed to render still more visible and dreadful. But my uncle, in order to calm the apprehensions of his friend, assured him that it was only the conflagration of the villages which the country people had abandoned. After this, he retired to rest, and it is most certain he was so little discomposed as to fall into a deep sleep; for, being corpulent and breathing hard, the attendants in the antechamber actually heard him snore. The court which led to his apartment being now almost filled with stones and ashes, it would have been impossible for him, if he had continued there any longer, to have made his way out. It was thought proper, therefore, to awaken him. He got up, and joined Pomponianus and the rest of the company, who had not been sufficiently unconcerned to think of going to bed. They consulted together whether it would be most prudent to trust to the houses, which now shook from side to side with frequent and violent concussions, or flee to the open fields, where the calcined stones and cinders, though levigated indeed, yet fell in large showers, and threatened them with instant destruction. In this distress, they resolved upon the fields, as the less dangerous situation of the two; a resolution which, while the rest of the company were hurried into by their fears, my uncle embraced upon cool and deliberate consideration. They went out then, having pillows tied upon their heads with napkins; and this was their whole defence against the storm of stones which fell around them. It was now day everywhere else, but *there* a deeper darkness prevailed than in the blackest night, which, however, was in some degree dissipated by torches and other lights of various kinds. They thought it expedient to go down further upon the shore, in order to observe if they might safely put out to sea; but they found the waves still running extremely high and boisterous. There my uncle, having drunk a draught or two of cold water, laid himself down upon a sail-cloth which was spread for him; when immediately the flames, preceded by a strong smell of sulphur, dispersed the rest of the company and obliged him to rise. He raised himself up with the assistance of two of his servants, and instantly fell down dead, suffocated, I conjecture, by some gross and noxious vapor, having always had weak lungs, and being frequently subject to a difficulty of breathing."

Notwithstanding the elegance and general accuracy of Mr. Melmoth's translation, there is room for doubting the exactness of that part which contains the closing scene of Pliny's life. The words of the younger Pliny are as follows: "Deinde flammæ, flammarumque prænuntius odor sulfuris, alios in fugam vertunt, excitant illum. Innixus servis duobus adsurrexit, et statim concidit, ut ego conjecto crassiore caligine spiritu obstructo, clausoque stomacho, qui illi natura invalidus et angustus et frequenter interæstuans erat." The more exact translation of this passage would be as follows: "Then the flames and the odor of sulphur premonitory of the flames put the others to flight and aroused him. He rose, leaning upon two slaves, and immediately fell dead, his breath being obstructed, as I conjecture, by the thick mist (caligine), and his stomach being shut up, which in him was by nature weak, narrow, and subject to frequent commotion." The fact here is that he fell suddenly dead. The theory of Pliny, his nephew, who was not present, and who was not much versed in anatomy, is, that he died from obstruction of his breath by the "caligo;" a word which means darkness, fog, mist, also metaphorically blindness, dizziness, and ignorance, but does not mean a noxious or irrespirable vapor.

That this "caligo" was not composed of materials necessarily destructive of life, there is abundant collateral evidence. Pliny had been attended to the spot by a considerable party, and two slaves were actually supporting him at the time of his death. Yet it does not appear from record that any of these persons suffered death or detriment from the inhalation of noxious gas on the occasion. The character of the "caligo" is further elucidated by the personal experience of the younger Pliny, who witnessed its effects during the same eruption, and has described its phenomena in a subsequent letter, the nephew being at Misenum, while the uncle was at Stabiæ, in the same vicinity to the mountain:

"It was now morning, but the light was exceedingly faint and languid. The buildings all around us tottered, and though we stood upon open ground, yet, as the place was narrow and confined, there was no remaining without imminent danger. We therefore resolved to leave the town. The people followed us in the utmost consternation, and pressed in great crowds about us in our way out. Being advanced at a convenient distance from the houses, we stood still in the midst of a most hazardous and tremendous scene. The chariots which we had ordered to be drawn out were so agitated backwards and forwards, though upon the most level ground, that we could not keep them steady even by supporting them with large stones. The sea seemed to roll back upon itself, and to be driven from its banks by the convulsive motion of the earth. On the other side, a black and dreadful cloud, bursting with an igneous, serpentine vapor, darted out a long train of fire resembling flashes of lightning. . . . . . Soon afterwards the cloud seemed to descend and cover the whole ocean, as indeed it entirely hid the island of Caprea and the promontory of Misenum. . . . . .

"The ashes now began to fall upon us, though in no great quantity. I turned my head, and observed behind us a thick smoke, which came rolling after us like a torrent. I proposed, while we had yet any light, to turn out of the high road, lest [we] should be pressed to death in the dark by the crowd that followed us. We had scarcely stepped out of the path when the darkness overspread us, not like that of a cloudy night, or when there is no moon, but of a room when it is shut up and all the lights extinct. Nothing then was to be heard but the shrieks of women, the screams of children, and the cries of men, some calling for their children, others for their parents, others for their husbands, and only distinguishing each other by their voices, one lamenting his own fate, another that of his family, some wishing to die from the very fear of dying. . . . . . At length a glimmering light appeared, ... then again we were immersed in thick darkness, and a heavy shower of ashes rained upon us, which we were obliged every now and then to shake off, otherwise we should have been overwhelmed and buried in the heap. . . . . . At last this terrible darkness [caligo] was dissipated by degrees, like a cloud or smoke, the real day returned, and even the sun appeared, though very faintly, as when an eclipse is coming on. Every object that presented itself to our eyes seemed changed, being covered with white ashes, as with a deep snow."

From these descriptions we are justified in believing that the "caligo" which pervaded the air during this eruption of Vesuvius was simply the darkness or dark haze existing in an atmosphere rendered nearly opaque by falling ashes. These ashes (cinis) appear to have consisted mainly of particles of solid substance, thrown out from the crater, or sublimed in the volcano and condensed in the atmosphere, such as now cover the ruins of Pompeii. As to the "odor sulfuris," mentioned in the first letter, it is not spoken of as a thing in itself deleterious, but merely as the forerunner (prænuntius) of the flames. Had the air been highly charged with sulphurous or hydrosulphuric acids, which are among the gaseous products of volcanoes, or even with the sublimed chlorides more common among volcanic gases, it is hardly probable that Pliny would have been the only sufferer on the occasion, or that eye-witnesses would have survived to be narrators of a catastrophe in which they themselves had no share, or even that the inhabitants of Herculaneum and Pompeii, which cities were buried in the same eruption of Vesuvius, would so generally have escaped as they appear to have done.

The important facts which belong to the object of the present inquiry may be summed up briefly as follows: Pliny the elder, a corpulent man, subject to laborious breathing and to other infirmities which had excited the notice, if not the apprehensions, of his friends, was, on the day and night preceding his death, exposed to unusual fatigue and anxiety. In the evening he had had himself carried to a bath, ate his supper, and went to bed, where he slept so profoundly as to be insensible to the noise and danger which kept his companions awake. At length, the danger growing more imminent, he was awakened, and with his companions fled from the house, the whole company carrying pillows on their heads to ward off the falling stones. In this way they groped their way through the darkness till the next morning (jam dies alibi, illic nox). He then lay down on a sail-cloth spread out for him, — a measure which, we may suppose, would hardly have been resorted to under the continuance of danger from the falling stones, except from want of strength on his part to proceed. Neither under the same circumstances would he have stopped repeatedly to demand cold water, unless suffering unusual thirst (Semel atque iterum frigidam poposcit hausitque). At length, under a fresh alarm, he raised himself up, and immediately fell dead while leaning upon his two servants.

A medical man may be excused for believing that Pliny died from apoplexy following unusual exertion and excitement, or possibly from a fatal crisis in some disease of the heart previously existing.

REMARKS ON PNEUMOTHORAX:

WITH CASES, AND AN EXPERIMENTAL INQUIRY INTO THE CAUSES OF THE METALLIC SOUNDS HEARD IN THAT DISEASE.

[From the American Journal of Medical Sciences, 1859.]

THE sounds which are heard during auscultation in cases of pneumothorax, especially when life has been prolonged for a considerable time under the disease, have a character, of which the term metallic is eminently descriptive. This character may be recognized not only in the respiration and cough, but frequently also in the voice and the succussion and percussion of the chest. The sound is either sharp and tinkling, or it is prolonged, reverberating and ringing, according to the kind of action under which it is produced. In both cases the mechanical condition of the chest is apparently the same.

The sounds of pneumothorax, as will appear from the experiments detailed at the end of this article, are divisible, with relation to their causes, into those of impulse and those of reverberation. The first requires the presence of liquid, the second may take place with only the presence of air. The first includes all the varieties of metallic tinkling which are heard in respiration, which also take place after speaking and coughing, and which may be abundantly produced in many cases by succussion of the chest. When well developed it is sharp, silvery and musical, resembling the note of short brass wires in certain children's toys. The second class, that of reverberating sounds, includes the varieties of amphoric breathing, and may be imitated by inflating a recent bladder to a considerable degree of tension while in contact with the ear, or less perfectly by blowing into a glass or metallic vessel. When a sudden impetus is given to it by coughing, this sound becomes more intense, ringing and metallic. The voice also at times acquires the metallic resonance. If percussion be performed on the distended chest, while the ear is applied to its parietes, a ringing sound is communicated, having more or less of a metallic character.

Metallic tinkling of the chest, although one of the most marked of the physical signs, appears not to have been fully explained in regard to the immediate cause by which it is produced. Various hypothetical solutions have at different times been offered, but all of them have been objected to, or seem liable to objections, on the score of insufficiency; and no one of them appears at this time to have obtained a general assent. A brief summary is sufficient to present the leading features of the different modes in which this phenomenon has been accounted for.

The only explanation given by Laennec of this sound is by him considered applicable to cases of what he calls simple hydro-pneumothorax, in which there is no communication with the bronchiæ; a form of the disease, however, the existence of which has been doubted by some subsequent writers. Laennec says that if a patient happen to raise himself suddenly in bed, and a drop of fluid fall from the upper part of the cavity of the pleura into the fluid beneath, it produces a sound like that occasioned by a drop of water let fall into a flask three quarters empty, and this sound is immediately followed by a distinct metallic tinkling. A similar sound, he says, may be heard by ausculting the epigastrium of a person who is swallowing water in minute quantities. This explanation has been adopted, by various subsequent writers, as a general mode of accounting for the phenomenon of metallic tinkling.

Dr. C. J. B. Williams, author of valuable works on diseases of the lungs and pleura, explains metallic tinkling on the principle of reverberation, or echo, produced in a cavity of uniformly reflecting parietes by the communication of a sound, or of a soniferous impulse, to the air contained within it. He considers that in common cases of pneumothorax communicating with a bronchus, if the fistulous opening be small, metallic tinkling will be produced, but if large, or if several such openings exist, there will be only amphoric resonance.

Dr. Thomas Davies, in his lectures at the London Hospital on diseases of the chest, says: "The metallic tinkling is caused by the resonance of air agitated upon the surface of a liquid contained in a preternatural cavity formed in the chest."* This explanation may have been suggested by a note of M. Meriadec Laennec in his edition of the great work of his relative, who says that the sound in question appears to depend upon the vibration of a gas upon the surface of a liquid.

Dr. James Houghton, author of the article Pneumothorax in the Cyclopedia of Practical Medicine, adopts the idea of an echo, which he derives both from the dropping of fluid in a cavity, and from the entrance of air through a fistulous opening. The latter variety, he says, appears to be manifestly the echo of the air forced into the cavity, reverberating against its hollow parietes; and the sound, he thinks, is more particularly caused by the bursting of minute air-bubbles at the orifice of the fistula, formed as the air traverses the latter by the entanglement of mucus. He thinks that the tinkling will be more or less loud and distinct in proportion as the fistulous opening is larger or smaller.

Mr. Guthrie, in the London Medical and Surgi

* London Medical Gazette, vol. xv.

cal Journal, 1833, asserts that Laennec, and also all who hold that metallic tinkling "depends entirely on the passage of air through a hole in the lung into the cavity of the thorax," have been mistaken; and in opposition to this he mentions that to produce the sound in question the air in the cavity must necessarily be compressed. "I do not," says he, "deny the facts of the air, the hole in the lung, or the fluid; but I believe that to produce the sounds of the Jews' harp (metallic tinkling) the air in the cavity must be greatly compressed."

M. Beau, a French writer on the causes of the respiratory *bruits*, is not satisfied with the explanation of Laennec, and contends that metallic tinkling is produced by a bubble of air, which, having traversed the fluid, bursts upon its surface. He founds his opinion on the fact that he has never witnessed metallic tinkling when the communication with the external air was above the level of the fluid. Dr. Spittal, of Edinburgh, seems to have suggested this explanation of metallic tinkling, by the bursting of air-bubbles, as early as 1830.

Magendie, in his lectures quoted in the Lancet

of 1835, says: "The causes which produce the *tintement metallique* are not by any means well understood. Suppositions have been made (they are made and abandoned with surprising facility in medicine), but when we come to examine them, we find nothing but mere theories without any shadow of proof." He tells us that the supposition that a drop of liquid sticks to the upper part of a cavity, and then falls into the fluid below, is mere hypothesis, which may or may not be true. He also denies the sufficiency of the explanation that the tinkling is caused by a bubble which traverses a fluid, and bursts upon its surface. His objections are grounded on an experiment, which he proceeds to repeat in presence of his class, showing the insufficiency of both these causes to produce metallic tinkling. In a dead subject, a quantity of fluid amounting to about half a pint was thrown into the chest. A perforation was then made through the pulmonary tissue, so as to establish a communication between the bronchi and cavity of the chest. A quantity of air was then forced in through the trachea, so as to enter the pleural cavity. No metallic sound was produced in the operation. Water was then dropped in through an opening in the upper part of the chest upon the fluid below, but this also produced no tinkling. Another orifice was made in the lung beneath the surface of the fluid, and air injected as before. A bubbling sound, or "craquement," was heard in the chest, but nothing of a metallic or tinkling character could be perceived. Magendie considers himself as having disproved the explanations to which his experiments relate, but he does not offer any new one of his own.

In regard to M. Guthrie's explanation, which supposes the necessity of compressed air being present, this has been effectually set aside by the fact, that, although in extreme pneumothorax the air in the pleura is moderately compressed, yet metallic tinkling is known to be also produced in large tubercular cavities of the lungs, which communicate freely with the atmosphere, and therefore are not subject to any compression whatever.

The solution of this phenomenon, given by Dr. Davies, and Laennec Junior, that it is caused by the resonance of air, agitated upon the surface of a liquid, seems to be too vague and unsupported to require particular attention.

In regard to the explanations given by Drs. Williams and Houghton, which ascribe metallic tinkling to an echo, or reverberation of air from the sides of a cavity, the solution seems to me to be neither adequate nor very probable. Echo is the secondary sound produced by the reflected vibrations of the atmosphere. It becomes powerful only when many reflections converge towards the same point. Air, moreover, is a feeble conductor of sound, when compared with liquid or solid bodies. It is unnecessary, therefore, to suppose that one of the most striking sounds heard in auscultation is produced by the secondary movement of a feeble conductor, when we have between the ear and the place of impulse the direct agency of a much more powerful conductor, namely, a liquid. To elucidate this point, let any one perform the following experiment: Into a large earthen or porcelain bowl, pour a few ounces of water. Then produce a slight and barely audible sound, by rubbing or snapping together the ends of the nails of the thumb and finger. If this sound is made in the air in any part of the cavity of the bowl above the water, it remains feeble, but if the nails be immersed below the surface of the water, the sound instantly becomes augmented to many times its former intensity, and it will be particularly intense to the ear of an ausculter applied to the outside of the bowl. Here, then, is a parallel case. The liquid in Pneumothorax, and not the air, as will hereafter be seen, conveys the sound of metallic tinkling to the walls of the chest, and these transmit it to the ear of the ausculter, constituting an uninterrupted chain of vibrations.

Considering the subject as being yet imperfectly explained, and therefore open to further inquiry, I have made some experiments in connection with the following cases, which I hope will not be found irrelevant to the question.

Case I. — J. B., cordwainer, aged forty-four, entered the Massachusetts General Hospital, December 28th, 1836. He had been troubled with cough and dyspnœa, during most of last year, increased during summer. Yesterday, after exposure to cold during perspiration, had a sudden increase of cough and dyspnœa with pain shooting from side to side, and hoarseness. Now, skin hot and dry, face flushed, pulse 98, respiration short, quick, 50 per minute, cough hard, with viscid frothy mucous sputa. Complains of pain in head and across hypochondria, increased by upward pressure or cough, tongue white, costiveness, dysury with frequent micturition.

29th, 31st. Percussion dull on right back, sufficiently resonant on left. Respiration very feeble in right back, with a slight bronchial sound opposite spine of right scapula. Bronchophony well pronounced in same place. Supplementary puerile respiration in left back. Hoarseness amounting to aphonia, cough frequent, painful, with dyspnœa. About ℥ii. of muco-purulent sputa daily. Costive; sleeps little.

January 2d, 1837. Has rested and felt somewhat better for two days. In right back respiration nearly inaudible, but voice and cough distinctly amphoric.

4th. By degrees the respiration in right back has grown more audible and amphoric. Percussion resonant. In left back voice natural, respiration puerile. Purulent sputa, one to three ounces.

5th, 8th. Metallic tinkling in right back, at lower edge of scapula, slight and few, heard on each day. Amphoric respiration; voice and cough audible from summit to base of right chest. Dyspnœa and cough more easy. Percussion of right back tympanitic to base of chest; right back when viewed vertically much more prominent to the eye than left; semi-circumference an inch greater; intercostal spaces prominent, the anterior ones level in supine posture. In erect posture, base of right chest less resonant than when lying on face or left side.

9th. Paroxysms of great dyspnœa, obliging him to get out of bed. Breath, voice and cough amphoric from summit to base of right back. Frequent metallic tinkling. Resonance of front and back, of right side on percussion. Purulent sputa, ℥iss.

11th. Rested better; pulse 104; anterior right chest tympanitic on percussion, with inaudible respiration from top to base; voice scarcely audible through parietes at same place, but towards base amphoric. Respiration in right back feeble, but amphoric, accompanied by continual metallic tinkling, frequent and rapid, resembling the boiling of a fluid in a glass retort or flask. Respiration highly puerile in whole left back; slight gurgling under clavicle. Very great exhaustion and anhelation, after rising to cough. Generally unable to expectorate unless he turns upon his left side, after which movement the pus flows freely.

12th, 13th. Many turns of violent and suffocative dyspnœa; metallic tinkling softer. Respiration in right back very feeble, in left back puerile.

14th, 16th. Breathes with more ease. Some ounces of purulent sputa raised each day. Amphoric or metallic respiration, voice and cough, with metallic tinkling more rare and feeble. Right anterior chest quite resonant on percussion, to the extreme base of the chest on inspiration, but about an inch less in extent at expiration.

From this time he continued delirious, with occasional twitching of muscles; respiration high and rapid; inaudible, or amphoric, in right front;

faint metallic impulses and mucous rales till the 21st, when he died.

Autopsy, two and a half hours post mortem.—Emaciation not great; right side of thorax enlarged; intercostal spaces obliterated, this side measuring an inch more than the left, opposite the lower end of the sternum. Percussion resonant, for a quarter of the semi-circumference, flat behind. Succussion of the chest gives a distinct metallic sound from the motion of fluid. The right chest, when perforated through water (see Experiment I.), discharged much air, and subsided gradually.

Thorax. Right pleura with strong old adhesions at apex, and along mediastinum; elsewhere covered with false membranes, mostly free, soft, whitish, recent. Its cavity contains nearly two quarts of opaque sero-purulent fluid, with detached flocculent masses of lymph. The lung being inflated *in situ*, air issued freely from behind the base near the spine, but the orifice could not subsequently be identified, on account of the rupture of cavities made in removing the adherent lung from the chest. Right lung greatly compressed, condensed, and nearly devoid of air, the upper lobe half destroyed by an abscess, a cavity an inch square in the upper part of the lower lobe, and tubercles scattered through all. Left pleura with some old adhesions. Lung large, somewhat emphysematous, upper and lower lobes tuberculous, a cavity capable of holding ℥i. in the upper part of the lower lobe. Air-passages of natural size, some redness in right bronchi. Glands at bifurcation of trachea healthy; those in upper part of thorax and the cervical, enlarged and moist, but not tuberculous.

Pericardium contained about an ounce of turbid serum, with flocculi of recent lymph; heart healthy; right auricle slightly adherent; blood in right side partly liquid, partly coagulated, with some fibrin; in left auricle the same, but no separate fibrin.

Abdomen. Liver of average size, rather dark and friable, pushed down so as to reach the umbilicus, compressed so that its superior and anterior surfaces formed a right angle. Gall-bladder containing ℥v. of very dark viscid bile. Stomach sufficiently healthy, except some small red spots about the small curvature. Mucous membrane of small intestines healthy.

CASE II. — I. C., aged forty-four, sailor, entered the hospital May 28th.* He was previously in the house, three months ago, with cough, and slight tuberculous signs. He now reports that he kept at work, continuing pretty well, until May 24th, when he had headache and dizziness in the afternoon, referred to having got wet in the rain the night before; in the evening fainted, and in the night had coughing and retching; raised without pain ℥ss. more or less of frothy blood; has had much cough since, mostly in the night, with scanty expectoration of frothy mucus; cough and long inspiration have caused pain in the right side, and across the chest; has had no other pain, no chills nor flushes; but has perspired considerably; has had little appetite and much thirst, bowels have been open daily; urine high-colored; feels very weak; tongue clean for most part, a little coated at roots; pulse 118.

29th. Slept better than out of house, but coughed considerably towards morning.

30th. Rested badly from great dyspnœa, which came on between nine and ten last night; bathed

* This case was most of the time under the care of Dr. Hale.

in a sweat; pulse 96; mucous rale in the throat; amphoric sound in respiration below left scapula; percussion resonant in the same place; respiration puerile on the other side; lies on the right; much distressed by lying on the back or left side. Half a pint of thin mucous fluid sputa, frothy on top and opaque.

31st. Rested badly from dyspnœa requiring him to maintain a stooping posture; five or six dejections; pulse 132 sitting up; dyspnœa now less urgent; a highly distinct metallic tinkle heard in the left chest, disappearing when he stoops forward, returning as he bends back. Just below the angle of the left scapula strong amphoric respiration with clear metallic tinkle. In axillary region sound as of striking a brass vessel with a nail; great resonance of the left chest, both behind and in front, on percussion. Strongly puerile respiration in the right back.

June 1st. Slept half the night, by intervals, sitting up and stooping forward. No dejection; pulse 144; tongue moist, thick coat on centre, livid; countenance distressed, anxious; respiration 32, laborious; no pain when at rest, but on motion sharp pain through the left chest, below the region of the heart; speaks only in a whisper; feet and ankles œdematous; whole left chest, both front and back, very resonant; respiration amphoric, with metallic tinkling loud and musical in the whole left back below spine of scapula, and whole left front from clavicle downwards.

2d. Slept pretty well in the same posture as last night; two dejections; countenance anxious; skin warm, with profuse perspiration; pulse 144; tongue white in centre, livid, moist; respiration 30, laborious; voice better than yesterday; amphoric resonance diminished; metallic tinkling as yesterday.

3d. Slept pretty well in his chair, as before; pulse 128; respiration 32, somewhat less laborious, except after coughing; unable to lie down; cough not frequent, but paroxysms long and severe; percussion everywhere very resonant in left chest except for a small space about spine of scapula, where it is only equal with the right; resonance continues to the very base of chest; respiration vesicular, but feeble about spine of scapula; amphoric in lower half of back; natural respiration without metallic tinkle; after coughing large and musical tinkle; in front no respiration heard below line one inch below nipple; above that metallic tinkle for the space of two or three inches, and above amphoric resonance in natural respiration; in forced respiration metallic tinkle over whole left chest; no resonance of voice; in right chest respiration puerile.

4th. Slept pretty well in posture as for the last four nights; countenance less distressed; pulse 124; cough less difficult, but still laborious; about ℥iss. of adhesive muco-purulent sputa; skin moist and warm; resonance of left back less than for some days past, though still greater than natural except about scapulæ; immediately over and above scapulæ, percussion nearly or quite equal in both backs; on two lower ribs of left back percussion resonant while leaning forward, flat on leaning backwards; respiration in left back vesicular about scapulæ and for an inch or two below, then amphoric for a space about the breadth of the hand, inaudible at base; no resonance or tremor of voice discovered either in back or side; metallic tinkling in front as before; also in back after cough. Sudamina above and about clavicles.

5th. In bed most of the night, lying on right side; slept two or three hours; four or five dejections; countenance improved; ℥ii. of adhesive muco-purulent sputa; pulse 108; tongue clear at edges, moist, coated in centre; percussion resonant down to sixth rib in left chest; flat immediately below; equal in both backs over scapulæ, and for two fingers' breadth below; below that much more resonant on left side, down to last rib, while leaning forward. When leaning back, more dull in the whole of the resonant space in back. Natural respiration vesicular about scapulæ, with sonorous rale; below scapulæ, amphoric resonance. In front, metallic tinkle after cough; metallic tinkle also in back. No resonance of voice at base of chest.

7th. In chair all night; slept three hours at intervals; five dejections; countenance more distressed; pulse 132; respiration 36, more labored than for the last two or three days. Tongue cleaner, rather less livid; nearly ℥ii. adhesive sputa; coughs, he thinks, about once an hour; percussion dull in back on lower rib, when leaning forward; respiration amphoric both in front and back; natural breathing unaccompanied by tinkle.

8th. Kept awake by difficulty of breathing. Cough less; expectoration about ℥i. adhesive purulent mucus. Countenance much distressed, pulse 132; tongue more coated; respiration 32, labored. Hair, skin and clothing wet with perspiration. In natural respiration very little sound perceived, except some amphoric resonance and occasional metallic tinkling. Percussion, when leaning much forward, flat on lower rib, resonant above; when sitting up, flat on four lower ribs. A peculiar metallic ringing sound perceived by ear applied to sternum, when the back is percussed.

11th. In the chair all night; slept none from dyspnœa; some pain in left chest; two dejections; countenance much distressed; coughs little; expectoration pretty easy; ℥ii. of adhesive muco-purulent sputa; pulse 144; percussion flat below nipple, also in back below corresponding line, resonant above; sonorous rale in whole front chest. No other sound in natural breathing. Amphoric resonance in back, feeble in natural breathing, loud and musical after cough. After speaking, metallic tinkling in front.

12th. Lay on couch all night without having head much raised. Could lie on left side as well as right, the first time for several weeks. Rested very well, but did not sleep much; one dejection; respiration 36, somewhat labored, but less so than for several days past. Countenance less distressed; pulse, after waking, 108; tongue much less livid, moist, with a broken coat in centre. Percussion of left chest (still lying on left side) quite resonant, except at most dependent part of side, where it is flat. In natural respiration, the only sound heard is sibilant rale both in front and back. Forced respiration, either in speaking or other effort, amphoric. Coughed but little; less than ℥i. adhesive, white, frothy, mucous sputa. Immediately after rising, loud, ringing, amphoric resonance in respiration, and especially in cough, heard both in back and front. Limit of flat sound on sitting, on a line an inch below the nipple. Same metallic ringing sound on percussion of chest as before.

13th. In erect posture most of night; slept little from dyspnœa; three dejections. Discharge from bowels thin and watery; countenance moderately distressed; perspiration not excessive; pulse 116, tolerably full; respiration 36, high, laborious. In erect position, resonance on percussion extends down to one finger's breadth below nipple. Below this line, intercostal spaces on a level with ribs; above, intercostal spaces projecting, resonant. In ordinary respiration, amphoric resonance loud and distinct in upper part of chest. A ringing sound, on percussion, as before. No metallic tinkling heard. Abdomen full, moderately resonant.

14th. Slept very well, lying down, on either side; four dejections. Countenance less distressed; feels better; pulse 108; respiration 36, moderately labored. Inspiration and expiration nearly equal. Percussion flat below line, a finger's breadth below nipple, resonant above. Same ringing sound as before, on percussion. Sounds of fluid readily distinguishable on succussion, heard with ear at a distance of a foot from chest. Moderate amphoric resonance in ordinary respiration. Two sides of chest nearly equal on measurement; left mamma more prominent to the eye than right, intercostal spaces protruding slightly. After some fatigue, amphoric resonance, ringing. Ribs of left chest scarcely raised in respiration.

15th. Slept pretty well, mostly in sitting posture; three dejections. Breathing more difficult when he attempted to lie down. Countenance anxious and distressed; skin quite cool, wet with perspiration; large sudamina about clavicles; respiration 36, laborious. Inspiration quicker than expiration. Cough little. Percussion about spines of scapulæ still equal on both sides. Ordinary respiration amphoric and ringing; when a little forced, voice and percussion ringing as before. Sound of fluid on succussion heard at a distance of several feet.

17th. Slept most of night in sitting posture and recumbent, lying on back or right side. Countenance much distressed; respiration quite laborious; inspirations quick; pulse 112. Tongue moist, slight coat on lobes, very slightly livid; skin cool and moist. Pain near left nipple if he lies on left side; no pain when at rest in any other position. Very little cough, ʒii. frothy mucous sputa. Line of flat sound level with nipple; respiration in right chest loud and coarse. Sounds in left chest as before. Ringing sound on percussion perceptible when percussion is on same surface with ear, in erect position.

18th. At six and a half A. M. found lying on back with shoulders raised, breathing quick and with tracheal rale. Eyes closed; pulse very small and feeble; extremities cold. Died soon after.

Autopsy, eight hours post mortem. — Body not much emaciated, skin livid, lower extremities œdematous.

Left chest quite resonant to a line with axilla, flat behind this line. Right side dull over whole space below pectoral muscles. The air rushed out from a perforation on left side, as detailed in Experiment I. Left pleura universally inflamed, mostly red and roughened, and lined with a soft, bluish-white false membrane of variable thickness, separable in some places into layers, containing about five pints of thin, purulent, inodorous liquid, with coarse masses of lymph lying loose in the depending parts. Left lung collapsed very small, fleshy, bluish-black, pressed against spine and ribs, and nearly destitute of air, having a coat of lymph, and adhering behind superiorly. A rounded fistulous opening was found, half a line in diameter, and situated on the posterior surface of the lower lobe, an inch and a half below its summit. Through this orifice air issued, if blown into the trachea, and a probe pressed upwards entered a large bronchus. This opening communicated immediately with a superficial cavity an inch long by half an inch broad, and which contained a whitish, friable, opaque substance. No other cavity was found, but small tubercles and gray granulations in various parts of this lung. The bronchi contained bloody fluid, were pale, thin and polished, excepting that which led to the cavity, and which was thickened, darker, and less polished.

Right lung universally adherent by pale, soft, friable, recent membrane, forming bands below, some of them an inch long, among which were cavities, containing ℥viii. of reddish fluid. This lung contained many tubercles, and a cavity an inch long at its apex.

In front of the neck was a tumor, occasioned by an abscess situated between sterno-hyoid muscles, containing ℥ss. of pus, with a lining of tuberculous-looking matter.

Pericardium pushed to the right side more than two thirds of it beyond the median line. Heart healthy, except perhaps slight hypertrophy of left ventricle, which measured five-eighths of an inch thick at base, and five-sixteenths at apex. Weight, nine and a half ounces.

Liver somewhat enlarged, rather dark, pushed down within an inch or two of the umbilicus. Small intestines tuberculous, especially on Peyer's plates, towards the end of the ilium, but no ulcers. Other viscera mostly natural.

Case III. — A. C., a young gentleman, aged twenty, called me to visit him June 28th, having just returned from a journey to the South. He reported that two years previously he had had a "lung fever," since which time his health has not been good. Last summer he was troubled with slight pains in the chest, emaciation, loss of strength, and some hectic symptoms, but does not recollect much cough. Being considered phthisical by his physician, he had been advised to pass the winter in the Southern States. My first visit was made to him on the second day after his return, and one day before his death. I found him thin and feeble, barely able to sit up, with a hot skin and circumscribed redness on his cheek. Dyspnœa by no means urgent, decubiture dorsal, pain and stricture across both hypochondria, and none felt elsewhere; pulse 80. Left chest tympanitic, respiration inaudible; a slight metallic tinkle heard singly at each inspiration and expiration. Pulsations of heart feeble in cardiac region, stronger on right side. On the following day, without any great aggravation of dyspnœa or distress, he became much prostrated, with a small, irregular pulse, cold sweats, and diminished sensibility, and died on the succeeding night. By his own testimony and that of his friends, his cough had been slight, and the dyspnœa at no time urgent.

Autopsy, sixteen hours after death.—The whole anterior chest resonant, the left tympanitic. On perforating the left chest through water, great quantities of air escaped. [See Experiment I.] The quantity of sero-purulent fluid was not estimated, water having been thrown into the chest for the sake of the experiment. The left lung was adherent superiorly and posteriorly, and had tubercles and cavities in its upper lobe. The lower part of the same lobe was indurated by tuberculous infiltration, and had about the color of gray hepatization. No communication between the bronchiæ and chest was detected except those produced in the cavities torn in the separation. Right lung healthy, excepting a few tuberculous lumps in its upper lobe. The heart was very small and flaccid, and was pushed almost wholly into the right chest. Mitral valves somewhat thickened at their roots with slight vegetation. Liver depressed, dark purple, flaccid. Gall-bladder healthy.

I consider the last case as noticeable for the absence of any great dyspnœa or distress, after the signs of pneumothorax were so distinct as to lead to an unequivocal diagnosis of that disease. I have seen similar cases where the pneumothorax was partial, owing to the adhesions of the lung preventing collapse, a case not wholly uncommon.

EXPERIMENT I.

Previously to the autopsies of the patients who were the subjects of Cases I. and II., a glass cylinder, open at both ends, was pressed into close contact with the chest, so as to hold water. Some ounces of that fluid were poured in, and a perforation was made through it into the cavity of the chest on the distended side. Immediately a large volume of air escaped from the chest, bubbling upwards through the water. In the third case, no cylinder being at hand, a superficial cavity was made out of the dissected integuments of the chest, and filled with water. Through this water a perforation of the chest was made on the left anterior surface. The air rushed out, producing strong ebullition, as in the former cases. The experiment was then repeated on the right side, and the perforation made through water as before. No air in this instance escaped, but the water was immediately sucked into the chest by the atmospheric pressure.

EXPERIMENT II.

Artificial respiration was produced in the

body of the subject of Case II., by inflating the lungs through the trachea, and expelling the air by pressure on the abdomen. At each inflation, a most distinct, clear and abundant metallic tinkling was produced, accompanied with more or less amphoric sound, and could be sustained *ad libitum* by repeating the inflation. The sound was recognized by several of the medical gentlemen attached to the hospital,* as being the same which had existed during the patient's life.

This experiment was repeated in the examination of the body of the patient in Case III. It produced amphoric sound, but no tinkling. The latter symptom, it will be observed, was but feebly perceptible in examinations during life.

EXPERIMENT III.

Through an aperture in the anterior part of the chest in the subject of Case II., a catheter was introduced, and air blown through it into the cavity of the left pleura. While

* Among the gentlemen present were Drs. Hale, Strong, Bowditch and Sargent.

the end of the catheter was above the level of the fluid, a strong amphoric buzzing was communicated to the ear of an observer in contact with the chest. But when the end of the instrument was pushed below the surface of the liquid, and the latter made to bubble by continuing the inflation, an exquisite metallic tinkling was heard at the explosion of each bubble resembling, as it had done in life, the sound of a little bell or musical wire. In the subject of Case III., this experiment was repeated, and varied by pouring into the chest different quantities of water. When a few ounces only were present, metallic tinkling was uniformly produced, but when two quarts or more were introduced, a bubbling only was heard, without metallic resonance. Similar results were also obtained by pouring a small stream, or letting fall drops of water from above upon the liquid in the chest.

EXPERIMENT IV.

Succussion and percussion were both found to produce the same metallic sounds in the dead body as during life in Case II. Metallic sounds elicited by percussion somewhat resemble those occasionally yielded by the heart, and, as has been observed by Bouillaud, these may be imitated by percussing the back of the hand pressed closely upon the ear, or by closing both ears with the palms of the hands, and walking on a carpet in a still room.

EXPERIMENT V.

In the body of a person recently dead from accident, having no pneumothorax, a repetition was made of several of the foregoing trials. Air and water were forced into the chest, the former so as to distend the cavity and render percussion quite resonant. Ebullition of the fluid was then produced by blowing through a tube inserted between the ribs and pushed below the surface. The only result was a bubbling noise, having not the slightest metallic character. It will be observed that this was nearly a repetition of Magendie's experiment, and it probably failed to produce metallic sound for the same reason as in that case, viz., that the patient was not pneumothoracic.

EXPERIMENT VI.

A bladder, and afterwards a stomach, each containing a few ounces of water, were inflated until thoroughly distended. Whenever the inflating tube was pushed below the surface of the liquid, and the inflation continued so as to produce bubbles, a sharp tinkling was heard, upon the explosion of every bubble, by the ear applied as in ausculting to the outside of the bladder. In this experiment the sound becomes more exquisitely metallic in proportion as the tension of the bladder is increased by further inflation. Succussion of the bladder produces a similar effect. It is necessary that a recent bladder should be used, the texture and elasticity of which are not altered by drying. When the orifice of the tube is above the surface of the water, also when no water is present in the bladder, an intense amphoric sound is produced during inflation; and if saliva or other liquid, in small quantities, is blown through the inflating tube, a more feeble, or *submetallic* tinkling is produced.

From the foregoing experiments and cases,

we may infer that the following agencies are concerned in producing metallic sounds of the chest.

1. There must be a cavity, the walls of which are preternaturally susceptible of vibration. This takes place when the pleura is pathologically distended, so as to overcome the obtuse or muffling effect of the contiguous soft organs, such as the lung, diaphragm and intercostal muscles. Some time is probably neccssary to prepare the parts for this pathological resonance, since it fails to appear *post mortem* in healthy chests submitted to experiment. It should be added, that, when metallic sounds appear in simple phthisis, there are cavities of the lungs, the walls of which are in a state of tubercular induration.

2. The immediate or exciting cause of metallic tinkling is a forcible or sudden disturbance of the liquid in a vibrating cavity like that described. The explosion of bubbles of air, from beneath the surface of the liquid, appears to be the most common cause of such a disturbance; but it may also take place when a part of the liquid is thrown upward in the act of coughing and falls back

upon the remainder. The same occurs in succussion of the chest.

3. The vibrations which yield metallic tinkling are transmitted from the liquid to the solid parietes, and thence directly to the ear, without any necessary agency of an echo, or reverberation of air in the cavity. This is shown particularly by the experiment of the bowl, page 218.

4. A minor, or *submetallic* tinkling, having no musical resonance, may be produced by slight impulses given to the air in the cavity, such as the breaking of bubbles of mucus at orifices above the surface of the liquid.

5. Amphoric resonance is produced by reverberations of the air in a vibrating cavity, without sonific impulse of the liquid. The same is true of metallic modifications of the voice, and of the cough when there is no tinkling. Metallic percussion seems also to depend upon the vibrations of air independently of liquid, and may be produced in some other cases when we strike upon a tense cavity in which a certain quantity of air is confined.

ON

THE PHARMACOPŒIA

OF THE

UNITED STATES OF AMERICA.

[From the American Journal of Medical Sciences for 1831.]

If the medical and scientific world were restricted to the most simple modes of expression and inter-communication, — if we possessed, for example, but one nosology, but one system of natural history, but one language of chemistry and pharmacy, — it is obvious that the books which treat of those sciences would be greatly simplified; that the labor of learners would be abridged, and much confusion prevented among those who respectively teach or cultivate these departments of knowledge. Of this fact the public are so well aware, that attempts have been many times made to establish in these sciences standards of definite expression. Sometimes under the sanction of governments, sometimes from the influence of popular writers or teachers in science, and sometimes from the conventional authority of delegated bodies, a common language has been introduced, and obtained a degree of currency, which, though seldom universal, has, nevertheless, been sufficiently extensive to produce a full proof and conviction of its utility.

Unhappily, however, in those studies, the subjects of which are most multifarious and complex, and which therefore stand most in need of precision in their nomenclatures, an inexplicable confusion of language still exists. Mineralogy, zoölogy, and botany, particularly the two latter, in themselves no trifling subjects of labor, have been rendered to most persons absolutely insurmountable, by the cumbrous load of synonyms, which has been gradually accumulating upon them, under the agency of successive reformers. The Latin language, once the common medium of intercourse for the learned of all countries, has itself become a sort of Babel, furnishing, not unfrequently, a dozen incongruous names for the same object. And since neither Napoleon nor Nicholas, nor any general congress for the pacification of Europe, has taken in hand the reconciliation of conflicting terminologies, the republic of names still remains at the mercy of every innovator whose new colors may attract partisans and disciples, and increase the anarchy already existing.

It is, therefore, sufficiently evident that the language of the sciences which we have mentioned needs retrenchment quite as much as extension; and were it not for the fact that certain nomenclatures have become incorporated with books more useful than themselves, it would be a happy circumstance, if all of them, save one, could be consigned to oblivion. To determine what one in each particular case should supersede all the rest, might be as delicate an affair as to elect a president of the United States. But it is not the less true, that one, even though deficient and unacceptable, would be far better than many.

Pharmacology, considered not only as a science, but as a medium of communication for two extensive professions, particularly needs simplicity and precision of language. It likewise requires that its expressions should be generally intelligible, an advantage which cannot be secured, except by the introduction of a general standard, regulating the names as well as the selection and modification of its subjects. On this ground, it is presumed, there is no variance of opinion. But when we arrive at the question, what the standard shall be, and who shall appoint it, the charm of unanimity is very apt to dissolve.

It is not difficult to frame a competent pharmacopœia, which shall be abundantly adequate to the wants of the medical community. But to devise a plan by which its general adoption shall be secured, is a task which experience has proved to be attended with no ordinary difficulty. Local partialities, and an unwillingness to receive the supposed dictation of others, have in more cases than one frustrated the best contrived plans for promoting a general accommodation. And since indisputable perfection is not to be expected in a pharmacopœia, there will always be found a spirit of hypercriticism, ready to consider trivial defects as reasons for rejecting a public good.

We hold it to be a maxim, that one standard

of pharmacy, if sanctioned throughout a whole country, even though it be an imperfect one, is far more promotive of public convenience than a number of more learned and perfect ones existing simultaneously. The late autocrat, Alexander, ordered his Scotch body-surgeon, Sir James Wylie, to prepare a Pharmacopœia Rossica, which he introduced by an ukase throughout his extensive dominions. This work, a copy of which has reached us, appears to be sufficiently respectable. But, without entering into its particular merits or demerits, we will venture to presume that the subjects of his hyperborean majesty have been enabled to compound and swallow their drugs with equal effect, and far less trouble, than those of the king of Great Britain, speaking in the tongues of three different colleges.

If the business of making a pharmacopœia could be commenced *de novo*, without reference to any of the standards now existing, the great question presented with regard to nomenclature would be, whether names should be scientific, that is, in some measure descriptive of the origin, character, and composition of medicines: or whether they should be arbitrary, having no such reference or import. In the former case, the names would be more expressive, and better suited to the dignity of science; in the latter they would be more permanent, from not being connected with any fluctuating medium.

To illustrate these positions, let us observe the revolution through which a single substance has been obliged to pass, in order to keep pace with the progress and improvements of science. Since the discovery of calomel, that article has been reformed by at least a score of successive appellations. In the figurative language of alchemy it was known by the names of *draco mitigatus, aquila alba, manna metallorum,* &c. As chemistry grew somewhat more definite as a science, this substance becomes *mercurius dulcis,* and *mercurius dulcis sublimatus.* Under the regime of Lavoisier and his cotemporaries, it was a muriate and a submuriate; and after Davy and Gay Lussac, became a chloride and a proto-chloruret. Lastly, as if the *gentleness* of its character was to produce a reconciliation of extremes, the *mitigated* dragon of antiquity has become a *mild* chloride of mercury.

On the other hand, when a nomenclature has been perfectly arbitrary and divested of scientific relations, it has been proportionally durable and constant. Like the words engrafted on a national language, its origin may be vague and accidental, yet the public convenience prevents it from falling into disuse; and though it might, perhaps, be susceptible of reform, yet the benefit would not compensate the trouble. In regard to pharmacology, there is one language alone which has remained permanent amidst mutations, and which a hundred years have not been able to shake from its basis, — we mean the language of commerce. This language, which is for the most part arbitrary and accidental, has seen many pharmacopœias rise and fall, and is now quite as likely as any one of them to last for a century to come. The simple names of opium and alum, of calomel and camphor, have never yielded to any periphrastic method of expressing the same things. Corrosive sublimate refuses to be modernized, and the salts of Epsom and Rochelle maintain their ground against all chemical interference. The combined learning of two hemispheres is unable to prevail against copperas and cream of tartar, and the manufacturer and merchant still continue to make, sell, and buy their tartar emetic, without troubling themselves to inquire whether it is a "tartrate," or a "cream tartrate," or neither. Nay, in some instances, the vulgar appellations have turned the tables upon the classical and scientific, and the homely name of potash has dictated to the learned their more elegant potass and potassium.

To combine in practice the expressiveness and precision of one language with the durability of the other, though very desirable, would, from the nature of the subject, be impossible. Yet an approach may be made to the advantages of both, by adopting, in the first instance, a descriptive language founded on the existing state of science at the time, and afterwards to declare it perpetual, or at least to establish it in force during a long term of years. We should thus possess a medium of communication in itself entitled to respect, and rendered more valuable by the prospect of being permanent.

It appears to us that the stability of pharmaceutical language is a consideration of quite as much importance as its improvement. Great changes in regard to any prevalent system can seldom be effected without doing violence to established habits and preferences of the community. An apothecary, whose drawers are labelled with the legitimate nomenclature of the day, and a physician, who for a score of years has employed a uniform phraseology in his prescriptions, are not compensated, by any trifling advantage, for the risk and trouble of an entire change. Wherever, therefore, it appears that a uniform system is extensively established in any country, it is incumbent on the friends of science to oppose all unnecessary deviation from the rules it prescribes. If the general progress of other sciences has been such as to require that pharmacy should be made to keep pace with them, its improvement ought to consist as far as possible in additions, synonyms, and commentaries, but not in great or violent changes. It is fortunate for the science of anatomy that its distinctive names have been handed down from one generation to another with so little alteration; and we believe no reformer at the present day would obtain many proselytes, who should propose to abolish its nomenclature, because *pia mater, os sacrum, ossa innominata,* and similar names, are absurd, misplaced, or unscientific.

In regard to preparations or compositions, it may often happen that improvements are necessary in pharmacy, to promote the economy and uniformity of certain results. Such changes are highly proper, provided they do not interfere materially with the standard of strength which has been previously current. But great changes in the strength of medicines may generally be regarded as pernicious, serving to perplex apothecaries and deceive physicians, if not to kill patients. It is to be regretted that, in the different pharmacopœias which have been published among us, there are operative medicines bearing the same name, in some of which the strength is double that of others. As to the more complex medicinal formulæ which crowd our books, it will be found that most of them owe their place in the shops to some fashion, or some traditional celebrity, rather than to any exclusive fitness or virtue; and we may perhaps get a true idea of their value from the consideration, that if, by any means, the knowledge of the whole of them should be lost, it is not probable, in the doctrine of chances, that one in fifty would ever be reïnvented. Yet, since the prevailing traffic requires that they should continue to be made and sold, it is important, for those who consume them, that they should be exempt from fluctuations of character.

In the United States, previous to 1820, there was no uniformity of pharmaceutical language. Pharmacopœias, indeed, had been adopted by medical bodies, in Massachusetts and some of the other States; and Dispensatories, both foreign and native, had been published among us. But, in the year referred to, an effort was made, by which the consent of a great majority of the medical institutions of the country was obtained, for a plan of a national pharmacopœia. This, it was confidently hoped, by introducing a current language throughout the country, would do away the confusion which then prevailed, and offered to the parties concerned a facility of intercommunication, corresponding to that which results from a common system of coinage, or of weights and measures. A numerous and highly respectable delegation was appointed, from most of the principal States, a part of whom met in the city of Washington, at the appointed time.

It may here be proper to inquire what such a convention could reasonably be expected to do, and what it was their duty to do, under the circumstances in which they were placed. Coming together from remote places, and holding their session at an inconvenient sacrifice of time and expense, it was not to be anticipated that they would institute an original investigation of the whole subject. The ordeal of an experiment upon every doubtful subject would have involved a labor of months, and perhaps of years. It would not reasonably be expected that they would produce a pharmacopœia which should be better than any which previously existed. A debating assembly would be far less likely to do this than a competent individual in his closet. Yet the convention possessed the power to confer a great good,—a power which no individual is likely to obtain,—that of introducing order in the place of confusion, and law instead of anarchy.

Under these circumstances, it was incumbent on them to produce, or sanction, some standard of pharmacy which should be adequate to the wants of the community. It was not very material what one, among many standards, they should adopt as their basis. They might have selected the Edinburgh Pharmacopœia, which, though prolix in its expressions, was at that time more current than any other in the country. Or they might have taken the London Pharmacopœia, dogged as it has been by Mr. Phillips, and this would have served very well as the groundwork of a useful book. Or they might endeavor to frame a system of their own, which, in some respects, might be superior to its predecessors, or at least better adapted to the customs and wants of our own country. The last plan was decided on by the convention, under the expectation, doubtless, that it would be more acceptable to their constituents. A programme of a pharmacopœia prepared by the College of Physicians in Philadelphia, was adopted as the groundwork, and, after being variously modified and augmented, was referred to a committee, with instructions to publish it.

It must necessarily happen .that a work emanating from so many disconnected sources, a part of whose contents must, from the nature of the case, be the result of compromise among the parties concerned, rather than of satisfaction to any of them, would be in some respects imperfect, disconnected, and redundant. Nevertheless, if it was, on the whole, better suited to the occasion than any other work actually existing, the public were bound to receive it with complacency, as the only standard which could ever become general among us. And if criticisms were needed to point out the faults which it contained, they should have been made in a spirit of manliness and liberality, such as would have promoted the gradual reform and perfection, rather than the overthrow of the work. But several of the journals thought otherwise, and the pharmacopœia was obliged to undergo an ordeal, the severity of which far exceeded its deserts. The spirit of criticism was pushed with a zeal not according to knowledge, and in many instances the ignorance of the commentator, rather than the defects of the book, produced a reprobation of its contents. Nevertheless, the pharmacopœia was received, willingly by some, and reluctantly by others, and became, we have reason to believe, the prevailing standard, or at least more prevalent than any other throughout the United States.

It was to be hoped that, when the period should arrive which had been assigned by the convention for a revision of this work, a sufficient unanimity of sentiment would have prevailed to direct into one channel whatever amount of skill and experience might be volunteered for its improvement, either by societies or individuals. It appears that numerous societies, in different parts of the Union, feeling an interest in the revision and confirmation of the pharmacopœia, had appointed delegates to attend the expected convention at Washington, in 1820. A part of the delegates thus designated were, agreeably to the provisions made in 1820, returned to the presiding officer of that year. But a greater number, who had not been formally returned, proceeded to Washington at the appointed time, and having organized a convention of such delegates as were present, and invited a coöperation of other medical gentlemen of eminence then in the city, proceeded to take measures for the republication of the work. In the mean time, a part of the delegates who had been officially returned to the former president, influenced either by convenience, or by the smallness of their numbers, determined not to convene at Washington, but held a meeting in New York, where they also proceeded to take measures for republishing the pharmacopœia, having likewise invited the coöperation of other medical gentlemen of note. Out of this want of concord have risen up two pharmacopœias, neither of which can strictly claim to be, by lineal descent, the legitimate heir of the original work; one, proceeding from a body not formally declared elected to the convention at Washington; the other, from a body who did not convene at Washington at all. We regret, during the long period of preparation, in which the proceedings of each party must have been known to the other, at least in a degree, that some compromise was not effected, so that the objects of both might be attained, with less trouble to themselves, and less expense to the public. It was not, indeed, in the power of the delegates at Washington to correct the original defect in their mode of election, but it was in the power of the delegates of New York to have gone to Washington, and there to have invited the coöperation of the other delegates present, especially as they appear not to have been afterwards fastidious in associating with their own body undelegated individuals. Even after the original meetings had taken place, a slight spirit of conciliation in one or both parties (we know not which was wanting in this respect) would have produced harmony and unity in the end.

As things now are, it appears to us that the two works must stand upon their respective merits as pharmaceutic compositions; and the public are called on to decide whether either, and, if either, which one, is entitled to be received as the national standard. And here, if it be asked what constitutes fitness or excellence in a pharmacopœia, we should answer, simply, that such a work ought to contain and identify the medicines which are commonly used by physicians, that its preparations should be scientifically composed, that its language should conform to the most current language of the day, and that it should be complete as a system in itself, that is, should have a correspondence between its own parts. In these respects we think the Washington Pharmacopœia has greatly the advantage of its competitor. We observe in its list of materia medica, comparatively few alterations of names, and these are made mostly in conformity to the present language of chemistry. In the New York edition the changes are exceedingly numerous, the new names being taken partly from the London Pharmacopœia, and partly invented for the occasion, so that the book has the aspect of an edition of some other work, rather than of the American Pharmacopœia. The references to authors, which are considered necessary by most pharmacologists, to identify the substances intended, are wholly omitted in this work. In regard to completeness and accuracy, the work of the Washington convention is prepared with much care and science, and with a correspondence of its different parts. In the New York edition we find a want of unity, such as attends hasty preparations, and a discordance often recurring between the names of the articles themselves and those of their preparations.

In regard to the latter work, knowing the difficulties which attend this species of composition, and entertaining a high respect for the character of the gentlemen concerned, we forbear to fill our pages with commentaries on its redundancies and discrepancies. We shall not therefore complain because Burgundy pitch is inserted twice under different names, in the materia medica, nor because the sulphates of quinine and morphine, figs, prunes, and some other articles required in the preparations, are not inserted in the materia medica at all. These things must be corrected with their pens by those who may employ the book. On the other hand, we are happy to perceive some improvements on the edition of 1820, in the greater accuracy of the chemical nomenclature, and in the introduction of some useful formulas. We think, however, that retrenchment in the old work was much more needed than augmentation.

Believing that the pharmacopœia produced by the Washington convention, being a more elaborate, accurate and finished work, will eventually become the standard of the country, we propose to enter somewhat more at large into the consideration of its contents. This we shall endeavor to do with the impartiality which the subject ought to receive.

In their preface this convention express their reasons for adopting as their basis the Pharmacopœia of 1820, a work having many inconveniences and defects, but at the same time many claims to approval. In its general outline, say they, and prominent features, it will bear a favorable comparison with the best pharmacopœias of Europe, and it is only in filling up, that improvement is demanded, or admissible. The changes, therefore, which have been made under the authority of the late convention, embrace the materials and minor arrangements, without extending to the general plan. In preparing for the press the present revised edition, the new convention inform us that much labor has been expended, and every part of the work submitted to the most strict and rigid scrutiny. Every accessible pharmaceutic authority has been consulted, and the accuracy of processes has been frequently tested by a practical investigation; the several departments have engaged the attention of individuals peculiarly qualified by their previous studies, and the whole has passed the examination of pharmaceutists of acknowledged eminence in their profession.

Considering how difficult it is to induce persons of the necessary competency to engage in gratuitous labors with perseverance and fidelity, we are happy that the individuals concerned in the present revision have devoted themselves with such singleness of purpose to the perfecting of the work. From our knowledge of the amount of labor actually bestowed on it, and from the internal evidences which it bears of extensive inquiry and precise examination, we doubt whether any future convention will present us with results more deserving of the public confidence.

In pursuance of the plan of the former edition, and for reasons which it is not necessary here to repeat, the pharmacopœia is written out on opposite pages in Latin and in English. The classical latinity of the London Pharmacopœia is adopted as a standard, and, by keeping this in view, a unity of style is preserved throughout the book. We see no cause to be dissatisfied with the general purity and elegance of this language, though in one case, we observe, the convention have erroneously followed the London example, in using the genitive "rosmarini," and ablative "rosmarino," instead of the undoubted *rorismarini*, and *roremarino*, sanctioned by Horace, Columella, and other classics.

In regard to names, the convention inform us in their preface, that, for reasons which they discuss at length, they have adopted the modern chemical nomenclature, in which the names are expressive of the composition of bodies. This was in most cases done by the framers of the former pharmacopœia, but in the present edition an attempt has been made to bring the nomenclature more completely in accordance with the best scientific usage. Thus we have *chloride of sodium*, instead of *muriate of soda ; ferrocyanate* of iron, instead of *prussiate* of iron, &c. In a few instances, however, to avoid great circumlocution, a pharmaceutical name is retained in the place of a more expressive chemical appellation, as in the case of alumen, hydrargyrum ammoniatum, &c. In conformity with the present language of chemistry, the proportional composition of bodies, it appears, is intended to be expressed, and we have, among other things, a *bicarbonate* of potass, and a *bicarbonate* of soda. But this intention is not always executed throughout the work, which seems to us a defect in uniformity. The substance called by this convention sulphate of copper is a bisulphate, and ought so to be called in a chemical nomenclature, since there is another sulphate, composed of one equivalent of acid and one of peroxide of copper, which is precipitated by adding pure potass to the solution of the bisulphate above mentioned, in a quantity insufficient for separating the whole of the acid.

We know not for what reason it has been thought proper to omit, as synonyms, certain commercial names of common usage, while others, of much less frequent occurrence, are retained. The student of pharmacy who would know what is meant by Epsom salt, Glauber's salt, blue vitriol, and other names which meet him in the daily price current, must seek for information in other books than the American Pharmocopœia. These names being international and long established, cannot, we think, with propriety, be given up in a work of general pharmacy.

In the nomenclature of substances derived

from the vegetable kingdom, the work before us adheres to the simple and appropriate plan of the first edition, that of using, in all practicable cases, a single word for the name of the drug, leaving its nature and origin to be defined in the opposite column. This peculiarity of the American Pharmacopœia is one of its leading excellences, and one which the New York convention seem to have acted unwisely in abandoning. Most of the names used in other pharmacopœias, to express vegetable substances, are either unwieldy in their length, or improper in their application. Thus the drug assafœtida is called by the Edinburgh college, gummi resina ferulæ assafœtidæ, a name which is highly descriptive, but inapplicable to common use. By the London college it is called assafœtidæ gummi resina; but as the term assafœtida alone is not the name of any plant, in any botanical system of the present day, the whole name is incorrectly composed. The simple name of the drug, assafœtida, is undoubtedly better than either. In like manner columbo may be called by the simple name colomba, or by the circuitous name cocculi palmata radix, but not calumbæ radix, for there is no such plant as calumba. The American Pharmacopœia has another advantage in using simple names, whenever the drug happens to be derived from several plants, as camphor, senna, rheum, and aloe, or from several animals, ichthyocolla. In the present edition a slight variation is made from the former, in using the Latin name of the article always in the singular number, as cantharis, caryophyllus, prunum, instead of cantharides, &c. This method preserves uniformity, and is supported by the usage of Celsus in similar cases.

As in the former edition, the materia medica list is divided into two columns, the first of which contains the officinal name of each article, in Latin and English, together with occasional synonyms, while the other defines the substance intended, and gives explanatory references. This part of the work gives evidence of a laudable degree of care and research, yet we notice a few minor things deserving of remark. The substance called lupulin, derived from the hop, is defined "strobilorum pollen." As the word pollen has, in vegetable physiology, a specific meaning, it would have been better to have used some other name to express powder. In the Latin, *lupulia,* as used by the New York convention, is more consonant to morphia and quinia than *lupulina.* We see no reason for giving up *spermaceti,* the universally-received name, both in chemistry and commerce, and substituting *cetaceum* of the London college, a word which is neither more classical nor more definitive. *Scabious,* applied to erigeron, is a provincial misnomer, that name belonging only to scabiosa.

In regard to the preparations, the convention, considering this the most extensive and important part of the work, have devoted to it a greater share of their attention. They inform us that examination has been carried into all its parts, and not a single process has been allowed to escape a close scrutiny. One of the most prominent defects of the original pharmacopœia was a want of uniformity, both in the manner of conducting the processes, and in the style of describing them. This arose from the variety of sources from which materials were drawn, and the want of due time to remould and shape them, so as to produce a harmonious whole. In the present edition an effort has been made to supply these deficiencies, and to produce uniformity of language, as well as correspondence and unity of design, in the different parts of the work. In the selection of the process for each preparation, two principles are stated to have governed the choice of formulæ, independent of their intrinsic merit, which, when superior, has always been allowed a predominating influence. When two or more methods of preparing the same compound, equally meritorious in themselves, have come under consideration, that has been preferred which has united in its favor the widest prevalence in this country, and the sanction of the majority of the British pharmacopœias. It is considered highly desirable that uniformity in the preparation of medicines should everywhere prevail, for the benefits accruing from the mutual interchange of the medical writings of different civilized nations must be greatly affected by any material difference in the nature or composition of the remedies employed. This remark is especially applicable to Great Britain and the United States, and to all countries where the English language is generally used. It is a duty, therefore, say the convention, which we owe to the cause of pharmacy, to throw our weight into the scale which already preponderates, and thus contribute to the production and maintenance of the desired uniformity.

In those cases where the chemical formulæ of the original pharmacopœia have been found to be defective or objectionable, their place has been supplied by more accurate and practicable rules, founded on a course of careful investigations. In this way the economy and uniformity of certain processes is greatly promoted. New preparations, which have been brought to light by the uncommon progress of pharmaceutic investigations, during the last dozen years, are, in various instances, inserted. Such are the preparations of iodine, quinine and morphine. The convention, however, have shown a wise forbearance, in not crowding their book with the host of new articles, often, we apprehend, more curious than useful, which modern chemistry has been enabled to extort from vegetable drugs. Retrenchment has been freely exercised in lopping off many of the superfluous formulas, which a necessity for hasty compromise had caused to be introduced into the pages of the old pharmacopœia; and, among other articles dismissed is the acetum opii, or black drop, a revived piece of antiquity, wasteful in its composition, and utterly uncertain in its strength, the place of which is now better supplied by the acetated tincture of opium, and the acetate of morphia. For ourselves, by the way, we lean to the opinion, that opium, to produce its full benefit, must be opium still, and we are not sure that any of the artificial salts of morphia are better than the natural meconate. We have seen delirium tremens brought on under the use of denarcotized laudanum. If the crude drug were cumbersome from the bulk necessary to form a dose, as in the case of cinchona, it would be highly useful to reduce its active ingredient into a smaller compass. But this is not the case with many of the narcotics.

Very complex medical formulas, such as abound among the old writers, and still encumber the pages of many of the pharmacopœias, we deem to be a superfluous appendage to medical science. One of the greatest modern improvements is found in the simplification of medical prescriptions. The art of prescribing appears to us a more simple affair than it has been represented by the hypercritical pedantry of Dr. Paris. We admit that adjuvants will help, and that corrigents will correct; nevertheless, we find that castor-oil, ipecac. and opium, will often do their duty without either. In admitting the influence of chemical considerations in the exhibition of medicines, it is important to recollect that the stomach has a chemistry of its own, and that the digestive organs exert a material control over the force of ordinary chemical agents, separating elements which have strong mutual attractions, and dissolving bodies which are insoluble in common menstrua. We ought by no means to consider medicines inert in proportion as they are insoluble, for we have a proof to the contrary in calomel. Nor are we to consider those substances medicinally incompatible, which, if mixed out of the body, occasion a precipitate, or a change of color. What incompatible, we would ask, destroys the effect of opium, strychnine, or cantharides?

Another consideration, which has great weight with writers on chemistry and pharmacy, is the exactness and precision of the quantities employed in their preparations. This circumstance, although of great consequence in strictly chemical compounds, is less so in arbitrary mixtures; and in the administration of simpler medicines its importance diminishes still further. Practical physicians know that a degree of accuracy, approaching nearer than within a fifth or sixth part of the amount desired for producing a given effect, is seldom attainable. Apothecaries divide their pills and powders by the eye, and patients take liquids by drops and spoonfuls. Nay, that physician must possess uncommon shrewdness, who, even after apportioning his dose by the most accurate weight and measure, can foretell with certainty how or when, how much or how often, it is going to operate. The stomachs of different patients, and those of the same patient at different times, vary more, if possible, than the samples of the same drug in commerce.

On these accounts we feel but little concern for the changes which the convention have thought proper to make in the character or strength of preparations and compositions, so long as they do not exceed the limits above mentioned. But in a few cases we observe that the strength has been altered in the proportion of two to one, or *vice versâ*, and of such changes we propose to take notice. The vinum antimonii, which in the old edition contained four grains to the fluid ounce, in this edition contains but two, and is therefore reduced in strength one half. We object to this change, because the stimulating character of the menstruum is incompatible with the indications for which antimony is generally administered, and we apprehend that a glass or two of Teneriffe wine would do no good to a man in apoplexy or incipient fever. The wine, indeed, ought to bear as small a proportion as possible to the operative medicine, and if the London college is followed in lessening the proportion of antimony, it should also have been followed in diluting the wine largely with water. The vinegar and syrup of squill are increased to twice their former strength, — a change in itself of no consequence, when the public shall have learned to regulate the dose. Liniment of ammonia is reduced to one quarter of its former strength. Can this preparation ever be too strong for the purposes to which it is applied?

In a work so generally uniform and consentaneous in its parts as the American Pharmacopœia, we would willingly have dispensed with such names as pulvis aromaticus and pilulæ catharticæ compositæ. These names designate nothing that is not common to a thousand other combinations.

A few things are omitted in this edition, which we would have willingly seen retained; but we are not disposed to cavil on this account, since in that instance, as well as in the case of objectionable formulas, the evil may generally be remedied by extemporaneous prescription. Every man has his particular taste and judgment, and *de gustibus non disputandum.* In the wine of antimony, to which we have objected, the evil is remedied by extemporaneous solutions in water, which are far preferable to those in wine. Even though a pharmacopœia should arrive at the highest and most unquestioned point of excellence, still physicians would suit themselves with formulas of their own, adapted to particular cases. We apprehend that most practitioners pass their lives in ignorance of half the contents of pharmaceutical works.

For ourselves, not being particularly given to hyper-practice, we should feel a strong sentiment of pity for the patients of that physician whose yearly rounds involved the application of the whole pharmacopœia.

To conclude, — having indulged somewhat freely in our remarks on the national work produced by the convention at Washington, — we proceed to make the *amende honorable*, by declaring our conviction that it is on the whole superior to any of the European pharmacopœias with which we are acquainted; that it is better suited to the wants of the American community than any work of the kind which has been published among us; that it has emanated from a larger delegation, and has undergone a more rigorous supervision, than any similar production of the day; and that, therefore, it ought to become the standard of the United States. In conformity with the views expressed in the first part of this article, we also hope that, to relieve the profession from the annoyance of incessant fluctuations, the contents of this book will be respected by all future conventions as something solid and permanent; and that if, as the edifice grows old, it shall be found to need repairs, enlargement, or modern decorations, still that its foundations may not be wantonly assailed, and that its walls may stand as a landmark and a barrier against the confusion of fluctuating language.

ON THE

MUÇUNA PRURIENS:

WITH REMARKS ON

THE IRRITABILITY OF DIFFERENT TEXTURES.

The Dolichos pruriens of Linnæus, now called Mucuna pruriens, and, in English, Cowhage, is a climbing-plant of the West Indies, the pods or seed-vessels of which are covered with stiff, sharp bristles, or spiculæ. I have examined these bristles in a microscope, and find them to be extremely acute, hollow, and apparently covered on the outside with little warts or vesicles.

It is well known that, when these bristles are rubbed on the skin, they excite an intense and violent itching, which lasts for a considerable time. They have been sometimes indiscreetly used as a counter-irritant, applied to the skin, by spreading from four to six grains on lint, and confining it with adhesive plaster. The result, within my observation, has been an exceedingly uncomfortable itching and burning of the part, which on the second day became universally red and inflamed. A copious eruption of papulæ followed, which increased in size for a week, and at length terminated in pustules, which required a second week to pass into scabs. In one patient two or three large prominences, like boils, continued for ten days after the rest of the part was well.

The irritation produced by cowhage appears to me greatly to exceed that which attends the application of flies or of tartar emetic. One patient, a woman, assured me she got no rest for two nights. On examining the skin, it was found in a state of great inflammation, exquisite tenderness, and stuck full of the spiculæ. After attempting in vain to relieve the trouble by a poultice, recourse was had to a mixture of Plaster of Paris and water, which was poured and suffered to harden upon the skin. When withdrawn from the skin, it extracted and brought with it the spiculæ, to the great relief of the patient. The same experiment, however, proved inapplicable to a man whose breast was covered with hairs, and did not admit of the process.

Cowhage was introduced into practice, I believe, by Dr. Chamberlain, who has published a small work upon it, strongly recommending it as a remedy for worms. Reasoning probably *à priori*, he supposed that a substance, which occasions so much irritation to the human skin, would act in a similar manner upon the bodies of worms in the alimentary canal. Finding that, when mixed with honey or molasses, it could be swallowed with impunity, this author, and subsequent writers of Dispensatories, have recommended its use as a remedy for worms, in the dose of from five to ten grains. When strong cathartics have followed its employment, worms in some cases have been brought to light, but I apprehend not more frequently than in cases where no cowhage has been given. Many years ago, having occasion to doubt the anthelmintic properties of this medicine, after it should have undergone the process of digestion in the stomach, I performed with it a number of experiments. A parcel of the spiculæ of full strength were soaked in blood-warm water for about ten minutes. On withdrawing them, they were found softened, apparently deprived of their venom, and wholly incapable of irritating the skin when rubbed upon it. Another portion was tied up in a muslin bag, and forced into the stomach of a cat. At the end of ten minutes an emetic was administered, which brought up the bag with the spiculæ so far digested that they could not be made to give the slightest irritation to the skin. I am therefore obliged to conclude that the vermifuge action attributed to cowhage was in reality due to the cathartics which followed its use.

Within a few weeks past,* I have noticed another curious property of the dolichos, that it stimulates the skin, but does not stimulate the mucous membrane. Applied to the hand, for example, it immediately causes violent itching; but if rubbed on the inside of the lip, or tongue, it excites no sensation beyond the ordinary mechanical stimulus. In like manner the effect on the outside and inside of the cheek are wholly different. It is this fact, probably, and not the sheathing quality of the mucilage or syrup in

* January, 1844.

which it is taken, that enables patients at all times to swallow it with impunity, as a medicine.

It is a field of interesting inquiry to ascertain how far particular morbid poisons and stimulants confine their action to particular textures. As far as my observation extends, the cutaneous poisons which produce eruptions on the skin, independent of any acrimony, or general stimulating quality, such as the Rhus vernix, &c., for the most part confine their action to the true skin or dermoid texture, and do not inflame the mucous membrane, so that they have often been eaten with impunity. Were it otherwise, effects highly dangerous to life would occur from the inflammation of the trachea and other mucous passages, if an action should take place in them at all correspondent in violence to that which is seen upon the skin. But there is another class of poisons which affects the mucous membrane, without incommoding the skin, at least by superficial contact. Such is the effluvium of roses and that of new hay, which always affect certain persons with catarrhal symptoms. Such is also the poison of syphilis and that of gonorrhœa, which are believed not to act through the cuticle, but which develop their activity as soon as they are brought in contact with a mucous surface.

There are other poisons, which seem alike to influence the dermoid and mucous tissues. The sting of a bee or wasp immediately inflames the skin, and it is said to have occasioned death by suffocation when applied to the fauces or throat. It is possible that the morbid poison of scarlatina, and of some other diseases which affect simultaneously the skin and mucous membrane, may possess the same universality of action.

ON THE

POISONOUS EFFECTS

OF THE

AMERICAN PARTRIDGE, OR RUFFED GROUSE.

The Tetrao umbellus of Linnæus, variously called Partridge in the Northern and Eastern States, Pheasant in Pennsylvania and the Western States, and "Ruffed Grous" by Wilson, Nuttall, and Audubon, appears to inhabit the continent from Hudson's Bay to the Gulf of Mexico, and from the Atlantic to the Mississippi. It is a handsome bird, of the Gallinaceous tribe, with mottled plumage, the tail eighteen-feathered, speckled, and barred with black, and with a black subterminal band. The male has a ruff of broad black feathers on the sides of the neck, the female a smaller ruff, of a dusky brown. Its favorite resorts are mountainous regions covered with evergreen trees, and in more cultivated countries it often frequents apple-trees, which are secluded or concealed by woods, having a fondness for the buds of this tree. It is well known, to residents in the interior, by the drumming noise which in the pairing season it makes with its wings, and also by the stratagem with which the mother protects her young by an illusive demonstration of surrendering herself in their place.

The partridge is quite common in the Eastern States, and constitutes one of the most frequent kinds of game in our markets. The flesh is much prized for the delicacy of its flavor, and is in its greatest perfection in September and October. It feeds in summer on wild berries, and at other seasons on the leaves, buds and seeds of various plants.

It is generally known, that although vast numbers of these birds are every year consumed with impunity, yet instances now and then happen of persons being apparently poisoned, or made sick with alarming symptoms, soon after swallowing their flesh. The following cases are selected from among a larger number, which have been observed by myself or my medical friends, and of which a part are in the records of the Society of Medical Improvement.

CASE I. — A gentleman of this city having dined at Worcester in part upon partridge, took the cars for Boston half an hour afterward. In an hour after entering, he was taken with sensations like those of sea-sickness, accompanied with dizziness and great prostration of strength. With difficulty he got his head out and vomited from the window of the car. He continued faint, cold, dizzy, and unable to sit up, with ringing in the ears and imperfect vision. He was conveyed to his house in a sinking and nearly insensible state. When I first saw him, he was cold and moist, with a slow, intermittent and very feeble pulse, difficult comprehension, and sluggish utterance. He had vomited again, with some relief. His vision was partially recovered. Stimulants had been given him, with hot applications and frictions to the surface, under which he gradually recovered.

CASE II. — A lady of delicate health took at

dinner a small piece of the breast and leg of a partridge. Two hours afterwards she became suddenly very faint, and her physician (Dr. Putnam) was called. She was found by him in a sitting posture on the bed, supported by two assistants, with the body bent forward. The surface was generally cold, countenance pale and sunken, and voice feeble. There was slight, frequent convulsive action of the muscles. The pupils were dilated, with loss of vision. Pulse irregular, feeble, at times nearly imperceptible. There was drowsiness approaching to insensibility, nausea and vomiting. Spirituous stimulants were given and ipecacuanha, with warmth, friction and sinapisms externally. Soon after free vomiting took place there was evident amendment. The sensibility returned, questions were comprehended, but the answers were slow and laborious. In the course of two or three hours vision was restored with contraction of the pupils and intolerance of light, with a remaining sense of numbness and uneasiness in the head.

Case III. — A man aged sixty, who had always

been healthy, but within a few months troubled with shortness of breath, which his physician attributed to some affection of the heart, ate the white meat of a partridge, avoiding the dark meat and the parts contiguous to it. About an hour afterwards he went to church, where he was shortly taken with a sensation of distress at the stomach, which he referred to the disagreement of his food. He endeavored to resist this annoyance, and kept his seat for some time, but at length his sight totally left him, he became faint, and fell. He was carried out of church, and laid on his back in the open air. At this time there was no pulse, and the respiration was hardly perceptible. These symptoms were at first attributed by those around to the suspected disease of the heart, but in the course of ten minutes he began to revive. The first word he uttered was "poisoned," and the second, "the partridge." He soon began to revive, sat up, got upon his feet with assistance, but had lost all power over his legs, and was unable to stand. He was now put into a carriage, some pressure was made upon the stomach, and he began to vomit. Ipecac. and warm water were given him until the stomach was fully evacuated. He remained somewhat delirious for a few hours, but on the following day was restored to his customary health.

Case IV.—A gentleman, twenty-six years of age, dined at five P.M. on soup, boiled tongue and potatoes, and ate the leg and part of the breast of a partridge. He afterwards went to a club-room, and remained till eight. On going out at this time he became chilly, and felt a sharp pain through the temples. He repaired to a shop for some soda-water, and, while standing there, was affected with vertigo and a "trance-like" feeling. This was followed by ringing in the ears, and a remarkable sense of coldness, mostly in the back of the neck and shoulders. He was unable to get warm at the fire, and the sensation given to bystanders by his head was compared to that of the contact of a stone jar. He had taken hot spirit and water, and was sitting up when seen by Dr. Holmes at nine o'clock. At this time the voice and expression were natural, mind a little excited, vision dim at times and once or twice quite lost, pupils widely dilated and equal, contracting but slightly on the approach of a light, hands rather cold, pulse 76, regular, small but not thready, no nausea nor vomiting. Took wine of ipecac., and threw off freely portions of food. In the course of half an hour was thoroughly relieved, but was languid and costive next day.

Two or three other persons, as it appeared, had partaken of the same partridge without obvious inconvenience.

CASE V. — A gentleman, aged seventy-four, of full habit and subject to gout, ate at breakfast the black meat of one partridge. In an hour or two he went to church, where he soon became sick, faint and dizzy. On being carried home he was found in a state approaching that of collapse, pale, livid, cold, nearly pulseless, and without vision. His appearance was that of a dying man, with glazed eyes and gasping for breath. Had repeated nausea, but vomited fluids only. Took stimulants, principally hot gin and water, and gradually recovered, after passing a restless night with much thirst. It was remarked that others of the family ate the white meat of the same bird without any disagreeable consequences.

Case VI. — A female, who had eaten at twelve o'clock of the white and black meat of a partridge, in half an hour was taken with pain in the chest and throat, nausea, weakness and loss of sight. Was seen by her physician at four P. M. Her pulse was 54, and hardly perceptible. After taking brandy and water and half a drachm of ipecac., her pulse improved in strength, but was still only 54. Her mind remained clear, and the most remarkable symptoms were the blindness and slow and feeble pulse.

Case VII. — An elderly gentleman, of full habit, breakfasted in part on a partridge. In two hours he was seized with a dizziness, partial loss of consciousness, and violent pain extending through the abdomen to the back. When visited by Dr. H. J. Bigelow, he was found on his hands and knees, cold, faint, partly insensible and nearly pulseless. The pain having subsided, returned at intervals, causing him to call often to have his back rubbed. After an emetic he was much relieved, and rallied slowly in the course of the afternoon.

CASE VIII. — For this and the two following, I am indebted to Dr. Morrill Wyman.

A very athletic and active man, aged fifty, at times making very great and long-continued exertion and eating freely, February 14, 1849, took supper at seven, P. M.; ate two roasted partridges, with ale and other liquors. At eight o'clock felt somewhat heavy, and, thinking he had eaten too much supper, proposed to go to the bowling-alley for exercise. In a few minutes perceived that the lights in the room had a blue tinge, — the fire also; asked if any new kind of burning-fluid had been used, and immediately fell, with loss of consciousness. Just previously to the loss of consciousness, had pain in the back of the neck, extending down along the spine and into the arm. In ten or fifteen minutes partially recovered, — then again unconscious; muscles of limbs completely relaxed; face very pale; respiration four to six times per minute; pulse 18 to 22; hands and feet cold and moist; groaned frequently; vomited freely and spontaneously, and afterwards under the influence of mustard-flour mixed with warm water. Warm blankets and bottles of hot water were applied to the epigastrium and limbs, and in the course of two hours he had recovered his consciousness and drank warm tea. Slept well during the night. In the morning was quite well.

CASE IX. — Same individual. February 23, 1850, went into the country in the morning and rode till three o'clock, P. M.; then sat down in the open air and ate a part of a partridge, but it was so bitter that the remainder was thrown away; drank a wine-glass of brandy. Took railroad train, and on leaving it in thirty-five minutes walked from fifteen to twenty minutes, when (about one hour after eating the partridge) had pain in the back of the neck and limbs. Passed a house, and observed that the lights appeared blue, and immediately suspected the partridge of being the cause of his trouble. Soon after, found himself at the bottom of a steep declivity, having lost his consciousness and rolled down a bank. Got up, and walked to a house; again noticed the blue lights. In attempting to take a glass of cold water again lost his consciousness and fell; was carried home, and, after taking mustard-flour, vomited, and was soon relieved. Before vomiting, respiration very slow, and not more than half the usual number of inspirations; pulse 42 per minute; hands and feet cold and the face pale. During the periods of loss of consciousness, which did not continue more than five minutes at a time, the limbs were quite powerless. The recovery was sudden, and the action energetic; speech impeded, apparently from want of muscular power. Time elapsed between first symptoms and relief by vomiting, from an hour and a half to two hours.

CASE X. — Mrs. W., aged forty-five, ate for dinner, two days before the date of the last case, a part of a roasted partridge, bought at the same time with that used by her husband. This, also, was extremely bitter, and only a small quantity eaten. After dinner walked a mile to a conservatory; when near the conservatory felt weak; pain in both back of neck and limbs. Felt faint in the conservatory, and obliged to return to the open air; was nauseated, but did not vomit.

Immediately walked towards home; found her limbs unsteady, obliged to run, and then stop and support herself by the fence; was compelled to lie down, but did not lose consciousness; was carried home. The pain in the back of the neck and limbs continued till nine o'clock, when she went to bed. Had occasionally some difficulty of breathing, a catching of the breath. In the morning was quite well.

Neither of these individuals have eaten partridges since.

The principal and most characteristic symptoms were loss of consciousness; relaxation of the muscles, and in one instance of the sphincters; paleness; cold feet and hands; slow and infrequent respiration, and slow and infrequent but regular pulse. The act of vomiting was followed by almost immediate relief.

To these cases may be added a number more, the outlines of which have been communicated by different medical friends.

From a general analysis of the symptoms produced, it appears that under certain circumstances the flesh of the partridge acts as a direct sedative poison, impairing the functions of the brain, and, in connection, those of the digestive and circulating systems. The cerebral symptoms, in a majority of cases, have been vertigo, loss of sight, tinitus aurium, and in bad cases general loss of the power of sensation and voluntary motion. Respiration has been slow, sometimes to a great degree. In the circulating system there has been syncope, feeble and sometimes irregular action of the heart; weak, slow, and sometimes imperceptible pulse; cold surface, and pale or livid complexion. In the digestive system there is oppression, nausea with tendency to vomit, and in many cases pain in the abdomen extending through to the back. In more rare cases pain has been felt in the head and limbs.

The foregoing morbid symptoms have mostly appeared within two or three hours after taking the food. But instances have occurred in which persons have been taken before leaving the table.

The poison of the partridge has never, to my knowledge, proved fatal. The remedies usually and properly resorted to, are a prompt emetic, accompanied or followed by stimulants, if the prostration is urgent. Free spontaneous vomiting not unfrequently removes the difficulty before the physician arrives. Acrid stimulants, such as a teaspoonful of mustard, may serve the double purpose of a quick emetic and an incitant to the depressed vital powers. Spirits, and other diffusible stimulants, are indicated by the sinking condition of the patient; but the anxiety of friends often leads to their excessive administration, for which the patient pays by a prolonged continuance of his narcotism. Friction and external warmth are indicated and generally desired by the patient.

The flesh of the partridge is justly esteemed as a great delicacy, and is abundantly sold in the markets of this and many other cities. Audubon says of it: "In my humble opinion it far surpasses as an article of food any land bird we have in the United States, except the wild turkey." It is in its best condition in the fall of the year, and continues to be common throughout the winter. We have hardly any species of game which is sought for with more avidity, or consumed, in proportion to its size, in greater numbers. As a general rule it is and may be taken with perfect impunity.

The fact that the meat of the partridge occasionally proves poisonous has given rise to much speculation in regard to the cause. The point most generally admitted respecting it, is, that its bad effects chiefly, if not always, take place in winter, when the ground is covered with snow. This circumstance has given rise to a popular belief that the noxious quality in the meat of the bird is attributable to some poisonous food on which, in winter, it is driven to subsist. And a prevalent suspicion has been fixed upon the mountain laurel (*Kalmia latifolia*), on the buds and leaves of which the partridge has been supposed to feed in cold weather. But this suspicion appears to be not well founded, since I have observed, in experiments made purposely, that the leaves of the kalmia are not particularly poisonous when taken into the human stomach in any quantity which the bird would be likely to devour; and the crops, when examined in winter, are found to contain leaves and fragments of most of the wild evergreen plants which are in verdure at that time. I have found, among other things, portions of leaves of Pyrola, Gaultheria, Smilax, Coptis, Mitchella, — also buds of Azalea, alder and apple tree, which latter appears to be a favorite food with the partridge.

It is, furthermore, not very probable that the common process of putrid decomposition is concerned in producing the noxious effects in question, for this circumstance would be generally detected by the taste, and the incipient putrescence so often recognized in game is usually corrected by the antiseptic effect of the gastric juice.

More probable solutions of the difficulty are, 1. That the bird is affected with some disease at the time of its death. 2. That some slow chemical change, not putrefactive, may take place when the flesh is long kept in cold weather, as observed by my friend Dr. Cabot. 3. That the idiosyncrasy of individuals renders some persons intolerant of this species of food. This latter supposition is sustained by the facts, that the same person has sometimes been affected twice, — that a majority of persons, partaking of the same partridge, escape unharmed, when others are poisoned,—and that individuals are found who cannot eat lobster, mackerel, and certain other kinds of food, without suffering symptoms approaching in character to those already described.

ON

COFFEE AND TEA;

AND THEIR

MEDICINAL EFFECTS.

THE articles Coffee and Tea have been so long and so generally introduced as luxuries of the table, that they are now viewed by the world as materials of diet and nutrition, and not in their proper light, as substances incapable of nourishing the body in any considerable degree, and depending for their value on an effect which is simply medicinal. If any one doubts whether they should be referred to the class of aliments, or to that of medicines, let him try the experiment of supporting life upon coffee or tea alone, and he would probably find that his term would not be much prolonged by such an expedient. Yet, when taken in combination with nutritious food, both these articles exert a salutary and useful influence upon digestion and health. The experience of all civilized nations has shown them to be innocent, when used at proper times and in moderate quantities, while, like all other medicinal substances, they are capable of abuse, if taken under improper circumstances or to an excessive degree.

As these two substances have a close affinity to each other, possessing properties not known to exist in any other plant, they are properly associated with each other as a class under the name of *anthypnotics*. Should any plant be hereafter found to possess qualities similar to those of coffee and tea, it would doubtless acquire an immediate value, and perhaps be in the same request as these imported articles. The subject is an interesting one for future inquiry, and already an identity in the active alkaloid principle has been asserted for some species of Ilex and Paullinia, consumed by the inhabitants of South America.

The prevailing fondness for coffee and tea is probably an acquired taste, like that for tobacco and alcohol. The flavor of both these articles in their crude state is disagreeable to most persons not already initiated in their use. But the discovery in modern times of their secondary effects, and the agreeable influence which they exert on the brain and nervous system, has created for them a general demand and consumption throughout the world.

COFFEE.

Coffee is the product of the *Coffæa Arabica*, a small tree which grows native in Arabia and several warm countries of the old continent, and is now cultivated extensively in the West Indies and tropical parts of the continent of America. The fruit of this tree is a roundish oblong berry, containing two seeds, the form and appearance of which are sufficiently familiar, constituting the common coffee which is brought to this country.

The use of coffee was unknown to the Greeks and Romans, and does not appear to have been known in the Asiatic countries as late as the time of the Crusades in the thirteenth century, although its first introduction into Europe was from Arabia. It seems to have been earliest in use in Ethiopia, where it has been drunk by the natives for a great length of time. Mr. Bruce, in his Travels in Abyssinia, states that the Gallæ, a wandering nation of Africa, in their incursions on Abyssinia, being obliged to traverse immense deserts, and wishing to be encumbered with as little baggage as possible, take with them a mixture of coffee and butter rolled up into balls, and carried in a leathern bag. One of these, about the size of a billiard ball, keeps them, they say, in strength and spirits during a day's fatigue. Coffee was introduced into Mecca, Medina and Cairo, about the middle of the fifteenth century, and two coffee-houses were opened at Constantinople in 1554. Both at Cairo and in Turkey it had to encounter political and religious opposition. The dervises affirmed that roasted coffee was nothing but a *coal*, and that the eating of *coals* was forbidden by the laws of their prophet. So that the coffee-houses were obliged to be shut up until "a more sensible mufti" succeeded in convincing the people that roasted coffee was not a coal; upon which they were again opened. In later years the use of coffee became extremely prevalent throughout the East. Houses for selling it were established in all parts of the Turkish empire; it was introduced into private families, and the refusal of a husband to supply his wife with coffee was reckoned among the legal causes of a divorce.

In Europe coffee was introduced into France and England about a century and a half ago. So rapid was the progress of a taste for it, after it became known, that, in eight years from its introduction, it had become in England a subject of public revenue.

Coffee has seldom been used in its raw state, except sometimes as a fanciful addition to certain *liqueurs* and ices. A decoction of raw coffee is disagreeable to the taste, but appears to possess properties analogous to those which it exhibits after being roasted. The roasting of coffee improves its flavor, and occasions considerable changes in its chemical constitution, without impairing its stimulant or medicinal activity. A peculiar alkaloid, called *caffeine*, is detected in both raw and roasted coffee. It is considered by chemists to be identical with *theine*, found in tea and in a few other vegetables. An aromatic oil, which has been called *caffeone*, is produced during the process of roasting.

During the extensive trial which has been made all over the world, as to the effect of coffee upon the health, no small diversity of opinion has existed in regard to its specific powers. Of the properties ascribed to it, two seem better established than any others. These are its property of assisting digestion, and that of obviating drowsiness. Coffee, when taken into the stomach, usually creates a pleasing sense of vigor in that organ; it moderates alimentary fermentation, takes off the feeling of distention and heaviness occasioned by over-eating, counteracts in some degree the fumes of wine, and produces a lightness and hilarity of mind, more moderate but more permanent than that occasioned by vinous or spirituous liquors. The custom, derived from the French, of drinking coffee after dinner, is beneficial, and powerfully promotes the process of digestion. It is known to epicures of most countries that a cup of strong coffee, at the end of some hours spent at the table, enables them to continue their functions, both of body and mind, to a greater extent than would have been done under any other assistance.

It is well known that coffee is strongly promotive of watchfulness, and enables us to resist for a long time the approaches of sleep. Students, whose lucubrations occupy a considerable portion of the night, find a great increase of the vigilance and vigor of their faculties, derived from the use of both coffee and tea. In fact, the long habit of drinking these articles renders us so dependent on them for the power of keeping the mind awake and active, that a change from them to any other kind of diet creates in most persons, at least for a time, a drowsiness and dulness of intellect. Hence it is common to hear milk and chocolate accused of creating sleepiness, — an effect which arises, not from any real soporific influence in those articles, but from the change of diet, and the want of the customary stimulus of coffee and tea. The Turks and Arabians consume large quantities of coffee, because it acts as an antidote to the stupefying effect of opium, to the abuse of which those nations are generally addicted. It has already been mentioned, and is a fact which every practitioner should remember, that perhaps no antidotal substance exerts so powerful an agency in counteracting the effect not only of opium, but of alcohol and the whole tribe of narcotics, as a seasonable draught of strong coffee.

Many complaints have been ascribed to the frequent and excessive use of coffee, such as tremors, headache, vertigo, and some more serious disorders. These complaints are most apt to appear when coffee has been taken alone, without a sufficient quantity of nourishment accompanying it. It is common for physicians, in the course of practice, to hear complaints of a sinking at the stomach, universal trembling of the limbs, and a loss of muscular power, coming on at eleven or twelve in the morning, and incapacitating the patient for business. These complaints I have, in more than half the instances which have come under my notice, been able to trace to a cup or two of strong coffee, or perhaps tea, taken for breakfast, without a particle of nourishment, or at least without a sufficient quantity to support the system, during and after the stimulant operation of these active liquids. I have generally found these complaints to be most effectually relieved by the simple remedy of eating, and cured either by increasing the quantity and quality of nourishment taken in the morning, or by exchanging the coffee for cocoa, chocolate or milk.

TEA.

The tea-tree, called by Linnæus THEA, is a native of Japan, China, Tonquin, and Assam. Linnæus believed that there were two distinct species of this genus, producing the green tea and the black, to which he has given the names of *Thea viridis* and *Thea bohea*, and distinguishes them by the number of petals in their flowers, the one having six petals, the other nine. But subsequent observers have found the number of these organs to be uncertain, varying from three to nine; and travellers in China and Japan, as well as various distinguished botanists, have arrived at the opinion that the different kinds of tea brought from those countries are the product of a single species, subject only to varieties from the influence of soil, climate, time of gathering, and mode of preparation.

The tea-plant is a small evergreen tree or shrub, of the height of six or eight feet. It grows in the valleys, and on the sloping sides of mountains, with a southern exposure. In

Japan it is planted around the borders of fields, without regard to the kind of soil, while in China, where it is an important article of commerce, whole fields are covered with it, and cultivated with the greatest care.*

* The origin of the employment of tea as a beverage, amongst the Chinese, is wrapped in the obscurity which generally belongs to ancient usages; and a fabulous tale is narrated, as to its introduction, which has had credence even amongst the better informed inhabitants of the empire, whilst, as is usual with fables, it has been imagined to have some allegorical allusion, which, if explained, would satisfy the lover of antiquarian lore. The tale is thus related by one of the compilers of a history of China:

"Darma, a very religious prince, and third son of an Indian king, named Kosjusvo, is said to have landed in China, in the year 510 of the Christian era. He employed all his care and thought to diffuse throughout the country a knowledge of God and religion; and, being desirous to excite men by his example, imposed on himself privations and mortifications of every kind, living in the open air, and devoting the days and nights to prayer and contemplation. After several years, however, being worn out with fatigue, he fell asleep against his will; and, that he might faithfully observe his oath, which he thought he had violated, he cut off his eyelids, and threw them on the ground. Next day, having returned to the same spot, he found them changed into a shrub which the earth had never before produced. Having eaten some of the leaves of it, he found his spirits exhilarated and his

When the plants have attained their third year, the collection of the leaves is commenced. It is repeated every year until the trees are seven or eight years old, after which they are cut down, that they may shoot up afresh from the roots,—a process which increases the quantity of leaves.

The leaves are carefully picked off, one by one. In Japan, the best kind, called imperial tea, is collected at the end of February, or the beginning of March, before the leaves are fully unfolded. This tea is scarce and dear, and is drunk by the grandees and rich people only. The second gathering is made a month later, taking indiscriminately the leaves that are unfolded and those which are not. Finally, a month after this, is made the third and last gathering, consisting of leaves fully grown, which furnish

former vigor restored. He recommended this aliment to his disciples and followers. The reputation of tea increased, and after that time it continued to be generally used. Kæmpfer, in his *Amœnitates Exoticæ*, gives the life with a portrait of this saint, so celebrated in China and Japan. There is seen at the feet of Darma a reed, which indicates that he had traversed the seas and rivers." — *Sigmond on Tea*, p. 12.

the poorest and lowest priced teas, consumed by the common people. It is now pretty well understood that the different sorts of tea imported into this country, from the finest green teas to the poorest bohea, depend for their difference of quality very much upon the time of their gathering.

The process of gathering, drying, and rolling the leaves is very laborious, and is in some instances conducted with the most superfluous nicety. In Japan, where a particular mountain is appropriated to raising tea for the exclusive use of the emperor, the shrubs are washed and cleansed from dust every day; the men employed in gathering the leaves are obliged to bathe themselves two or three times a day, and to wear gloves in the performance of their occupation.

The drying and rolling of the leaves is performed by the Chinese in buildings erected for general use. Several pounds of the leaves fresh gathered are placed in a large, shallow pan of thin iron, and heated over a furnace, the operator shaking and turning them with his hands until they begin to crackle. The heat thus applied deprives the leaves of their juice, and with it of the inebriating and deleterious properties which they possess while green. After the leaves are thoroughly roasted, they are taken out with wooden shovels, and delivered to the rollers. These persons roll them rapidly and with a regular motion, with the palms of their hands, upon tables covered with fine mats, until they acquire the form in which we see them imported. This operation produces an almost insupportable burning in the hands, which is aggravated by a yellowish inflammatory juice pressed out from the leaves. Nevertheless, it is necessary to continue the operation until the leaves are completely cold, for they cannot be rolled except when hot, and, in order that they should not unroll, it is necessary that they should cool under the hands. The more rapid the cooling, the better they are rolled, and on this account the workmen agitate the air with a kind of fan. But, in spite of this precaution, a great number of the leaves unroll themselves, and are obliged to be separated and roasted, and rolled several successive times before they are in order to be packed.

In order that the tea should keep well, it must

be inclosed in vessels which are air-tight. Kæmpfer assures us that the tea brought into Europe is always injured in quality, and never retains the fine flavor and delicate perfume which it has in its own country. The Japanese inclose their tea in vessels of tin, which, if large, are placed in savin boxes having their cracks closed with paper within and without. The tea imported to this country from China, it is well known, comes in tight wooden chests, lined with sheet-lead hermetically soldered. It is packed in these chests, by the Chinese, by stamping it down with their bare feet.

Some writers have asserted that the tea is roasted upon plates of copper, and that its color is owing to verdigris, with which it thus becomes impregnated. But those travellers who are most entitled to credit, affirm that the plates are, without exception, of iron; and Dr. Lettson, after a great number of experiments made with chemical tests, never detected any trace of copper; so that this suspicion appears to be void of foundation.

Among the Chinese tea is drunk in a variety of ways. Some use it as we do, in the form of an infusion; others take it in the form of fine powder, mixed with boiling water. The common or laboring people are said to use it in decoction, several handfuls of the ordinary kinds of tea being boiled in a kettle of water until the strength is extracted. This is taken by them as their common drink for assuaging thirst, and diluting meals.

Tea was first introduced into Europe by the Dutch, before the middle of the seventeenth century; and several physicians of eminence, either from conviction of its utility, or perhaps for the more substantial reason of a pecuniary reward, published warm eulogies in its favor. From this time its adoption was rapid in all the countries of Europe, and it is now a common article of diet with both rich and poor.*

* Nicolaus Tulpius was about the first medical man who wrote professionally upon tea, but his were not original observations; they were the opinions of the most eminent men he had collected to give to the world. But in 1678 appeared the first edition of a book, which speedily ran through three large impressions, and had a considerable influence upon the introduction of tea. It was entitled *Cornelio Bontekoe, Tractaat van het excellenste Kruyd Thee.* Although this work was, from the extravagance of its commendations on tea, severely handled by some of the critics, it

In regard to the medicinal qualities of tea, and its general influence upon the health of those who take it, reports and opinions are various and

was translated into many languages, and quoted as the highest authority. He pronounced tea to be the infallible cause of health, and that if mankind could be induced to drink a sufficient quantity of it, the innumerable ills to which man is subject would not only be diminished, but entirely unknown. He thinks that two hundred cups daily would not be too much. He is said to have been rewarded for his judgment by the liberality of the Dutch East India Company. Heydentrik Overcamp, who wrote the life of Bontekoe, states that his inducement to write was to recommend himself to his fellow-citizens, and to defend himself against his colleagues, who did not follow his theory or his practice. Etmüller recommended tea as a fine stomachic cephalic and anti-nephritic. Pechlin wrote a dialogue on tea, which he entitled *Theophilus Bibaculus*, and several poets indulged themselves in its praise. Petit wrote a poem; Peter Francius, two Anacreontics; Heinrich, a Doric Melydrion; and our poet-laureate, Tate, joined the melodious bards. Whilst it met with so much approbation, there were likewise those who were not equally satisfied with its merits. Boerhaave, Van Swieten, and others, attempted to stem the tide that was setting in its favor, but they have proved themselves incapable of resisting the general impression; for no beverage that has ever yet been introduced sits so agreeably on the stomach, so refreshes the system, soothes nervous irritation after fatigue, or forms a more grateful repast. It contributes to the sobriety of a nation; it imparts all the charms to society which spring from the enjoyment of conversation, with-

contradictory. Such is the diversity of temperaments and constitutions, that it cannot otherwise happen than that an article of diet which is taken

out that excitement which follows upon a fermented drink.—*Sigmond*, p. 94.

The introduction of tea-drinking into England has been ascribed to Lord Arlington and Lord Orrery, and the year 1666, the *annus mirabilis* of Dryden, has been assigned as the exact date; but in the diary of Mr. Pepys, secretary to the Admiralty, the following is registered: "I sent for a cup of tea, a Chinese drink, of which I had never drank before." In the diary of Henry, Earl of Clarendon, there is a memorandum: "Père Couplet supped with me, and after supper we had tea, which he said was really as good as any he drank in China." The first historical record, however, is an act of Parliament, passed in the year 1660, 12 Carl. II. c. 23, which enacts that a duty should be laid of eight pence per gallon on all tea made and sold in coffee-houses; which were visited twice daily by officers, whose duty it was to ascertain what quantity had been made.

From *An exact Description of the Growth, Quality, and Virtues of the Leaf Tea*, by Thomas Garway, in Exchange Alley, near the Royal Exchange, in London, Tobacconist, and Seller and Retailer of Tea and Coffee; published about 1660:

"Tea is generally brought from China, and groweth there upon little shrubs and bushes, the branches whereof are well garnished with white flowers, that are yellow within, of the bigness and fashion of sweet-brier, but in smell unlike, bearing thin green leaves about the bigness of scordium, myrtle, or sumack, and is judged to be a kind of sumack. The said leaf is of such known

by one person with impunity, and even with benefit, shall in another occasion disagreeable and even serious consequences. Dr. Cullen con-

virtues, that those very nations, so famous for antiquity, knowledge and wisdom, do frequently sell it among themselves for twice its weight in silver ; and the high estimation of the drink made therewith hath occasioned an inquiry into the nature thereof, amongst the most intelligent persons of all nations that have travelled in those parts, who, after exact tryal and experience by all wayes imaginable, have commended it to the use of their several countries, and for its virtues and operations, particularly as followeth, viz. :

"The quality is moderately hot, proper for winter and summer. The drink is declared to be most wholesome, preserving in perfect health until extreme old age.

"The particular virtues are these :

"It maketh the body active and lusty.

"It helpeth the headache, giddiness and heaviness thereof.

"It removeth the obstructions of the spleen.

"It taketh away the difficulty of breathing, opening obstructions.

"It is good against tipitude, distillations, and cleareth the sight.

"It removeth lassitude, and cleanseth and purifieth acrid humors, and a hot liver.

"It is good against crudities, strengthening the weakness of the ventricle or stomach, causing good appetite and digestion, and particularly for men of corpulent body, and such as are great eaters of flesh.

sidered tea as decidedly narcotic and sedative in its effects; but the most superficial observer must see that tea has very little in common with

"It vanquisheth heavy dreams, easeth the frame, and strengtheneth the memory.

"It overcometh superfluous sleep, and prevents sleepiness in general, a draught of the infusion being taken ; so that, without trouble, whole nights may be spent in study without hurt to the body, in that it moderately healeth and bindeth the mouth of the stomach.

"It prevents and cures agues, surfeits and fevers, by infusing a fit quantity of the leaf, thereby provoking a most gentle vomit and breathing of the pores, and hath been given with wonderful success.

"It (being prepared and drank with milk and water) strengtheneth the inward parts, and prevents consumption ; and powerfully assuageth the pains of the bowels, or griping of the guts, and looseness.

"And that the virtues and excellences of this leaf and drink are many and great, is evident and manifest by the high esteem and use of it (especially of late years) among the physicians and knowing men of France, Italy, Holland, and other parts of Christendom ; and in England it hath been sold in the leaf for six pounds, and sometimes for ten pounds the pound weight ; and in respect of its former scarceness and dearness, it hath been only used as a regalia in high treatments and entertainments, and presents made thereof to princes and grandees till the year 1657. The said Thomas Garway did purchase a quantity thereof, and first publicly sold the said tea in leaf and drink, made according

other narcotics. The excitement which it produces upon the mind and upon the organs of digestion is of a durable and permanent kind, and it never, like other narcotics, leaves the system in a state of somnolency and intoxication. These

to the directions of the most knowing merchants and travellers in those eastern countries; and upon knowledge and experience of the said Garway's continued care and industry in obtaining the best tea, and making drink thereof, very many noblemen, physicians, and merchants, and gentlemen of quality, have ever since sent to him for the said leaf, and daily resort to his house in Exchange Alley *aforesaid, to drink the drink thereof.*

"And that ignorance nor envy may have no ground or power to report, or suggest, that what is here asserted, of the virtues and excellences of this precious leaf and drink, hath more of design than truth, for the justification of himself and the satisfaction of others, he hath here enumerated several authors, who, in their learned works, have expressly written and asserted the same and much more, in honor of this noble leaf and drink, viz., Bontius, Riccius, Jarricus, Almeyda, Horstius, Alvarez Semeda, Martinivus in his *China Atlas*, and Alexander de Rhodes in his *Voyage and Missions*, in a large discourse of the ordering of this leaf, and the many virtues of the drink; printed at Paris, 1653, part x. chap. 13.

"And to the end that all persons of eminency and quality, gentlemen and others, who have occasion for tea in leaf, may be supplied, these are to give notice that the said Thomas hath tea to sell, from sixteen to fifty shillings in the pound." — *Sigmond*, p. 96, &c.

remarks are to be understood of tea in the state in which we consume it, that is, the state of perfect dryness. In its green or recent state, it is said to possess a decided narcotic quality, capable of producing intoxication and other deleterious consequences. This property, however, is of a volatile nature, and is lost in the process of drying and by a few months' age.

A crystalline, volatile, salefiable substance has been found in tea by chemists, and by them named *Theine.* It is said to exist in combination with tannic acid in the leaves, and to be identical in its chemical composition with *caffeine*, the alkaloid found in coffee. Its chemical character has led Liebig to suppose that, when used as an article of diet, it may promote the formation of *taurine*, a peculiar compound in the bile.

Tea, as it is brought to us in its dry state, has the effect of creating a lightness and exhilaration of mind, an increased action of the stomach in the process of digestion, and, above all, a vigilance and increased power of mental exertion. Dr. Johnson is recorded to have made the teapot the companion of his lucubrations, and to have taken immense quantities of its contents, to sustain the energies of his powerful mind during the prodigious labors which he accomplished. In its other properties tea is astringent and antiseptic. It visibly produces no injurious effect upon the generality of persons who take it from infancy to old age. It is remarked by Desfontaines, that no vegetable is known, the infusion of which can be drunk so often, and in such large quantities, without disgust. The Chinese regard it as highly salubrious. They mix with it neither milk nor sugar, but drink it pure, sometimes holding a piece of sugar in the mouth. The constant use which this people have made of it for so many ages seems to prove that, when rightly prepared, it is destitute at least of injurious properties. Professor Kalm states that tea is the best corrector of bad water, and that he derived from it great comfort and benefit during the illness and inconvenience of a long sea-voyage. It is, in fact, one of the best remedies for slight sea-sickness. An extract made of tea is in high repute as a medicine in China, and is said to remove obstructions and promote perspiration. Dr. Lettsom states that tea given in fine powder, in doses of thirty grains once in three or four hours, produced nausea and diaphoresis, and appeared to diminish the heat accompanying inflammatory complaints. The finer and more green is the tea, the more powerful are its specific effects.

Nevertheless, a variety of injurious consequences have been ascribed to tea, and many no doubt *have* arisen, either from its abuse or from the idiosyncrasies of those who have been the subjects of its influence. Some persons complain that, after taking freely of tea, a nervous agitation of the whole frame commences. The hands tremble, so as to be incapable of writing; the limbs experience a loss of power, and perform their office with difficulty; at the same time a confusion of ideas incapacitates the mind for any close or active train of thinking. There are even some persons in whom tea produces great nausea and sickness, with spasmodic pains of the stomach and bowels, and an uncontrollable agitation of spirits on the least hurry, noise or disturbance. These symptoms, however, are the effect of some peculiarity in the constitution, a great mobility of the nervous system, and generally of a slender, enfeebled or effeminate frame. They may, however, arise in all persons from an excessive use, either as it respects the quantity or strength of the tea, or the want of nourishment taken at the same time. I believe the number of persons will be found to be exceedingly small who cannot take tea in moderate quantities, and accompanied by food, without any inconvenience whatever.

The inquiry is very often made of physicians, Which is the most wholesome article of food, coffee or tea? The prejudices of most persons are ranged on one side or the other of this question, and even practitioners themselves are apt to fall into one or the other extreme. One of the oldest and most distinguished physicians of this city,* being asked what was the difference in effect between tea and coffee, replied, that "one is poison, and the other not." A physician of equal eminence, in Philadelphia,† decided on the properties of the two with equal positiveness, taking, however, the opposite side of the question. The truth is, that there are scarcely any two substances in the materia medica which bear

* Dr. S. Danforth. † Dr. B. S. Barton.

a closer relation, or more nearly resemble each other, in their properties, than coffee and tea. Tea is more astringent than coffee, and coffee of the strength commonly used is somewhat more stimulating than tea, — otherwise the differences which have been ascribed to them have mostly arisen from the accidental opinions of individuals, whose taste and idiosyncrasies have rendered them fond of the one and averse to the other.

REPORT

OF THE

ACTION OF COCHITUATE WATER ON LEAD PIPES,

AND THE INFLUENCE OF THE SAME ON HEALTH.

[From the American Journal of Medical Sciences for 1852.]

THE committee appointed by the Society of Medical Improvement in Boston, for investigating the question of the occurrence of any diseases attributable to the presence of lead in the aqueduct water introduced into the city from the Cochituate Lake, report as follows: —

That from an extensive inquiry among physicians, and also from the bills of mortality, they are led to believe that the health of the city of Boston has been uncommonly good during several years since the introduction of Cochituate water; and they have not learned that any well-marked cases of the diseases usually attributed to lead, have occurred, which were not traceable to some other cause than the use of Cochituate water drawn from leaden pipes.

It appears, from the experiments of Professor Horsford, that the water of the Schuylkill and Croton rivers, and of Jamaica and Cochituate lakes, acts upon the surface of lead so as to take up a small portion of that metal during the first two or three days of its contact. But after a few days the surface of the lead becomes coated with an insoluble compound which protects the lead for the most part from the further action of the water. Nevertheless, traces of lead are reported to have been found by various chemists in specimens of some of these waters, when greatly reduced by evaporation.

In consequence of the extensive use made of lead for various economical purposes, no person in civilized society can expect to escape from the reception of that metal in minute quantities into the body. The presence of lead in the paint of dwelling-houses and furniture, of water-buckets and other culinary apparatus, in vessels made of leaden alloys or soldered with the same, in the lining of tea-chests, in flint-glass, and in the glazing of coarse pottery, furnishes but a part of the examples which indicate our exposure to receive this metal in our daily food. To these examples it may be added that physicians give lead to their patients sometimes for weeks successively, and apply solutions and solid compounds of the metal to absorbing surfaces for longer periods; that persons are known to carry shot and bullets in their flesh during a long life; and, finally, that reliable chemists testify that lead naturally exists in the solids and fluids of man, and in those of some of the animals on which he feeds.

From all these facts we are authorized to draw the conclusion that, in the present state of our knowledge, the presence of lead in a very minute amount, like the presence of other substances in infinitesimal quantities, is inoperative upon the living body.

It is a general law, known to medical men, and to which there are not many exceptions, that diseases and symptoms produced by specific metallic agents, such as mercury, lead, and arsenic, do not cease until after the withdrawal of those agents. But it appears from the records of the Massachusetts General Hospital, during the last twenty years, as well as from the private experience of physicians, that many cases of lead colic and paralysis, acquired by persons who work in that metal, have got well under the daily use of water delivered from leaden pipes. This would not probably have been the case did the water contain any deleterious amount of lead in solution or suspension.

The principal diseases ascribed by Tanquerel, and some subsequent writers, to the presence of lead, are colic, paralysis, arthralgia and encephalopathy. Of these the committee have not been able to learn that there has been any sensible increase in this city since the introduction of Cochituate water. Of lead colic, but one case has entered the hospital during the last two years, which is a smaller proportion than the average of the preceding twenty years. Of lead paralysis there have been but two cases within the same period, both occurring to workmen in lead. Of arthralgia, or pain in the joints or limbs directly traceable to lead, it is believed there have not been a sufficient number of cases at any time to attract extensively the notice of our physicians. As to encephalopathy,—a general term used by some writers to express cerebral disease, and including coma, delirium, convulsions, &c.,—there is apparently no more reason for attributing it to lead, than consumption, fever, or any other common disease which may happen to occur among lead workmen.

It is obvious, to a medical reader, that many of the cases detailed by writers on lead diseases are coïncidences rather than consequences; and therefore do not furnish a ground for general laws. Such is the case when persons have been supposed to have contracted lead diseases by sleeping in newly-painted apartments, where, unless the lead were volatile, it could not leave the walls to enter the bodies of the patients. It is also the case when solitary examples of common diseases are ascribed to lead, when it is known that they more frequently result from different causes. It is also often the case when the reports of credulous and incompetent observers are received as scientific authority.

In a late "English Report by the Government Commissioners on the Chemical Quality of the Supply of Water to the Metropolis" of London, made in 1851, by Drs. Th. Graham, W. A. Miller, and A. W. Hoffman, men of high standing in the scientific world, an investigation is made of the condition of the various waters now supplied to that city. In this Report, the commissioners state (page 32) that "no recent or authenticated case can be cited of the health of any of the numerous towns, lately supplied with soft water, being affected by the use of leaden distributing-tubes." Again, on page 33, the commissioners say: "We are disposed, therefore, to conclude that the danger from lead, in towns supplied with water, has been overrated; and that, with a supply from the water companies, not less frequent than daily, no danger is to be apprehended from the use of the present distributing apparatus, with any supply of moderately soft water which the metropolis is likely to obtain."

On the present occasion it is by no means intended to deny the well-known fact, that certain acid liquors, also that the water of certain springs and wells, may and do act upon and even dissolve lead in such quantities as to prove injurious to human health. It is also possible that, at certain seasons, and under certain circumstances, the soft water of lakes and rivers may contain organic or other products, which may take up in solution a minute portion of the pipes through which they pass. And it may even be conceded as possible that a few susceptible and predisposed individuals will get lead diseases while using this water. Nevertheless, lead is a very convenient material to be used in aqueducts. It is more cheaply manufactured, more conveniently applied, and more readily repaired, than any other material; and while this is the case, mankind will not be prevented from employing it. The general law derived from the experience of the large cities of this country and of Europe is, that its employment for the conveyance of soft water is safe. To this law the few recorded cases of disease, if genuine, must be regarded as exceptions. And it should be borne in mind that nearly all the great agents which minister to the physical happiness and improvement of man are fraught with more or less danger. Ships and railroads, fire and water, food, drink and medicine, destroy annually multitudes of our species. Nevertheless, all these agents increase every year in use, with the increase of wealth and civilization. And as a humble example under the same law, it is not probable that the leaden aqueduct will be abandoned, on account of the inconsiderable risk which it may involve of occasioning disease. From the present state of our knowledge, we are authorized to conclude that the insurance on a citizen of Boston, New York, Philadelphia, or London, against lead colic, is probably worth much less than his insurance would be on a voyage across the Atlantic, or on a railroad for twenty miles.

ON

THE POISONOUS PROPERTIES

OF

CERTAIN AMERICAN SPECIES OF RHUS.

SEVERAL species of Rhus, or Sumac, growing in the United States, possess a peculiar property of exciting, by their contact, a specific cutaneous disease in certain predisposed or susceptible persons. A great majority of persons are exempt from liability to this disease; yet some individuals receive from the contact, and even the exhalation of those shrubs, a serious and distressing eruptive affection of the skin.

The *Rhus vernix* of Linnæus, called by Decandolle *Rhus venenata*, is a handsome shrub, with smooth foliage and reddish leaf-stalks, common in swamps and low grounds throughout the United States, and rising to the height of ten or fifteen feet. It is variously denominated Swamp Sumac, Poison Ash, Dogwood, &c., in different parts of the country. A figure and description of it are given in Bigelow's Medical Botany, vol. I., p. 96. It so closely resembles a tree growing in Japan, from which the varnish is made which bears the name of that country, that botanists are not agreed on the question of their identity. Both are poisonous, and both are capable of affording a black varnish.

If an incision be made in the bark of the American shrub, in spring or autumn, a quantity of thick viscid fluid immediately exudes, and sometimes with such rapidity as to drop off before it can be collected. This juice has an opaque, whitish appearance, and a strong, penetrating, disagreeable smell. On exposure to the atmosphere its color soon changes to a deep black. It is extremely slow in drying, and permanently retains its black color. It is, for the most part, insoluble in water, but dissolves partially in alcohol, and still more in ether. Spread upon surfaces of wood or cloth, it gives them a black appearance; but, in my experiments, it did not dry in exposure to the atmosphere for two summer months. But if boiled until its volatile part is expelled, and then applied warm with a brush, it assumes a glossy jet-black appearance, and is durable, firm, elastic, and not affected by moisture.

A distressing cutaneous disease ensues in many persons from the contact and even from the effluvium of this shrub. The poisonous influence which produces this affection is common to several other species of Rhus, also to the Cashew-nut, the Manchineel, and some other vegetables. The poison is extremely various in its action upon persons of different idiosyncrasies. Some cannot come within the atmosphere of the shrub without suffering violent consequences. Others are but slightly affected by handling it, and some can even rub, chew and swallow the leaves without inconvenience.

The most formidable cases in persons subject to this poison usually commence within twenty-four hours after the exposure. The symptoms are generally ushered in by a sense of itching, with a tumefaction of the hands and face. If the skin be examined at this stage, a minute vesicular eruption, like eczema, can be discovered in different places, particularly between the fingers. The swelling gradually extends over various parts of the body, affecting most those parts which have been exposed to the poison. The inflamed surfaces become elevated, acquiring a vivid redness, attended with a painful burning sensation. The vesicles enlarge and run into each other. The fluid which they contain is at first transparent and watery, but soon becomes yellow and purulent. As the vesicles and pustules break, and at length dry, they give rise to a yellowish and brownish incrustation. The swelling is greatest where the cellular substance is loose, so that the eyelids are frequently closed by it. When the eruption is confluent it gives to the whole countenance a shapeless and cadaverous appearance. The disease is usually at its height from the fourth to the eighth day, after which the skin and incrustations begin to separate from the diseased parts, and the symptoms gradually subside. I have never known it to terminate fatally, and it is not usual for scars or permanent traces of the eruption to remain. Some persons, however, are said to have recovered with the loss of the hair and nails.

The *Rhus radicans*, like the *Rhus vernix*, is regarded with aversion as a poisonous plant, and frequently furnishes cause to be remembered by susceptible persons who become exposed to its influence. It is a common plant, about the borders of fields and road-sides, running over walls and climbing trees, and usually known by the names of Poison ivy, Poison vine, Poison creeper, &c. It climbs upon tall objects in its neighborhood by means of strong lateral rooting fibres, which project in great numbers from its sides, and attach themselves to the bark of trees and the surface of stones. The adhesion of the vine to the bark of trees is frequently so strong that it cannot be torn off without breaking, and sometimes the stems are completely buried in the trunks of old trees, the bark having grown over and enveloped them. When it does not meet with an elevated prop, the plant becomes stunted in its growth, is more branched, and affects a spiral mode of growth, or falls to the ground, takes root and rises again. The erect variety is the *Rhus toxicodendron* of some botanists.

If a leaf or stem of this plant is broken off, a

yellowish milky juice exudes from the wounded extremity, which, after a short exposure to the air, becomes of a dark-black color. If applied to linen, it produces a dark spot, which is not afterwards eradicated by washing.

The contact of this vine produces in susceptible persons an eruption similar to that caused by the *Rhus vernix*, though it is believed that fewer individuals are affected by it. A particular account of this disease is given in the third volume of American Medical Botany, already referred to. Some other species of Rhus, such as *Rhus punilum* and *Rhus aromaticum* are considered as possessing a poisonous quality of the same character.

The disease has an average duration of a week, more or less. It does not appear to be shortened by medical treatment, but the patient is rendered more comfortable by soothing emollient applications. It sometimes returns on the trunk and limbs after having disappeared from the face.

I apprehend that a majority of persons are not liable to the injurious effects of the poisonous sumacs. Among persons residing in the country, exposures must occur very frequently, from the abundance of the shrubs, especially of *Rhus radicans*, by road-sides and elsewhere. Very few, however, in proportion to the number exposed, have personal experience of their deleterious effects. In those, on the contrary, in whom a constitutional liability to the poison exists, the disease frequently returns several times during life, notwithstanding the utmost caution in avoiding exposure to its causes. A gentleman residing in the country informed me that he had seven times been poisoned in the most violent degree. In such constitutions a slight exposure is sufficient to excite the disease. I have known individuals badly poisoned in winter from the wood of the *Rhus vernix* accidentally burnt on the fire; and others have made the same observation.

ON THE

HISTORY AND USE OF TOBACCO.

[Mostly from the American Medical Botany, vol. I.]

IT is a law of the animal economy, that the power of use and habit is capable of reconciling the system to bear with impunity what in its unaccustomed state proves deleterious or even fatal. It is a well-known fact that many substances in the Materia Medica lose their effect after the continuance of their use for a certain length of time, so that, if we would realize their original operation, we must increase their dose in proportion as the body becomes accustomed and insensible to their stimulus. This is particularly exemplified in the narcotics. Several of these substances, which at first are not only nauseous and disgusting in their sensible qualities, but highly injurious in their influence upon health, are so changed in their effect by habitual use, as to become to those who employ them an indispensable comfort and a first-rate luxury of life.

In its external and sensible properties, there is no plant which has less to recommend it than the common tobacco. Its taste in the green state is acrid, nauseous and repulsive, and a small quantity taken into the stomach excites violent vomiting, attended with other alarming symptoms. Yet the first person who had courage and patience enough to persevere in its use until habit had overcome his original disgust, eventually found in it a pleasing sedative, a soother of care, and a material addition to the pleasures of life. Its use, which originated among savages, has spread into every civilized country; it has made its way against the declamations of the learned, and the prohibitions of civil and religious authority, and it now gives rise to an extensive branch of agriculture, or of commerce, in every part of the globe.

Tobacco was in use among the aborigines of America at the time of its discovery. They employed it as incense in their sacrificial fires, believing that the odor of it was grateful to their gods. The priests of some tribes swallowed the smoke of this plant to excite in them a spirit of divination, and this they did to a degree which threw them into a stupor of many hours' continuance. When recovered from this fit of intoxication, they asserted that they had held a conference with the devil, and had learned from him the course of future events. Their physicians also got inebriated with the smoke, and pretended that while under the influence of this intoxication they were admitted to the council of the gods, who revealed to them the event of diseases.

In 1559, tobacco was sent into Spain and Portugal by Hernandez de Toledo, and from thence it was carried into France as a curiosity by Jean Nicot or Nicotius, ambassador at the court of Lisbon, whose name is now immortalized by its application to this genus of plants. From this period the use of tobacco spread rapidly through the continent, and in half a century it was known in most countries in Europe. The rich indulged in it as a luxury of the highest kind; and the poor gave themselves up to it as a solace for the miseries of life. Its use became so general and so excessive, that in many countries the constituted authorities, both of church and state, found it necessary to interpose, and to stop the extravagant indulgence in it by severe prohibitions. James the First of England, besides writing a book against it, called his "Counterblast to Tobacco," gave orders that no planter in Virginia should cultivate more than one hundred pounds. Pope Urban the Eighth published a decree of excommunication against all who took snuff in the church. Smoking was forbidden in Russia under penalty of having the nose cut off. In Switzerland a tribunal (*Chambre du tabac*) was instituted for the express purpose of trying transgressors in tobacco. A Turk, who was found smoking in Constantinople, was conducted through the streets of that city with his pipe transfixed through his nose.

Even in this country, where the use of tobacco was originated, we find our puritanic ancestors guarding against its abuse by salutary statutes. In the old Massachusetts colony laws is an act laying a penalty upon any one "who shall smoke tobacco within twenty poles of any house;" or who shall "take tobacco in any inn or common victualling house, except in a private room, so as that neither the master of the said house nor any other guest shall take offence thereat." In the earliest records of Harvard University, soon after its foundation, is a regulation of this kind: "No scholar shall take tobacco, unless permitted by the president, with the consent of their parents and guardians, and on good reason first given by a physician, and then in a sober and private manner."

While the legal authorities in various parts of the world took upon them to control the abuse of this fascinating weed, the literati of different countries entered warmly into the discussion of its merits and its faults. Among its advocates were Castor Duranti and Raphael Thorius, both of whom wrote Latin poems expressly in its praise. The performance of the latter is entitled a "Hymn to Tobacco," and is very lavish in ascriptions to this plant, which he styles the "gift of heaven and the ornament of earth." So warm were the prejudices of its advocates, that it obtained the reputation of a general panacea, and the catalogue of diseases which it was announced to cure amounted almost to a complete nosology.

But the opinions of its adversaries were not less extravagant upon the other extreme. It is remarkable that, in the days of its first general introduction, no man spoke about it with coolness and indifference, but every one warmly espoused its censure or its praise. Camden, in his Life of Queen Elizabeth, says, that men used tobacco everywhere, some for wantonness and some for health's sake; and that, "with insatiable desire and greediness, they sucked the stinking smoke thereof through an earthen pipe, which they presently blew out again at their nostrils; so that Englishmen's bodies were so delighted with this plant, that they seemed as it were degenerated into barbarians."

Dr. Venner, in a work entitled *Via recta ad vitam longam*, published at London in 1638, gives a brief summary of the injuries done by tobacco. "It drieth the brain, dimmeth the sight, vitiateth the smell, hurteth the stomach, destroyeth the concoction, disturbeth the humors and spirits, corrupteth the breath, induceth a trembling of the limbs, exsiccateth the winde pipe, lungs and liver, annoyeth the milt, scorcheth the heart, and causeth the blood to be adusted. In a word, it overthroweth the spirits, perverteth the understanding, and confoundeth the senses with sudden astonishment and stupiditie of the whole body."

A poetical philippic, called "Tobacco Battered," was published in the reign of King James, by Joshua Sylvester, in which he compares tobacco to gunpowder, and pipes to guns; making the mischief of the two equal. But the most celebrated of all invectives against tobacco was the "Counterblast" of King James I. That weak monarch gave vent to his prejudices against this herb in a publication, in which he professes to disprove all the alleged grounds for the toleration of tobacco, and warns his subjects in a most earnest manner not to sin against God, and harm their own persons and goods, and render themselves scorned and contemned by strangers, who should come among them, by persevering in a custom "loathsome to the eye, hateful to the nose, and baneful to the brain."

Such were the commotions excited by the introduction and spreading of an article, the use of which has now become so common as scarcely to attract notice. This article is the product of several species of Nicotiana, but chiefly of the *N. tabacum* or Virginia tobacco, and the *N. rustica*, sometimes called English tobacco, and being the sort which Sir Walter Raleigh introduced at the court of Queen Elizabeth. Another species, *N. fruticosa*, is said to have been cultivated in the East prior to the discovery of America. The Indians on the banks of the Missouri and Columbia rivers cultivate for use the *N. quadrivalvis* of Pursh and Nuttall. It has been remarked that the tobacco of warm climates is more mild in its flavor, while that raised in colder latitudes is more strong and pungent. The Bengal tobacco, of which the sheroots are made, is one of the most mild in its properties. After this is the West India tobacco, which affords the Havana cigars. Next is the tobacco of our Southern States, and, lastly, the tobacco raised in the northern parts of the Union, which is the most acrimonious and pungent of all.

Chemists have extracted from tobacco a colorless liquid alkaloid, which they have called *Nicotine.* It is acrid to the taste and smell, forms neutral compounds with acids, and is intensely poisonous in minute quantities. *Nicotianine*, another product, is a concrete volatile oil, like camphor, and resembles tobacco in its properties.

Among the substances used by Sir Benjamin Brodie in his experiments on vegetable poisons, was an empyreumatic oil of tobacco, prepared by Mr. Brande by distilling the leaves of tobacco in a heat above that of boiling water. A quantity of watery fluid came over, on the surface of which was a film of unctuous substance, which he calls the empyreumatic oil. Mr. Brodie found that two drops of this oil applied to the tongue of a young cat, with an interval of fifteen minutes, occasioned death. A single drop, suspended in an ounce of water and injected into the rectum of a cat, produced death in about five minutes. One drop, suspended in an ounce and a half of mucilage and thrown into the rectum of a dog, produced violent symptoms, and a repetition of the experiment killed him.

Tobacco has been used both as a luxury and prophylactic, and as a medicine. In the former cases it has not been taken internally, but only kept in contact with absorbing surfaces. It is well known that to the mouth it is applied in substance and in smoke, and to the nose in the form of powder. The opinion, which at one time prevailed, of its power to prolong life and to secure immunity from diseases, is now pretty fully abandoned. It has no prophylactic reputation, except as a preservative for the teeth, and in some degree as a protection against the contagion of epidemics. In both these cases it has acquired a certain degree of confidence, though it is probably inferior to many other substances for both these purposes.

As to its effects upon longevity, the great frequency of its use, and the facts and observations of Sir John Sinclair, render it improbable that, when moderately taken, it has much influence in wearing out the constitution, or abridging the usual period of life. But, like all other narcotics, its excessive use or abuse must impair the health and engender disease. Of the different modes of using tobacco, it is probable that smoking is the most injurious, and the most capable of abuse, since in this process the active principles of the tobacco are volatilized with the smoke, and are extensively applied to the lungs as well as the mouth and nose and fauces.

As a medicine, this plant has been employed in a variety of ways for the alleviation and cure of diseases. Externally it has been applied with benefit in tinea capitis, and in some complaints occasioned by the presence of insects. In the form of a cataplasm applied to the pit of the stomach it occasions severe vomiting. The prostration of strength and other distressing symptoms which attend this application must prevent its general employment. Still it may be remembered as an auxiliary in some cases where other emetics have failed to operate. A surgeon in the United States Army informed me that the soldiers had an expedient to exempt themselves from duty, by wearing a piece of tobacco under each armpit, until the most alarming symptoms of real illness appeared in the whole system.

Dr. James Currie has recorded a case of epilepsy cured by the external use of tobacco. A cataplasm was applied to the stomach for several days, about half an hour before the expected return of the paroxysm. A violent impression was produced each time upon the system, the paroxysm prevented, and the diseased association apparently broken up. Two cases of obstinate and dangerous intermittent were intercepted in the same manner by a decoction of half a drachm of tobacco in four ounces of water, thrown up as an enema, a short period before the time of the expected paroxysm.

The tobacco enema was formerly recommended in colic, nephritic complaints, &c. In later years it has been extensively employed in aiding the reduction of strangulated hernia. But since the introduction of ether and chloroform in the treatment of this disease, the use of tobacco has been little resorted to.

When the infusion is not used, an injection of tobacco-smoke into the rectum frequently produces the same consequences. The smoke may be made to penetrate further than any liquid, and it is equally efficacious, from the activity of the volatile parts. It was formerly much used in the restoration of persons apparently dead from drowning, but of late years it has gone more into disuse. From the sedative effect of tobacco, the tendency to syncope and the great prostration of strength which it occasions in ordinary cases, it is probable that its employment, in cases of asphyxia from drowning, must assist in extinguishing rather than in rekindling the spark of life.

Tobacco has been employed with some success in the locked jaw, both of warm and cold climates, by enemas of the infusion and of the smoke. These applications generally produce syncope and deathlike sickness in the patient, but, by prudent management of them, the disease has sometimes been overcome.

This powerful medicine is reported to have been also employed with some palliative effect in hydrophobia, and certain other spasmodic diseases. Its internal use, however, requires great caution, since patients have in various instances been destroyed by improper quantities, administered by the hands of the unskilful or unwary. Notwithstanding the common use and extensive consumption of tobacco, in its various forms, it must unquestionably be ranked among narcotic poisons of the most active class. The great prostration of strength, excessive giddiness, fainting, and violent affections of the alimentary canal, which often attend its internal use, make it proper that so potent a drug should be resorted to, by medical men, only in restricted doses, and on occasions of magnitude.

ON THE

EARLY HISTORY OF MEDICINE.

[From a Review of Miller's Disquisitions on the History of Medicine, published in the New England Journal of Medicine and Surgery, April, 1812.]

It is commonly understood that the history of medicine has already been traced with sufficient accuracy in all ages and countries where authorities for its elucidation are extant. The labors of Le Clerc, Friend, Haller and Cabanis, seem to have left very little to be wished in this department of science. But, although a general history of medicine is by no means a desideratum at the present day, yet there are undoubtedly parts of it which are still susceptible of correction or enlargement. Dr. Edward Miller, the author of the present disquisitions, apprises us that he has been induced to attempt them, partly from some singular traits which he thought he had discovered in the medicine of the early Greeks, and partly from the extraordinary advancement made of late years in Sanscrit literature. By means of this last we are informed that, long previous to its introduction into Europe, the science of healing had made very considerable progress in Hindostan; yet to commemorate its details, or appreciate its merits, has never yet been the task of any historian in medicine. This new field of research Professor Miller has attempted to cultivate, and the fruits of his oriental inquiries are to constitute a second volume of Disquisitions. In the mean time, the present volume, containing general archæological remarks, with speculations on the primitive physic of Greece and Egypt, is submitted to the ordeal of the public.

It must be exceedingly obvious that, prior to the introduction of letters, no very definite information can be expected with regard to the state of medical practice in any country. If the traditionary account of the most important and notorious events, such as battles and sieges, the rise and fall of heroes and of empires, is involved in necessary uncertainty; we cannot expect that a complex science, closely interwoven in early ages with mystery and superstition, should reach us in a state capable of affording much satisfaction. The few traditions handed down to us from the primitive ages afford matter for speculation to the curious, but yield no certainty to the accurate.

Dr. Miller, seemingly aware of the difficulties attendant on this part of his subject, has thought it proper to commence the present undertaking with a sort of history *à priori*, or *presumptive history*, of medicine in its primeval state. He begins with stating the progress of observation and reasoning, which would naturally be made by the early and rude nations, in regard to the phenomena of life, health, disease and death. He details the manner in which a gradual acquaintance would be formed with the nutritious, medical and deleterious effects of the various productions of nature; and from hence assigns to the Materia Medica the supreme honors of antiquity. Afterwards comes the knowledge of practical physic, of anatomy and of surgery, in proportion as men became habituated to watch the progress and cure of diseases, to butcher and dissect brute animals, to sacrifice, eat, or embalm their own species, and to inflict or remedy the wounds and injuries occasioned in war or elsewhere.

After this we are presented with an interesting account of that tract of territory, which we have reason to believe contained the earliest tribes of our species. To this region, composed chiefly of Egypt, Ethiopia, Turkey, Arabia, Persia and India, Dr. M. gives the collective name of the *Primæval Chersonese.** He expatiates on the exuberance of its soil, the variety and value of its productions, its inducements for agriculture, and facilities for commercial intercourse. He represents that six races or stems have, from time immemorial, occupied this ample and favored portion of the earth's surface. These are the Chinese, the Hindus, the Tartars, the Iranians (or Assyrians), the Arabs, and lastly the Nilotic tribes, or those of Egypt and Ethiopia. Among these he assigns an undoubted claim for priority of civilization to three nations, the Hindus, the

* This application of the term *Chersonese*, we think, rather stretches its ancient signification.

Iranians, and the tribes inhabiting the banks of the Nile. The individual claims of these three he compromises by endeavoring to prove, from tradition and history, from identity of language, &c., from conformity of religious and philosophical opinions, and, lastly, from similitude of corporeal structure, that they were only separate branches of one and the same individual family or race of men. In this investigation the author gives proofs of extensive and assiduous research.

Before quitting the general subject of the Primæval Chersonese, we are made minutely acquainted with its natural productions, or those articles which must have constituted the earliest food and medicine of man.

We now come to the particular history of medicine in early Greece, as it existed during the traditionary ages. On collecting the scattered rays of information respecting this period, chiefly from the poets, our author alights on a curious circumstance, which he makes the basis of this chapter, viz., "That, for its first discoveries and improvements, medicine in Greece appears indebted almost wholly to two orders of men, from whom such benefit was not likely to be derived, viz.:

"1. The chiefs or sovereigns of its different small communities.

"2. The priests or ministers of religion."

Upon this ground the author proceeds to give us two dissertations on the heroic and the priestly medicine of Greece;—and, first, of "heroic medicine."

On this subject we are told that scarcely a royal or distinguished personage, during the traditionary period, can be named, to whom some degree of medical skill has not been accorded. The ascription of this honor is traced to several causes, such as the obscurity which hangs over the beginning of all arts; the veneration which savage tribes entertain for the character of their leaders; and the policy which would lead these chiefs to maintain their ascendency by the display of every species of personal merit or skill, that of medicine being not the least imposing. The practice of these heroic physicians, which the author believes to have been chiefly surgical, is illustrated by various accounts of the therapeutic exploits performed by several individuals.

These are Chiron, Esculapius, Machaon, Podalirius, Achilles, Teucer, &c. &c. &c. The claims for medical distinction are, indeed, so numerous that they may be said to amount to no distinction at all, since every man whose name has been handed down to us as holding a rank in a tolerable degree above the vulgar, would seem entitled to enrolment among the faculty. Chiron the Centaur is stated to have been preceptor to nearly all the heroes who figured in the Argonautic and Trojan expeditions. Now, as Chiron was one of those universal geniuses, who was competent to exercise the arduous and multiform functions of warrior and necromancer, of horse-breaker, musician and doctor, it must be supposed that those who received the supreme honors of his school were not ushered into the world without a smattering of these various accomplishments. Hence the crew of the Argo might, on emergency, be considered a crew of the faculty ; and the council of warriors in Agamemnon's camp required only a change of occasion to resolve them into a jury of doctors.

We have already intimated that any accounts now extant respecting the medicine of the *early*

Greeks must be extremely unsatisfactory. We may now add, that, from the few authorities we have, it may be doubted whether any proficiency in medicine was ever made among them, beyond what a rude individual would naturally attain in the science of self-preservation. The boasted achievements performed by their distinguished personages apparently consisted in some trifling and obvious operations, or else in such exaggerated and miraculous performances as distance all possibility of belief. The heroic or surgical practice among them was confined chiefly to the extraction of weapons and the dressing of wounds. The highest praise which Homer has bestowed on the medical or surgical profession is contained in the following lines:

> *'Ιητρος γαρ 'ανὴρ πολλων, 'ανταξιος αλλων,*
> *'Ιυς τ' εκταμνειν, 'επί τ' ἤπια φαρμακα πασσειν,—*

which amount to simply this,—that "one doctor is worth a host of other men, to cut out arrows, and apply mild dressings." And, indeed, whenever he tells us of such a man being actually engaged in practice, it is commonly in one or the other of the above processes. Now it could require no great depth of intellect to discover, that if a barbed arrow stuck in the flesh, it could most easily be removed by excision, and that if a wound became dry and painful from exposure to the air, it might be made more comfortable by covering it with emollient applications.

But, with such humble and obvious operations as these, the ancient physicians could not have sustained their elevated rank in society, and substantiated their claims upon immortality. It became necessary, in order to secure complete ascendency over the public mind, that they should profess an intercourse with the gods, a knowledge of mysterious charms and incantations, and other special gifts peculiar to jugglers in all nations since their time. Very surprising stories are told of Melampus, Polyidus, and Chiron. These, however, are small when compared with the feats of Esculapius, the prince of physicians, and the deified inventor of medicine. Esculapius, in addition to many other astonishing powers, was gifted with a very remarkable faculty, peculiar to himself, of raising at pleasure the dead to life. Not less than six or seven instances are on record of distinguished corpses that were benefited by the exertion of this happy talent. It is impossible to say how far the bounds of science might have been enlarged by so mighty a genius, had not *Pluto* taken alarm at his progress, and presented a memorial to Jupiter, humbly showing, that if a stop was not put to the career of this officious mortal, people would soon cease to die, and hell would become a desert ; whereupon Jupiter interposed, and killed the wonder-working doctor with his thunderbolts.

There is reason to believe, from what has been said, that the cures effected by these medical worthies were either inconsiderable and real, or else preternatural and counterfeited. We have additional ground for this belief, on finding that frequently, when emergencies occurred opening a fine field for medical practice, the champions of physic were totally idle or inefficient. When a pestilence broke out among the Greeks at the Trojan war, we find them, with all their heroic and priestly medicine, resorting, not to their drugs and preparations, not to any regular system of practice, but simply to superstitious prayers, rites and atonements. The Argonauts, with Esculapius at their head, required the aid of a sorceress, before they could administer an opiate to the dragon that watched their fleece. Chiron died of a wound or ulcer in the leg, and Achilles of one in the heel. Such disasters as these last were not to be expected, after what Dr. Miller tells us in his account of Chiron:—"So celebrated was he in tradition for the cure of ulcers, as we are informed by Galen, that when a sore was obstinate and could not be healed up, it was customary in later times to call it a *Chironian ulcer;* intimating, by the expression, that it was an ailment of such malignity as to baffle the skill even of Chiron himself."

Now, we conceive, it was no compliment to the Centaur to name only incurables after him. We also conceive that, between Galen and Dr. Miller, the origin of the term Chironian ulcer may have been mistaken, and that it may be derived, not from the skill of Chiron in curing malignant ulcers, but from the circumstance of his having languished and died under a malignant ulcer. Galen informs us, on this subject, that of the phagedæna, or eating ulcer, there were different species, called the Chironian and Telephian: "Harum species quædam sunt, quæ Chironia et Telephia dicuntur." In another place he tells us that the Telephian ulcer was so called from Telephus, who was afflicted with it. Now the case of Chiron was not dissimilar to that of Telephus, as both their maladies were occasioned by the wound of a spear, only Telephus got well, whereas Chiron, after languishing with his lame leg for nine days, either died, or was made into a constellation; for all which the reader may consult Ovid. Fastorum, V. 379—414.

Machaon, the son of Esculapius, when wounded at the siege of Troy, retired with Nestor to his tent, where they took from the hands of a woman a farrago of onions, cheese, meal, honey and wine. From Pope's translation of this account in the Iliad, which Dr. M. has quoted, we are led to suppose that this potion was a *prescription* of the physician himself for his own case. Witness the following lines:

"The draught *prescribed* fair Hecamede prepares."

And again,

> "This *for the wounded prince* the dame prepares."

Unfortunately, however, there is no sort of authority in the original for the above expressions, and it appears that Hecamede prepared the draught, probably of her own invention, to treat her master Nestor, as well as his guest Machaon, and this, too, for the sole purpose of assuaging their thirst.

> *Τοῖσι δὲ τεῦχε κυκειω 'εϋπλόκαμος 'Εκαμήδη.* Il. λ. 623.
> *Τω δ' ἐπεὶ οὖν πίνοντ' ἀφέτην πολυκαγκέα διψαν.** 641.

It is a little remarkable that the learned professor should copy out the whole Greek passage for his book, and overlook such words as *τοῖσι*, *σφῶϊν*, *σφι* and *τω*; or imagine them to be meant for Machaon individually. We are much inclined to suspect that he placed undue reliance on the translation, when we find him leaving off his Greek in the middle of a sentence, and observing that "It might be difficult in English poetry to discover a translation more distin-

* The translations of this passage by Cowper and Dacier are correct. Chapman has the same inaccuracy with Pope.

guished for a happy mixture of *precision* and elegance, than the above version of Pope."

One more of these worthies, and then we have done with "heroic medicine." We presume that the name of Achilles will not yet descend to oblivion, even though our author should fail in his attempts to dub him also a doctor of medicine. Nevertheless Achilles, it seems, was a pupil of Chiron. He cured the wound of Telephus with the rust of his spear; and the plant Achillæa, or yarrow, had the honor to be named after him. But it ought not to be forgotten that the circumstance of his pupilage was common to most of the preëminent heroes of his time, and that in the cure of Telephus he had scarcely any merit. Telephus consulted the oracle, and was told that his wound could only be healed by the same *spear* which had occasioned it. Accordingly he applied to Achilles, whose spear had done the mischief, and requested his medical assistance. Achilles at first refused, saying that he was no physician; but afterwards was prevailed on to scrape the rust of his spear into the wound, which, in due time, got well. With regard to the plant Achillæa, we presume its name has as much to do with medicine as that of the plant Jeffersonia.

We now come to consider the second department which Dr. Miller has made in the physic of Greece, namely, his Priestly medicine. As he has shown that the medicine of heroes was chiefly surgical, he now makes it equally clear that that of priests and conjurers was mere "practical physic." For this he gives us all the presumptive evidence which can arise from the natural ascendency of priests and wizards over the public mind, and from the analogy of customs in all the barbarous nations in the world. He gives us, however,* only two instances of priest-physicians in Greece, namely, Melampus and Orpheus; of whom Melampus appears to us to have been only a fortune-hunter, who cured the daughters of Prœtus of real or pretended madness, that he might gain the hand of one of his patients, together with her kingdom, in marriage; while with regard to Orpheus, there is very little authority for his having practised physic in any particular instance, and his high reputation is sufficiently supported by the established fact, that

* "He *played* so well, he moved Old Nick."

On considerations like the foregoing we are disposed to ascribe to the ancient Greeks the credit of very little real proficiency in the art of healing. From similar motives we doubt the correctness of Dr. Miller's belief, that Greece was indebted for its first discoveries and improvements in medicine solely to two classes of men, namely, the chiefs or sovereigns, and the priests or ministers of religion. Unwilling, however, to interfere with the doctor's ardor for classification, we only suggest, for a second edition of his work, the propriety of adding a new class or department in primitive physic, to be called the department of *old women*, or of *female medicine.* These early practitioners of physic, we think, he has treated with unmerited neglect; for we will engage, where he produces one instance in Greece of a priest skilled in medicine, that we will furnish two of females possessing the same accomplishment. It is sufficient now to mention only the names of Circe, Medea, Angitia, Agamede, Helen and Œnone.*

* "In these early ages all the knowledge of the tribe formed a common stock; and their imperfect arts might be exercised by all

The last portion of our author's work embraces the history of medicine in Egypt and the East; and on this subject our limits compel us to be more brief. The advantages possessed by the Eastern countries over European Greece for the early cultivation of science, are said to have been the coalition of their inhabitants into large and mighty empires, instead of petty states and communities; and also the peculiar nature of their ecclesiastical institutions, in which an hereditary priesthood was placed in possession of all the facilities and inducements for scientific speculation. The invention of letters, or alphabetic characters, was among them an early auxiliary to the cultivation of the sciences, and medicine was not the last to profit by so signal an advantage. Some of the earliest lettered productions contained copious treatises on the healing art as an integrant portion of their contents.

The very ancient and celebrated personage *Thoth*, or, as he is called by Dr. Miller, *Tot*, and

those who were endowed with a certain portion of intelligence. Medicine, therefore, existed before there were any regular physicians." — *Cabanis's Revolutions of Med. Science.*

who is the same with Hermes, or Mercury of the Greeks, seems to have been the founder of medicine in Egypt. His writings, afterwards held sacred, were divided into forty-two books, six of which treated of medical subjects, namely, one of anatomy, one of diseases, one of instruments, one of medicaments, one of disorders of the eyes, and one of diseases of women. While the higher orders of Egyptian priesthood were employed in the study and execution of religious and philosophical offices contained in the former books, a second or inferior class were busied in the study and practice of healing. The Pastophori, for so the cultivators of physic were called, were bound to make themselves intimately acquainted with the medical scriptures of Thoth, and so long as their practice was strictly conformable to these, no blame was incurred by them. On the contrary, if any practitioner ventured to deviate in the least from these sacred rules, he became responsible with his own life for the safety of his patient. This circumstance must have furnished a powerful check to improvement, and kept the science of medicine long in a state altogether stationary.

Of the other peculiarities in Egyptian practice, the following are among the most remarkable: The art was made altogether hereditary, so that "he who was born a physician was prohibited equally by Heaven and by law from abandoning the occupation of his ancestors." The profession was also subdivided into minute departments, so that each particular disease had a separate healer. Some took charge of disorders of the eyes, some of the head, some of the teeth, some of the abdomen, &c. The vast number of individuals who were engaged in some branch of medical practice led to the assertion of Homer and Herodotus, that in Egypt every man met with was a physician.

What were the particular modes of practice enjoined by Thoth it is impossible now to know, for the books of the Pastophori have long since been lost. Dr. Miller, however, has industriously attempted to glean whatever authorities were afforded respecting them, from their successors in art and science, the Greeks. He has told us that the Pastophori, and even the kings, were wont to immolate and dissect beasts and human victims, but with what proficiency in anatomy it is not known. In the science of diseases they appear to have had some idea of critical days, to have divided disorders into acute and chronic, and to have ascribed their pestilential distempers to a morbific principle in the air. In the Materia Medica, they seem to have been acquainted with many efficacious articles, together with their most useful forms of composition.

Having now run through the contents of this volume, we would observe that, in general, it is far from being an uninteresting production. The extent of the author's researches, and the ingenuity of his deductions, will afford some novelty and instruction to most readers. His predominant fault is a disposition to annex an undue consequence to circumstances which are doubtful or unimportant. We think he might profit by the observation of Cabanis, that, in a subject where materials to compensate inquiry are wanting, "the friends of truth should not lose their time in forming vain conjectures, however *learned* they may happen to be."

ADDRESS

DELIVERED BEFORE

THE AMERICAN ACADEMY OF ARTS AND SCIENCES,

AT THE OPENING OF THEIR COURSE OF LECTURES, OCTOBER 27, 1852.

At a meeting of the American Academy of Arts and Sciences, June 22, 1852, —

Mr. Agassiz, in behalf of the committee appointed to consider the best means of increasing the Academy's publication fund, reported, — that the committee were unanimous in recommending that a course of public lectures of a popular character be given by Fellows of the Academy during the ensuing winter; that the President be requested to commence the course by an Address setting forth the objects and aim of the course; and that each section of the Academy appoint one of its number to deliver one lecture upon some special subject belonging to, and prominent in, the section's sphere of research.

It has been a serious question whether, amid the general sadness which hangs as a cloud over our city, which has seemed to check the ordinary current of affairs, and to darken the very atmosphere of social intercourse,* the preärranged exercises of this place should not be suspended in solemn and silent respect to the unusual occasion. But we are bound by circumstances to perform that which at this time we would not have wished to do. And leaving to the public voice the expression of that general emotion, to which no limited occasion can afford utterance, we shall proceed in the attempt to execute the more humble duty that has been set before us.

I am instructed, in behalf of the American Academy of Arts and Sciences, to report to you this evening on the character and condition of that institution, and the objects of the present course of lectures. If it were possible that a society which has existed in your midst for two or three generations, and which from time to time has numbered among its members many of the most enlightened and valuable of our citizens, could be in any measure unknown, I might safely rely on the more gifted laborers, who are

* The death of Daniel Webster.

to follow me in this field, for the vindication of its character and name. And if the present occupation of this lecture-room were a question of doubtful propriety, I might briefly say that the Academy needs, nay, more, that it deserves your countenance and support, and that this is the place and the manner in which your kind regards have been solicited towards the encouragement of its labors. But as the quiet operations of Science have not that wide-spread notoriety which attends the more absorbing questions of peace and war, of property and privilege, of safety and of danger, there is reason for attempting a more detailed consideration of the objects and results of our Academic Incorporation.

Academies in the higher use of the term, philosophical and learned societies, exist and have long existed in every country of civilized Europe. In common with Colleges and Universities, they are designed to cultivate and disseminate scientific truth; but unlike those institutions, the usual province of the modern Academy is to investigate rather than to teach; to bring together experts from the various walks of science, literature and art; to accumulate for the benefit of the whole the researches and observations of all, to aid and to encourage the different inquirers on their respective tracks, and to furnish vehicles for what is true, and ordeals for what is unsettled, in the progress of human knowledge.

One of the early fruits of the restoration of arts and letters in Italy was the perception of the great advantage attending the combination of effort in academic institutions. In that country were the first efficient examples of learned bodies coöperating for their common good, and bringing their united efforts to bear in the promotion of the arts and sciences. From Italy the principle of academic association spread to England, Germany and France, and in all those countries, noble institutions, having their foundation in the earnest quest of truth, and supported by the zeal and learning of the best men of their times, have been sent down to the present age, marking their way by many high developments of human intellect, and noble achievements of human science. Some of them, which for two centuries have enjoyed the sunshine of royal and public patronage, now find themselves intrenched in ample halls, surrounded by the machinery of modern science, dispensing rewards with princely prodigality, offering seats, of which the prospective vacancy fills with ambition the learned of foreign countries, throwing lustre on the cities of their respective establishment, and connected by little resemblance, save that of etymology, with the simple preceding groves of Plato and Arcesilaus.

Academic institutions have differed widely from each other in the object as well as the comprehensiveness of their pursuits. Not only does the history of literature furnish many examples of Academies of Sciences and the Arts, but there are well-known like institutions of Belles Lettres, of Language, of Inscriptions, of Painting, Sculpture and Architecture, of Music, of Antiquities, and of many subordinate branches of useful and of elegant learning. Of course, the value of membership in any of these bodies has depended on the character of the institution itself, and the principles on which it is conducted. The Royal Academy of France, often known *par excellence* as *the Academy*, not only under its original name, but under the subsequent appellations of National and Imperial Institute, has, during a long period of years, sustained an almost uninterrupted preëminence in the republic of letters. The labors of this body have cast a flood of light on modern science, and its assembled savans have formed a tribunal from whose scientific sentence there seemed no appeal. Yet, even this institution, under the occasional supineness of its members, and the influence of royal favoritism, has more than once been a mark for the shafts of cotemporaneous criticism. The poet Piron, affecting to define his own humble position by an epitaph, says, "Here lies Piron, who was nothing at all, not even an Academician."

In the year 1779, in the midst of the exhausting and yet unfinished contest of our Revolution, with humble resources, but with confidence of future promise, the American Academy of Arts and Sciences was founded by an association of citizens of Massachusetts. The fathers of our Commonwealth, well aware that the lights of liberty and learning are jointly conducive to the stability of free government, gave their sanction and in many cases their individual efforts to construct the foundation of an ample edifice. Among the constellation of worthies enrolled as the first members, we find the names of the two Adamses, of Bowdoin and Cushing, of Chauncey and Cooper, of Hancock, of Lowell, of Sedgwick, Strong and Sullivan, and about fifty others, all of them names already registered in the annals of their country's service, or distinguished as proficients in the learning of their time.

The preface to their first publication states that the Legislature was called on to sanction the society on a liberal and extensive plan, and to establish it on a firm basis. "And to the honor of our political fathers," say they, "be it spoken, that although the country was engaged in a distressing war, — a war the most important to the liberties of mankind that was ever undertaken by any people, and which required the utmost attention of those who were entrusted with our public concerns,—they immediately adverted to the usefulness of the design, entered into its spirit, and incorporated a society with ample privileges."

But the approval of the Legislature was but a small offset to the difficulties against which the new association had to contend. "The country being young," say they, "few among us have such affluence and leisure as to admit of" our "applying much time to the cultivation of the sciences." And in another place, "Many important European discoveries have been in a great measure useless to this part of the world, in consequence of a situation so remote from the ancient seats of learning and improvement. And of such publications as have reached this country, the smallness of the number has greatly limited their usefulness, as but few have had the opportunity for perusing them."

Under such disadvantages, so unlike the state of things now, well might our courageous predecessors solace and assure themselves by a prospective view of the harvests they were sowing for their descendants. "Settled," say they, "in an extensive country, bordering upon the ocean, and opened to a free intercourse with all the commercial world,—a country comprehending several climates and a rich variety of soils, watered and fertilized by multitudes of springs and streams, and by many grand rivers,—the citizens have great opportunities and advantages for making useful experiments and improvements, whereby the interests and happiness of the rising empire may be essentially advanced. At the same time enjoying, under a mild but steady government, that freedom which excites and rewards industry and gives a relish to life, — that freedom which is propitious to the diffusion of knowledge, which expands the mind and engages it to noble and generous pursuits, — they have a stimulus to enterprise which the inhabitants of few other countries can feel."

Such were the principles and the auspices under which was kindled the small, dim light of our Academy. Although it was not often overfed with fuel, nor at all times watched with vestal vigilance, it has at least never been suffered to go wholly out, and, after glimmering with uncertain yet increasing rays for two thirds of a century, it has at length grown to be an acknowledged beacon in science, a light to the philosophic of our own country, a western star to whose unshadowed brilliancy and true monitions the European world now looks with interest and respect.

The early labors of the Academy were in keeping with its early professions. They did not trench deeply on fields appropriated by foreign explorers, but rather turned their inquiries to the capacities of their own country, to the improvement of its practical advantages and the knowledge of its natural history. With the exception of a few limited papers in mathematics and astronomy, the first volumes of the Transactions are occupied with such objects as the cultivation of corn and the engrafting of trees, examination of springs of water, and reports on diseases of cattle, speculations on natural caves, recorded earthquakes and conjectured volcanoes. Narratives are given of the appearance of water-spouts, and of remarkable devastations of lightning on trees, rocks and dwelling-houses. Fossil frogs, "that under the cold stone" were believed to have passed monotonous ages of incomprehensible existence, are presented, in these memoirs, living and jumping before the reader. Flocks of swallows, blackening the air with their numbers, abandon the joyous, twittering, feather-chasing career of their summer life, and with ominous solemnity assemble on the banks of some stagnant pool, rendered famous perhaps with the tradition of former engulfments of their species, and then are seen no more. A cloud settles on the mystery of their wintry existence, and the wonder was that, when they appeared in the following spring, their sleek and glossy plumage bore no traces of the deep mud under which they were believed to have slept out their hybernation.

The riches of our vegetable kingdom and the importance of establishing a more thorough and practical knowledge of its different portions, did not escape the attention of the pioneers of our natural history. Great difficulties beset the early botanists in the prosecution of their inquiries, from the novelty of the subject, the paucity of books, and the difficulty of maintaining correspondence with foreign scientific authorities, in those cases where books are insufficient and knowledge, to a certain extent, must be ocular and traditionary. Yet, the Rev. Dr. Cutler, of our State, has culled for himself an enduring garland from a field in which it would appear that the harvest was plenteous, but the laborers were few.

The valleys of New England are not the seat of antiquities and hieroglyphic records, yet, in the earlier volumes of the Transactions, there is more than one account of the memorable inscription on our far-famed Dighton rock. This curious relic of the scattered and now fast disappearing aboriginal inhabitants of our country, is copied and described by various persons, and hypothetically explained by the late excellent Judge Davis, of this city. Whatever be the mystery it involves, a hunting scene or a religious rite, an achievement of war or of conquest, the pages of the Academy offer a faithful facsimile for the use of foreigners and of posterity, who may happen to find themselves called and competent to its perusal.

But by far the most ambitious among the early speculations of the Academy is the theory of Governor Bowdoin, then President of the Institution, on the existence in the universe of an all-surrounding orb. That distinguished gentleman and scholar, after various speculations on the supposed waste of material light from the surface of the sun, and the danger to all material bodies from their own unresisted gravity attracting them towards each other, published an elaborate memoir, entitled "Observations tending to prove by phenomena and Scripture, the existence of an

33*

orb which surrounds the visible material system, and which may be necessary to preserve it from the ruin to which, without such a counter-balance, it seems liable, by that universal principle in matter, gravitation."

The author satisfies himself, by a train of ingenious reasoning, of the sufficiency of his theory to prevent the apprehended catastrophe. He deals not only with the necessities of such an arrangement to produce stability in our universe, but draws supernumerary arguments from the presence of the milky way, the blue color of the firmament, and lastly from various corroborative texts of Scripture.

History is silent in regard to the extent of the impression made upon the world by the promulgation of this comprehensive theory. The orb is supposed to have been standing several years after the announcement of its character and office; and when it fell, the Academy, nothing daunted, proceeded to prosecute its celestial investigations with a zeal and tenacity of purpose prophetic of its future more elevated destiny.

——— tenacem propositi ———
——— si fractus illabatur orbis
Impavidum ferient ruinæ.

Should any one incline to disparage the labors of our predecessors on account of their honest and earnest, though sometimes misdirected, inquiries for truth, he will find parallel examples in the early history of every learned body in Europe of a century's standing. The first publications of the oldest philosophical societies contain speculations on the transmuting of metals, projects for perpetual motion, schemes for raising water without power, and for flying in the air by machinery, credulous inquiries about secret poisons and fabulous natural productions. They did not think it beneath them to investigate extravagant rumors, and they often propounded interrogatories, with this view, to foreign ambassadors, missionaries, merchants and navigators. The Royal Society of London sent many grave inquiries to Sir Philberto Vernatti, then resident in the Indies, in hopes to solve some of the difficulties which were weighing upon them. The first of these was, "Whether diamonds and other precious stones grow again after three or four years in the same places where they have been digged out?" The categorical answer to this question is, "Never." Another inquiry is, "Whether, in the island of Sombrero, there be found such a vegetable as Master James Lancaster relates to have seen, which grows up to a tree, shrinks down when one offers to pluck it, and would quite shrink unless held very hard?" Sir Philberto replies, that he "cannot meet with any that ever heard of such a vegetable."

Again they inquire, "Whether the Indians can so prepare that stupefying herb Datura, that they may make it lie several days, months, years, according as they will have it, in a man's body, and at the end kill him without missing half an hour's time?"

The twenty-ninth question is, "Whether there be a tree in Mexico that yields water, wine, vinegar, oil, milk, honey, wax, thread and needles?" The answer here is more encouraging: "The cocos-trees yield all this, and more."

In the inquisitiveness and credulity which marked these early stages of scientific inquiry, we have at least the gratifying assurance that our philosophic fathers did not close their ears against the reception of knowledge, from whatever quarter it might proceed. They were just emerging from the deep intellectual darkness which for long ages had brooded over the world. They were the survivors of many generations, among whom to inquire had been a crime, to reason had been a heresy, and to experiment a satisfactory evidence of intercourse with the powers of darkness. Secretly, and by stealth and stratagem, the germs of science had here and there been nourished into visible life, but the air and the sunlight of heaven were denied to their upward expanding tendencies. And when at length, with the Reformation, the revival of letters and the introduction of the printing-press, a veil was lifted from the moral and material world, no wonder that inquiring eyes were dazzled and strong heads were turned with the startling developments of the solar system, the circumnavigation of the globe, and the practicable intercourse of men and nations with each other.

The comparatively short period during which the American Academy has existed, has been one of advanced and rapid progress in the history of science throughout the world. It has been the era of the Herschels and Laplace, of Lavoisier and of Davy, of Cuvier, of Watt, and a host of gigantic minds, whose conquests over unknown regions will never be obliterated from the map of science. During this period of progress, the small number and limited opportunities of the scientific men of our own hemisphere have been such as to render them lookers-on, recipients and dispensers, rather than originators of new discovery. For many years the publications of this Academy were so sparse and inconsiderable as to induce serious question from some foreign scientific bodies, whether the usual exchange of printed transactions were worth keeping up. There was a long period, during which the late venerated Bowditch seemed to be the almost solitary pillar on whose support the Academy relied for its character and position in the philosophic world. And to his praise be it said, that while engaged in the surpassing labors which have constituted the monument of his living and posthumous fame, he never shrunk from identifying his name with a small, and then almost obscure institution of his native country. Punctual in his attendance on its meetings, earnest in his appeals to the lagging industry of its members, foremost in every movement for its prospective welfare, pouring into its vacant pages the overflowings of his own exuberant mind, he was not only a centre, but a central fire; not only attracting but exciting, warming, illuminating all within the circle of his influence. By his side walked the accomplished Pickering, laborious, erudite, modest, a votary of learning for its own sake, whose capacious and cultivated mind, affluent in various lore, seemed poor only to his own aspiring and comprehensive genius.

By these men, more than all others, in the day of its obscurity, was this Academy cherished and upheld. They did not feel authorized to boast much of its history, nor of its existing performances. They were not vainglorious of their own share in whatever of reputation it might have happened to acquire. But they felt and expressed that in it was contained the germ of future development; that to a certain extent it had books, and endowments, and position; that it was their duty and that of their cotemporaries to cultivate its capacities, to improve its condition, and at least to preserve it unimpaired, until the increasing population and wealth in our country, and correspondent increase of the men and means of science, should impart to it a vigorous vitality, like that which sustains the older institutions of Europe.

We do not assume too much in saying that this period has at length arrived. The thinly attended meetings, few and far between, in which a quorum was with difficulty convened, perhaps only to spend an hour in debating a by-law or electing a foreign fellow, have been replaced by monthly and semi-monthly gatherings, in which the time is often too short to give utterance to the accumulated researches of the members. The demand for publication of new and important matter outstrips the limited resources of the treasury, and now brings the institution before the public of this city, a solicitor for the hearing of its claims. What is it that this Academy, through its members, is now performing? What is it that it asks the means of publishing to the world? Not the meagre and uninteresting record of every-day phenomena. Not the premature speculations of unqualified reasoners on more expanded subjeets. Not the repeated lessons reeeived with unquestioning doeility from the higher sourees of transatlantie wisdom. It now rather sits in judgment on unsettled questions of European science, and pushes its own unaided investigations beyond the previous bounds of human knowledge. Its researehes during the last five or six years have been sueh in magnitude and importanee that they may without disadvantage be brought into eomparison with those of many of the time-honored institutions of the Old World. Closely eonneeted with our distinguished University, numbering among the teaehers of that seminary a large portion of its most accomplished and effieient members, making the pages of its publieations a vehiele for the light whieh emanates from the observatory, the apparatus, the eolleetions of that venerable seat of learning, aided moreover by the naturalists, the philosophers and the annalists of other soeieties among us, it has established an influenee which eould not well be now spared from the republie of seienee.

We may say, without fear of eontradietion, that there are few branches of physieal knowledge which have not been illustrated or enlarged by the members of this body, and when difficult labors are to be performed, or difficult problems to be solved, no source of information in our country has been deemed more reliable, or more frequently been put in requisition, than the authority of this Academy. The plants of California and New Mexico have repeatedly come here to be named and described. The late exploring expedition sent to this city a large portion of its collected treasures, for investigation and judgment. The fossil bones of gigantic quadrupeds are accumulated in our midst with a completeness and abundance such as is found in no other place; and they are presented to the world with an amplitude of scientific delineation, seldom, if ever, surpassed. Huge limbs and heads of undescribed troglodytes, exceeding those of man which they counterfeit, and whose race is now living in African forests, have received their first description in this city.

The pages of our Transactions offer the faithful impress, not elsewhere found, of the foot-prints of colossal birds and mysterious reptiles, transferred from the banks of our own rivers, where, awaiting the perusal of the naturalist, they have lain for unknown ages, stereotyped in stone. It is fresh in our recollection, that when the credulity of the popular voice, not without the assent of men of science, had given a fictitious reality to a monster compounded of contributions levied from many individuals, and when this deception gained foothold not only in our own greatest city, but afterwards in one of the enlightened capitals of Germany, the doubt was removed and the deception made manifest by the scientific sentence of one of this Academy.

A few years ago a call was made by the Legislature of this Commonwealth for researches into the various departments of its indigenous natural history. This call was promptly and ably responded to, and the reports returned on the geology, the forest-trees, the fishes, the insects, and the other invertebrata of Massachusetts, were in the highest degree creditable to those academicians from whose labors they emanated. Some of these subjects are yet waiting the results of this course of lectures, to give their illustrations to the public.

The incipient mysteries of organic development, the structure and transformations of the animalcular world, the scarce visible organisms which fill our waters with busy and effective life, the unknown generations which have written with their own remains the history of preceding nature, have often been drawn from obscurity, their laws and limits studied, and many of their new and unknown forms for the first time described and arranged by one of our adopted members, whom we may well place in the foremost rank of living naturalists. And, as if to indicate the claim to notice of what might seem a humble department of zoölogy, we have been taught, from the same indefatigable source, that, since the period of man's existence on this globe, a vast peninsula, constituting nearly an entire state of this Union, has been raised from the bottom of the ocean, and added to the previous continent, by the silent conspiring agency of coral polypes.

When we turn our inquiries in another direction, we find that the study and knowledge of the electric power has not deserted the country of Franklin. This mighty agent, before which men trembled in former ages, believing, in their alarm, that Jove was wielding his bolts, or "that spirits were riding the northern light," has become, in philosophic hands, the docile messenger of thought over our vast country, and the faithful monitor of danger in our cities, and seems about to reveal the very measure of its velocity to the persevering interrogations of members of this Academy.

I should weary you with detail, were I to recount the various contributions made among us to mathematical, chemical, economical, mechanic, and microscopic science, and to the natural history of the globe and of its inhabitants. I might say that the tornado which last year swept over a neighboring district, has left on our pages an impress more minute than ever whirlwind left before. I might say that the forthcoming nautical almanac, the joint and arduous production of our mathematicians, will stand in the foremost rank of similar authorities. I might bring before you the perfected turbine wheel, and the elaborate cordage machinery, as examples of the mechanical ability and inventive genius of our academicians; and I might cite many instances of energetic coöperation with other bodies, in the magnetic observations, in meteorology, in the coast survey, and in the general advancement of geographical and philosophic knowledge.

Conspicuous above other sciences, for the vastness of its objects, and the amount of intellectual effort which it has called into being, stands Astronomy, one of the earliest, the most difficult, and most successful studies of the human mind. For many years the discoveries of its observers, and the results of its analysts, have, by the common consent of central and northern Europe, been chronicled in one place, in the city of Altona, in the astronomical journal of the eminent Professor Schumacher. But Schumacher is dead, and his divided mantle has fallen upon the shoulders of more than one competent successor. The only journal in the English language, now devoted to pure astronomical science, regularly reporting, with discriminating exactness, the advances made in that department of knowledge, and enriched by contributions from both sides of the Atlantic, as well as from its own editor, is now published in this country, and issues periodically from the press of Cambridge in Massachusetts.

It has not been in vain that public liberality has provided our University with instruments capable of penetrating the depths of space. It has found in that place eyes adequate to perceive, and minds competent to analyze, the abstruser revelations of astronomical science. The meetings of this Academy have heard the announcement of new celestial bodies, and the assignment of unexpected laws to others already familiar to the European world. Who is there, from the schoolboy to the sage, who has not dwelt and gazed and speculated on the mysterious ring that surrounds the planet Saturn? Who has not wondered at this exceptional feature of the known universe, and planted himself in imagination on the surface of that distant sphere, that he might seem to contemplate the radiant arch that spanned its unknown firmament? Yet this remaining anomaly of the visible creation, this marvel and study of modern astronomy, has been destined to reveal its structure at our own observatory. And the necessity of its fluid nature, and the laws by which it is sustained, have been deduced from the observations, and established by the profound analysis, of our own astronomers.

Need I call up before this audience the recent fame of that far ulterior planet, which, since the creation of the world, has held its dim and undetected course around the verge of our solar system, until at length its remote presence so weighed upon the instructed sense of the Parisian philosopher, that it was felt and known even before it was seen? And need I say that this object of absorbing interest, this wonder of its time, after justifying in some measure the rival claims to its discovery of the three most enlightened nations of Europe, came at last to receive the determination of its true orbit, position, mass and motion, from the geometers of our own Academy?

I have said enough to show that the American Academy of Arts and Sciences has earned for itself a position among similar institutions of the world; and although, from the necessary limits of the occasion, I have not been able to take fitting notice of other investigations made here for the advancement of knowledge and other worthy achievements in the parallel walks of literature, yet without arrogance I might assert that, in the different sections of this Academy, embracing the great departments of modern research and cultivation, men are now found competent to perceive truth, and qualified to return light, on the varied objects of human science.

It is not necessary to say that the meetings of such a body afford a nucleus, around which are attracted and concentrated the contributions of most of our scientific men. And the regularly published proceedings of this body are the vehicle through which are given to the world the results of their labors.

It ought not then to be said that, in this enlightened community, the efforts of so active and efficient an institution should be embarrassed by financial deficiencies. Yet such is the uniform excess of its expenditures over its limited income, that the Academy is not able to procure the books wanted for the information of its members, nor to issue the publications which should give utterance to its own investigations. So far from enjoying the promptness and amplitude of appearance which attend the productions of similar institutions abroad, it has happened, more than once, that the discoveries of our scientific men have had to wait, until they were actually superseded by the same discoveries abroad, because the printed pages and the illustrations of the engraver could not be commanded at the requisite time.

As a nation we are proud of whatever contributes to our national glory. We are boastful of our growth, our political progress, our victories, our annexations. We are proverbially sensitive, even in small matters, to questions of precedence and subordination, and we give our undivided sympathy even to a national contest of lock-smiths. The triumph of nautical skill in a distant boat-race binds this Union more firmly together, by the common thrill of exultation which vibrates from Maine to Texas.

Have we then no place for the rising star of science? Shall we avert our eyes from the dawning light, because its rays do not fall on us from the accustomed east? Have we no encouragement for those, our countrymen, to whom the Old World is beginning to yield its reluctant honors? Are we incapable of appreciating the value of scientific progress, and the importance that our own country should not be last in the general march of improvement which characterizes the present age? Such has not been the character and usage of this our city. Such could not have been the expectation of those who, in adverse times, planted and nourished among us seeds capable of a redundant harvest.

I have thus, ladies and gentlemen, endeavored to present to your favorable notice the character and claims of the Academy of Arts and Sciences. In the course of lectures which is to follow, the Academy will speak for itself. I am aware that it is presumptuous for one absorbed in the cares of a responsible profession, who has added little to the common storehouse of indigenous science, to appear as the advocate and representative of so distinguished a body. But I am impressed with the importance of the occasion, and obey the commands which have been laid upon me; and I will shelter myself under the belief that it may sometimes be permitted, even to the drone in the hive, to cause the air to vibrate in honor of the labors of his more efficient colleagues.

INDEX.

CPSIA information can be obtained
at www.ICGtesting.com
Printed in the USA
LVHW101232230223
740172LV00006B/415

9 783382 304263